Daffodils
in the
SOUTH WIND

A NOVEL

PATRICIA A. GREEN

This is a work of fiction. All of the characters, names, incidents,
organizations, and dialogue in this novel are either the products
of the author's imagination or are used fictitiously.
The book is set against a historical backdrop, therefore some of the
historical references are based on actual events or persons.

Archway Publishing books may be ordered through booksellers or by contacting:

Archway Publishing
1663 Liberty Drive
Bloomington, IN 47403
www.archwaypublishing.com
1 (888) 242-5904

Scripture taken from the King James Version of the Bible.

ISBN: 978-1-4808-6087-2 (sc)
ISBN: 978-1-4808-6088-9 (e)

Library of Congress Control Number: 2018903659

Print information available on the last page.

Archway Publishing rev. date: 1/30/2020

To Mom and Dad
with love and gratitude

Acknowledgements

First, I would like to express my love, appreciation and gratitude to my husband, **Leon Green**, for reading and editing the first draft of this novel, and for his subsequent constructive input, dialogue and endearing support; and to my daughter, **Briyonna Joi**, who always believed in me and in the worth and significance of this work.

I would also like to acknowledge my editor, **Crystal Daniels**, whose technical and editorial skills, thoroughness, thoughtfulness, candor, and sense of humor made the end process smooth sailing.

Special thanks to **Dr. Rosemary Smith** for her time, careful reading, literary review, suggestions and support which were critical in bringing this work to fruition.

I thank my friend, **Jill George**, for reading various drafts of this book and sharing her sage comments.

I appreciate **Anne Marie Oborn** for her patience, superb artwork and cover design for the book.

Thank you to my sister, **Wilma Mikkelson** and to my niece/cousin, **Ahmani Daniels Fritz**, for their unwavering belief in me and for their encouragement.

Heartfelt thanks to friends, **Jerrina McKinney, Michael Chambliss**, and **Dr. Jacqueline Parson-Barker,** whose generosity and encouragement afforded me the opportunity and inspiration to focus on putting the final touches on this novel.

Contents

"In the confrontation between the stream and the rock, the stream always wins, not through strength but by perseverance."

H. Jackson Brown Jr

Pillsbury Landing

Boisterous claps–quick and loud- erupted like the sudden scattering of a school of wild geese. The blast resounded clearly and could be heard outside of the sanctuary's half-opened windows. It was offering time, and this was the congregants' usual response when it came time to pay their tenths. They were eager to show the Most High that they were givers and not just takers.

It was high noon at Travelers Rest Baptist Church. Well-dressed old men and women, mid-lifers, young adults, teens and children adorned the usual Sunday morning bouquet of worshippers. A creek, arrayed with occasional water lilies, ran alongside the church. In the sanctuary, some had come out of duty and tradition, others had come to be social, and then some had come to lift Him up!

At offering time, they came down the aisles in double rows. Parishioners—the favorite sons and daughters, the well-connected, the hangers-on, and the ordinary—strutted in their Sunday best past the table to drop their offerings or just to be seen. There was no pause in worship as the choir melodiously sang an upbeat song, and the musicians strummed, played, blew, or beat their instruments inducing a toe-tapping sound. Some congregants tapped their feet and others nodded to the rhythmic beat.

Oblique rays shone lightly through the antique, stained glass windows, warming the inner sanctuary and providing what Pastor

Brewster called "beams of hope". The sun's glow produced soft, slender rays of light that ricocheted throughout the congregation, radiating a rich prism that appeared to emanate from the glittering hats of the ladies. There were pillbox hats, veiled hats, brimmed hats, jeweled hats, and even fruit-looking hats in a combination of colors. Hats crowned the heads of the pillared elect women, the aspiring missionaries, the fashion conscious, and the humble.

Up front, a few steps below the pulpit, sat the church mothers. Some rocked slightly and watched reverently as the offering proceeded. Miss Paisley, one of the priceless treasures of the church and community, was one of these mothers. Well-regarded, she was a fixture at Travelers Rest. A seasoned church mother, she was a stalwart who had the distinct ability to encourage and inspire perseverance despite life's difficulties.

As the offering continued, a few of the mature women twinkled and flashed sweet smiles and adoring looks at the young children who walked by the offering table. Their joy was sparked by little lads and lasses who tiptoed and reached up with their short stubby fingers to place their offerings on the table.

"Such good training," whispered Mother Rollins. Her eyes danced and her round cheeks brightened when she saw the children give their offerings.

A few of the mothers and churchwomen briefly, but deliberately, looked down as Jenay passed by the offering table. Most parishioners looked straight ahead or whispered softly to those seated next to them, oblivious to her presence. The average Sunday church-goer did not know her. Some pretended not to notice her. But the long-time "traveling" faithful, especially Bessie, stole solemn side looks as she walked down the aisle. She remembered. Bessie, who never wore a hat so she could show off her long, pretty, brown hair, had been born and raised at the Landing. She claimed to know which way the water wound down the back creek—and, to let her tell it, "It flowed down to the ocean floor." She knew the twists and turns within the church and along the adjacent creek, where the skeletons lay; the surprise turns; and, generally, everybody's business. She prided herself for knowing the latest church news and possessing the longest of memories. While others guessed, Bessie knew. She thought of herself as a church historian of sorts.

"Ain't nothin' wrong with knowin' de news. What you don't know can cost you!" Bessie would sometimes exclaim emphatically. While Bessie thought she was just being herself, others saw her as a gossip and feared for her soul.

Miss Paisley was enjoying the worship service, but as she scanned the church's congregation, her eyes fell on Bessie's mocking face. She stared at Bessie, tilted her head, and looked at her over her eyeglasses. She then turned her attention to the pulpit.

This Sunday morning, Bessie was seated in the pew where she had sat for the last ten years. A perennially late arriver, she usually took her seat on the pew four rows from the back row on the left side of the sanctuary. When she was a younger woman, she had marked a seat for herself in the very last row on the right side and had sat there for seven years, that is, until the outspoken Deacon Henry Stepp, from the Methodist church around the way, joined Travelers Rest. Deacon Stepp, a large white-haired man, was a church trustee, and he was also a member of the ushers' board. He was as direct as he was faithful and timely for every church service. On his third Sunday at Travelers Rest, he had summarily done what no other member of the usher board had ever dared to do. He told Bessie Slack that the last row in the church was reserved for the church ushers, and he had directed her to sit elsewhere.

Bessie had given Deacon Stepp a dark, lingering look and

snapped under her breath what she really thought, "He ain't been here ninety days and askin' people up out de seats. He don't know nothin' about this church, no how," Bessie said to herself and to those within an earshot of her. From then on, however, she took a closer seat on the other side of the main isle, perfectly situated so she could take in the service and watch the comings and goings of the saints at an angular view. So, she had decided not to make a fuss about it. She huffed on numerous occasions that the old man, Deacon Stepp, had done her a favor anyway, but she still voiced displeasure about the deacon, - "Smokin' self, like don't nobody know it. We don't do that ovah here. Naah, what he needs to do is come clean or stay away dirty!" She delivered her angry asides in hushed tones.

But, on this luminous third Sunday in April, Bessie Slack's disdain was directed at Jenay Morgan, who was about to walk by her after giving her alms. At first, she managed to give her a sunny, but quick, welcome-home smile. A few observant, distracted choir members, whose eyes were perpetually on the front door or elsewhere, took note of Bessie's fleeting smile. They watched her nudge her seat neighbor, June, and noted how quickly the pair surveyed Jenay from head to toe and then looked at each other and snickered before shooting a perceptible look of disapproval her way, as she returned to her seat. The had known her all of her life, during both her mountain and valley days. When they heard that she had changed her name to LéJenay, while starring as an entertainer on Shaker's Island, they took it in stride because they had known her first as just Jenay, Jinger Rose Keys' wayward daughter.

Jenay felt their watchful eyes, sighs, and silence. Always a sensitive soul, she felt her face burn and her armpits itch and tingle as she walked by the offering table. The slight discomfort she felt did not deter her from looking straight ahead. She tilted her head a bit to the right and wore the most pleasant look she could muster. She even offered smiles to a few parishioners. After all, this was her church. It was right there on the front row that she had learned from Sister Satterfield in her kindergarten class that "a merry heart makes a cheerful countenance." Once she reached her seat, she let out a long, silent sigh. It was true, she thought: "Home is where the heart is."

She began to reminisce and fleetingly remembered how she had been christened in the church with her parents and godmother looking on. Then, later she had transitioned from the Little Sunbeam class to the Little Lilies singing group, youth choir, young adult choir, and finally to the Young Women's Christian League, right before she had departed Troutdale. No matter how far she wandered, "Creekside", as the teenagers called their church, always clung to her heart. And here she was, home at the Landing, at last.

Looking up, she noticed the polished wooden anchor planks that sectioned off the ceiling, adorned with seven matching, semi-fancy hanging light fixtures, which gave the small church a magnificent, airy look. She was pleasantly surprised at the lofty sight, as there had been serious talk of replacing the hanging lights with more ornate lighting fixtures. Personally, she thought this would sacrifice the quaint beauty of the sanctuary. She took in the raised fountain inset behind the pulpit, the neat and tailored drapes, and the image of a dove centered in the large, colorful stained-glass window–positioned above and behind the choir stand. Pastor Brewster and the ministerial staff sat in their high-backed designated places, before the choir, the mother's board, trustees, deacons, ushers, congregants, saints, and sinners.

It was a familiar scene; one she had spent a lot of time observing as she grew up and before she left the Landing. As Jinger Keys' daughter and only child, she spent more time than most at the church because she had accompanied her saintly mother to 9 a.m. prayer three days a week throughout her early childhood and on Saturdays as a teen. She took stock of those around her and decided that no matter what they thought of her, this was home, and your home was the place where they had to accept you as you are—or as you had been, anyway.

After the message and as the choir sang one of its closing selections, Jenay did what the wounded soul who had left Troutdale seven years before would never have done. She lifted her head and rose to her feet with her fellow parishioners, and gently swayed and clapped to the syncopated beat of a favorite gospel spiritual:

> Have you got good religion?
> Cert'nly, Lord!
>
> Have you got good religion?
> Cert'nly, Lord!
>
> Have you got good religion?
> Cert'nly, Lord!
>
> Cert'nly, cert'nly, cert'nly, Lord![1]

"Yes! I am home!" she whispered excitedly to herself. She was home to rest and renew her life in Pillsbury County, Troutdale. Unbeknownst to others, she was also home to move into her place as the new Mrs. John Taylor Barlow.

Jinger Keys, who sat near the front row, gazed into the audience and stretched to see her daughter. She was glad to see her getting into the church service. She smiled and just marveled at Jenay with a warm, glazed look. She recalled their times together and what had brought them to the present moment. Although she had had her share of life's ups and downs, she shook her head and reflected how she "wouldn't take nothing for her journey."

Pastor Brewster's post-sermon remarks of greeting and preaching at the same time broke off her thoughts, "We just so thankful and honorin' God for the return of Brother Simms and Brother Johnson. They put themselves in harm's way for you and me." The two uniformed soldiers rose to a round of warm handclaps. Pastor Brewster continued, "Next Sunday we will have Heroes Day to honor those who served us overseas. While we're thankful for the freedoms we enjoy, we know we got a long way to go yet. Aaah, we not gone talk about the gravity of winning the war or about how much things have *not* changed for our people. No, today we just glad the war is ovah and that we have mor'n what we had when the war broke out. Howsoinever, I submit to you, my brothers and sisters, that there is yet more to come— has to be. I just don't' believe He brought us this far to leave us lacking. Weah just have to wait on His timing and trust Him for a 'new normal' for our people. Can I get a amen? If I cain't get that, I'll take a 'Hep 'em, Lord.'"

"Amen!" peppered with a few "Hep 'em, Lord!" responses, rang throughout the congregation.

He continued, "We're glad also to see the return of Miss Jenay Morgan, our own sister Keys' daughter, back in the Sunday service." This brought a soft, polite congregational applause; whispers; turned heads; and some plain stares, all of which was ended when Pastor Brewster commanded, "All rise for the benediction! We gone ask our visiting minister, Reverend Wheats, to come and send us home."

Cyrus Wheats gave the closing prayer as the choir softly sang a benediction hymn. He then dismissed the congregants with the familiar edict - "What I say unto one, I say unto all, watch and pray."

At the close of the Sunday service, the parishioner's shook hands and greeted each other. Some hugged and made dinner arrangements; others caught up on church and community news.

Jinger looked eagerly over the heads of the exiting churchgoers and spotted Jenay. She greeted those around her, including one of her longtime, close friends, Miss Paisley.

Miss Paisley smiled warmly at Jinger, joyfully squeezed both of their hands together and said, "I saw Jenay in the service. She made such a fine young lady!"

Jinger, glowing, smiled and nodded to her friend, heartily acknowledged those in her path, spread around a few hugs, and patted a few little ones on the head as she walked toward the doors of the church.

Jenay greeted some of the churchgoers, but no one really held a conversation with her. She received a few hugs from exiting parishioners, hand waves, and smiles. She was thankful for these brief gestures because, as she recalled, most Travelers did not really know how to speak just for the sake of saying hello or to inquire about one's general well-being. Instead, they were inclined to ask intrusive or obnoxious questions and, as the old folks would say, "get in yo' business." For this reason, she was content with the few pedestrian greetings that came her way.

Jinger met her Jenay in the foyer and gave her a sweeping hug and a loving up-and-down look before the two of them descended the outside church steps. Brother Colbert, noting Jinger's stilted descent, interrupted his conversation with two deacons, and rushed to assist. "Watch it, naah, Mother," he said as he helped Jenay deliver her mother to the ground level. She flashed a warm grin and thanked Brother Colbert, who smiled and nodded in return. He gave a brief, shy, tentative nod to Jenay, tucked his head, squeezed his hat, walked a few steps backward, and rejoined his deacon brothers.

Jinger gave her daughter a bright Sunday-morning smile and a cheek kiss before they looped arms. The two headed for her neat, small home, which was located a fourth of a mile from the church, near the Parson's Row. Chatting parishioners kept up their conversations, but some stared as the two women headed home arm in arm past a swath of golden, gently swaying daffodils, stirring in the Sunday-afternoon breeze.

2

Mulberry Ash

Jenay had left Troutdale searching for her own way as an aggrieved twenty-year-old. Although this had distressed Jinger at the time, she decided not to dwell on the past, since it was her daughter's homecoming. She focused instead on the joy of her return and the special Sunday supper she had prepared. Having been away from home for seven years, Jenay looked forward to her mother's cooking.

After they sampled a homemade supper of snap peas, stuffing, yams, potato salad, roasted herb hen with gravy, peach tea, and peach cobbler à la mode, Jinger offered her daughter a bowl of berries. She declined, however, stating that she was already too full. Jenay thanked her mother for such a tasty, wonderful dinner. She heartily poured them both a cup of coffee and pretended not to notice the disappointed look that crossed her mother's face.

"Well, we can eat it later. I got a pound cake coming from Flossie's, so we'll eat this and that later," she said.

"Sounds good, Momma," she replied, in spite of the fact that she knew she had eaten her last morsel for the day.

As she cleared the table, Jinger quietly observed her daughter, pondering a difference of some sort in her. "Well, I know you're trying to keep your schoolgirl figure and all, but a little meat on those bones won't hurt," she said playfully.

Jenay blushed, because even as an adult, she found that she was still not able to hide anything from her mother. As she watched Jinger replace the berries into the icebox, she surveyed her mother's comfortable home and longed for a home of her own. She reminisced about her days as a young girl. She vaguely remembered when they had first moved to their house at 900 Mulberry Ash. The bare, seven-room house that she remembered had blossomed into a homey, unforgettable dwelling. She smiled at the familiar surroundings about her that held so many memories. Jinger caught her wistful reverie.

"And what does my tea cake find so amusing?" she inquired, smiling.

Before Jenay could share her pleasure of all things good with her mother, there was a ring at the front door. Noticing her reluctance to see who was buzzing, Jinger coaxed her.

"Go on, Jenay. Open the door."

When she answered the door, she was relieved to see a young boy of about nine years old bearing a covered plate. He asked for Miss Rosie, the name his grandmother called Jinger, and Jenay asked him to come in and go back to the kitchen.

"Well, hello, Gregory. How are you?" Jinger sweetly inquired.

"Um all right. My grammy sent you this cake."

"Oh, how nice. You tell your grammy I said thanks for me, you hear? And here are some nickels to go into your camping fund."

"Thank you, ma'am!" he responded as his innocent, gleeful eyes opened wide.

He took a small cloth sack out of his pocket and happily deposited fifteen silver nickels, thanked Miss Rosie again, and surveyed his coins as he left.

"You're welcome, child…and don't forget to tell your grammy hello and thanks for the cake."

"I won't!"

Jenay watched and listened to the exchange. She then showed the boy to the door and walked onto the front porch. As Gregory

scampered away, she instinctively peeked both ways down
Mulberry Ash. Jinger saw her street-ward glance but said nothing.

Having arrived late at night the day before, Jenay had only
spent a brief time with her mother before they retired. So, after
dinner, they moved to the parlor, opened the front door, but kept
the screen door shut in order to let in a cool breeze. Jenay was
brimming with family, church, and community inquiries. Jinger
was happy to share news of the past seven years, pausing at times
to share programs, newspaper clippings, and obituaries.

"Oh, look. You have the news story about Marian Anderson
singing at the White House!"

"Yes, that was really something that she had the opportunity
to sing in such a high place. They tell me our late president's wife,
Eleanor, had a lot to do with it. My, how she has shown herself to
be a friend to all people," Jinger smiled and nodded.

"I was in Saint Martin when I heard about it, and it just made
me smile with pride."

"Yes, that was a great day. It's not every day that people get a
chance. I always say just be ready to shine in case you are called
upon to share your gift," responded Jinger as she quietly studied
her daughter during the light banter. But she tired long before
Jenay could ask all of her questions and before she could learn
about her daughter's sojourn since she had left Troutdale. Jinger
indicated they would have a long time to catch up and that she
needed to lie down for a spell.

"This is what happens when you get older. You just don't have
the stamina that you once did—enjoy your youth while you can,"
she instructed, cheerfully.

As Jenay rose to walk her mother to her bedroom to lie down,
she surveyed her surroundings again and yawned because she,
too, was tired from her train journey. She helped her mother to
her place of rest; propped up her pillows, just as her mother had

done for her as a young girl; closed the door halfway; and went to her familiar bedroom to rest. Before lying down, she gazed at the flower-edged wallpaper and the few stuffed animals perched on a corner shelf. She looked around the room and noted the stillness of the black-and-white photos of singers, old school and family photographs of times past. A necklace, half-placed in a jewelry box on the dresser, caught her eye. She remembered both the pearls and the matching dollies beneath the jewel case and antique lamps. Although the contents of the room were dated, the air was fresh with the scent of pine oil. Looking around, she mused to herself that the room was too pristine for someone not to have dusted it recently. She imagined her mother had deep cleaned the room just as she had done every spring, and fall, from the time when she was just a little girl. Her doll-filled rocker swayed softly, stirred by a crisp breeze from the slightly opened bedroom window. Other than the rearrangement of an old trunk that doubled as a hope chest, she detected that things hadn't changed much. She sat on the bed, took in a deep breath, and exhaled.

She instinctively took out a small case from her purse and studied the bronze face on it. John Barlow smiled at her from the locket. She looked at the picture of her husband, admired his handsome features—his short-cropped hair and the smooth texture of his tanned skin—and smiled sentimentally. She read gentleness and a quiet determination into his arresting face. She then closed the trinket, lay down, and pondered over how she would break the news to her mother.

She shifted, stretched her body in bed, and luxuriated at the thought of being back in Troutdale. She missed the folksy ways of the people and the innocent, simple way they lived their lives. She thought of how she used to jump rope with her neighbor Penny Poteet and how she had missed her so badly when her mother abruptly sent her away to live with her sister upstate for some reason. She still wished she could have had a chance to say good-bye to her playmate.

She reveled deeper into her childhood and thought of the cool summer evenings when she and her new best friend, Nina, played on the front lawn in their bare feet, doing cartwheels as they ran. Nina was never as much fun as Penny, but she was an appealing companion to spend time with, nonetheless. She remembered the fragrant smell of freshly planted flowers, especially the work required to grow them; the colorful flowerbed near the porch; the smell of the red-clay earth; and the static sounds of her mother's radio. Jenay recalled how Jinger and her friend Ms. Cozy Lee, who lived around the corner on the next block, would visit, and then the women would walk each other home on summer evenings, never, seemingly, running out of things to talk about. She also recalled how she and Nina would laugh at the high-pitched cackling sound that Miss Cozy made when she was tickled. Her laughter could be heard halfway down the block. And she relived the feeling of cool drops of water on her face from the water sprinklers. When they came on, this meant their playtime was over and that they would be turning in for the evening soon.

As the breeze softened, tossing the lace linen curtains, Jenay did what was natural. She fell into a sound sleep and she dreamed:

It was a silky night at dusk in Saint Croix—or was it Saint Thomas? The long rehearsals had paid off. The audience was attentive and responsive. The patrons' eyes were fixed on her. They watched with a low glow in their eyes as they drank their champagne, scotch, and hard liquor. They spoke in low tones and gently swayed to the tempo of a medley of familiar songs. Heads bobbed; toes

*tapped; romantics whispered. The club room was elegant
with sparkly platinum chandeliers. There sat Joe Robinson
"Rob", the piano player, who followed her lead nightly. It
was he who had taught her to let her voice flow. She read
the patrons. Caucasians and Negroes dotted the audience.
The two races, mostly people of means, were elegant in their
dress, manners, and taste—separate in most ways but with
a common purpose, to hear cool jazz and a little blues to
drown out the tensions of daily life. By letting them listen
to her soothing voice, if only for a few hours, she felt like
she was helping them cope with life. She aimed to please,
singing lyrical, soulful tunes of their liking as she had so
many nights before.*

She was in the middle of singing a popular ballad in her
dream when she was awakened by the sound of a closing door.
Jinger had looked in on her as she napped and tried to quietly
close her slightly cracked bedroom door, but over the years, the
door had never been repaired, and it closed, as usual, with a clack.
Jenay checked the clock, and it was half past five. She lay for a few
moments and then washed her face, combed her hair, brushed her
teeth, and rejoined her mother in the dining room in hopes that
she would be regaled once again of missed moments.

Jinger had other plans, though, and she asked her daughter to
join her for a walk. She brought along a rainbow-colored basket
so they could pick spring wildflowers and berries on the way,
just as they had in times past. As they began their deliberate trek
around Mulberry Ash, Jenay recollected the lavender, the crepe
myrtle trees and the golden irises, lilies, violets, daffodils, and
feather grass that lined the neighborhood pond. Just as vivid and
visible in her mind were memories of the ever-flowing fountains
and of the European figures that graced the waterfall at the park.

The "Europeans," as they were called, displayed a stark contrast to the actual people and surroundings of Mulberry Ash. The elevated statues, situated in front of the waterfall, was that of a French gentleman placing a gilded pair of slippers on the perfect, tiny feet of a lady socialite. There was an airiness in their manner, almost arrogance, as the gentleman placed the once-shiny slipper on the coy woman's foot. Jenay had imagined they had been preparing for a ball where they could flaunt their affluence and position in life in front of those who were less fortunate.

"They must not know they're in the Ash," she had said to herself, chuckling, in times past.

"Ash" was the slang term for Mulberry Ash, which she and her friends called their close-knit community. She delighted in the vibrant, fragrant flowers and the culturally and economically misplaced European figures.

As they approached the roundabout, she recalled past days of frolicking on the greens until dusk most summer evenings. She gaily recalled the games, hunts, parties and fun in the Ash.

As they walked past the park fountains, both commented on the playfulness of the little ones, consumed in their games of tag and hide-and-go-seek under their parents' watchful eyes.

Just then a gaggle of girls and young boys ran toward the pond blossoms.

"Would you look at those little daffodils?" Jinger noted as they both looked on with delight. "They're having themselves a ball, just a-running in the wind. Reminds me of when you were little like that. You all were busy, but you were easy to look after at that age…"

"Till we grew up and went from kid games to the game of life," retorted Jenay cheerlessly.

"Yes, then it's a different story. Life has a way of blowing us to and 'fro, but we just have to keep moving, whether the day is sunny or blue. We must always put our trust in Him. If we do that and persevere through the storms of life, we can snap back, run our race, and look good doing it. Kind of like those free-running daffodils streaming in the breeze around that fountain; they're not worried about a thing." Jinger paused and then continued, "When children are young, it is such a precious time. As a matter of fact, I ran across some Easter pictures of you, Penny, and Wyatt the other day."

The mention of Wyatt's name drew discernible silence from Jenay. Mother and daughter remembered those pictures but seemed stunned by the sudden recall. Sensing a staggering quietness on her daughter's part at the mention of Wyatt, Jinger spoke again of nature and the weather as they continued their casual walk around the Ash.

Jenay did not mind her mother's somewhat deliberate gait. Jinger Rose was not an old woman, but she had fallen from a short ladder while cleaning the year before, which left her with an ever-so-slight limp in her walk. Jinger never dwelled on it, since she was not one to draw attention to herself. Seeing her mother again, new limp and all, Jenay managed to enjoy the familiar beauty of Mulberry Ash with joyful revelry.

Their home—located near their church and the town square—was near a lively, center section of Troutdale. When she was growing up, this location was seen as an advantage by their friends and relatives, as many of them had to traverse miles to get to town from rural areas for business, shopping, church, and pleasure.

As the two completed their flower-and blueberry-gathering errand, they began the short walk back home. Looking down at their basket, they laughed at their sparse gatherings of flowers and berries. Looking up, they could not help but notice the alluring sky composed of the setting sun and the slow moving, thinly stretched clouds which were tinged with an apricot hue. The splendor of the scene was made vibrant by the backdrop of the green Carolina hills which were speckled with brilliant lavender and light pink streaks, modeling perfectly the representation of a prize water-colored painting. Mother and daughter marveled at the beauty of the time and place.

As they neared their home, they spotted Miss Paisley sitting on her front porch. She waved and beckoned for them to stop by. Jinger waved and returned a warm greeting but said she needed to go home but would return soon. She had a home errand to attend to but encouraged her daughter to spend a while and visit Miss Paisley. Jenay agreed, as she had always been fond of and admired their neighbor. Jinger then left the younger and older woman to visit as she made her way home five houses down the street. It was time to soak and "rest off of her feet" awhile. First, though, she would lay out the ingredients for a small batch of blueberry jam.

3

Island Blues

As Miss Paisley waited for her erstwhile young neighbor to come up to the porch, she was going through her normal process of deep reflection. "Over the years, this I have learned for sure… to 'not be weary in well doing, for we will surely reap, if we faint not.' True that," she thought, nodding as she referenced a familiar Galatian scripture.

"Welcome back home, Miss Jen. It is so nice to see you. I was wonderin' if you all might have a lil' time to visit, and here you are."

She was happy to sit and talk to Miss Paisley again, as she had when she was younger. She waved to her mother and gave her hostess a big hug. Then she sat in one of her "visiting chairs" on the front porch.

"Well naah, it's been a long time since I saw ya. What on earth have you been doing since ya been gone?"

"I have been just trying to get my life together since I left here, but I am really happy about this trip home. There is so much beauty here and so many memories…good and not so good… you know?"

"I know what ya sayin'. We just have to take the bitter along with the sweet in life. I always knew things would work out for you."

"There is so much to tell you. Let's see where should I begin?" she thought aloud.

"Well, why don't you tell me about some of your most

memorable experiences while you were away. That way you might get your mind wanderin' and ya mouth talkin'," she said with a comforting grin.

Miss Paisley had a way of making people feel at ease and talkative. She was one of the best listeners in the community, and she never seemed to pass judgment on anyone. Even though she had only finished nine grades in school, she was a wise woman and she was sagely aware of how to weather challenges. She let others know she had trials in life and enemies like others, but she would say in the same breath that their importance to her was "teeny tiny".

Jenay thought about this respected matriarch's love for her neighbors and their children. Over the years, more than a few individuals in the community sought her advice, so she felt comfortable sharing with her.

"After me and my sweetheart, Wyatt, broke up, I had to get away. I had to work awhile and save in order to do it, but I was determined to leave and see what else life had to offer besides Troutdale. The thing that made me determined to leave was the uncomfortable way people, especially church people, made me feel after me and Wyatt parted ways. The stares and the silence were hard to take. And then there was the attention from Bousley. Oh, my goodness…I just had to leave after that one." She shook her head and remembered in disgust. "I knew I wouldn't be here long after that. I really felt betrayed and shocked by the suddenness of the breakup with Wyatt, so I wanted to get as far away from the Landing as possible but without hurting Momma. I tried to stay after I graduated. But after a while, I just had to move on."

"I understand. Jes' what did you move on to?"

"Well, I'm not sure how to tell you. A lot has happened that

I have not even shared with momma yet. I want to sit and talk with her, but maybe I can share with you first."

"It's okay. Jes' start talkin'. I'm listening."

"I know you have probably heard things about me from the gossips in town."

"That doesn't matter any. I'm hearing what you want me to hear from your angle. It really doesn't matter what anyone else has to say!"

"Without going into much detail, I'll start with the beauty I found abroad. I didn't ever think that I would wind up on a beautiful island in the Caribbean Sea. There is something about an island that is magical, even mystical, but definitely soothing. Miss Paisley, you would enjoy sitting on a porch on the island of Saint Croix. You would love to feel the ocean breezes on your face and the warm white sand under your feet. And Miss Paisley, the people...the people are beautiful too, inside and outside. Even I felt creative and very peaceful."

"Umm hum, I can feel the breezes now." She listened with visions of the young woman's reflection.

"This beautiful island was the result of the first, most important experience I had while I was away. It is a little harder to talk about. Oh, nothing horrible happened or anything; it is just troublesome because of my upbringing. As you know, I love music. I love to sing whether I am alone or in a crowd. In Saint Croix, I wanted to explore new ways to improve and use my singing talents and explore new places."

"I hear you, and I understand. Keep on."

"I met some wonderful people before I went to Saint Croix. We all became friends. To get right to the matter, the people were talented musicians who entertained people in... well... nightclubs! They liked my singing, they asked me to join the group, and I did just that. Now Miss Paisley, I want you to know that I did not take on any bad habits of any kind or become a wanton woman or anything like that, but I sang in nightclubs where people smoked cigars and cigarettes, drank liquor, and danced boldly. But whenever I sang, they would slow down or sit down and listen. The words of the ballads I sang seemed to reach them. It's funny, but most of the time, I could tell what kind of songs the people wanted to hear. I felt good when I sang and even better when people enjoyed the melody's I chose for them…I also had true friendship with the band members, and that made me feel comfortable. I really enjoyed these two experiences. However, deep down, I always worried about how my singing in nightclubs might affect Momma. You know there are big gossips in church, and someone was bound to see me and distort the facts. I could tell Miss Bessie had been running her mouth because she had a big smirk on her face when she saw me in church that told everything."

"Now, don't you go gettin' all upset about that busybody. She doesn't have much of a life for herself, so she makes up stuff about other folks. She doesn't matter much. Make Miss Bessie and those like her, teeny tiny in ya life! Go on with your story. I'm pleased so far."

Feeling reassured, she continued. "As for the third experience, this is where it gets to be difficult, because I haven't even told Momma yet. I am somewhat nervous about telling her, but I know I must. You see, I fell in love again. I fell in love with a wonderful man, and I never thought I could be this happy again…with anyone or anything in my life."

"Why, that's wonderful!" Miss Paisley stopped rocking and beamed at her young guest. "I sense that there is more that you want to say. Please, go on, but I want you to think about if you really want to tell me first. Are you sure ya don't want to tell your momma first?"

"I understand the position this puts you in, so I guess I will wait and share the news with the both of you together," she said thoughtfully. Miss Paisley nodded her agreement.

"At this point, I'm apprehensive because it is not so much that I am in love again, it's who I am in love with that may cause Momma some surprise."

"Sure enough?" Miss Paisley wondered aloud in suspense. She resumed rocking in her chair and pondered quietly.

The younger woman then inquired about Miss Paisley's health and well-being. The matriarch briefly shared a few of her trials and joys from previous years. There was a natural pause in the conversation and Miss Paisley began to softly hum a familiar hymn. This tune wafted through the air to the approaching Jinger. She almost stopped in her tracks. She vividly remembered a similar song from her childhood.

As Jinger ascended the porch steps, Jenay anxiously waited to share the news with her. This discernment was bolstered as Miss Paisley mentioned that she had seen Townley Jacobs walking down the street in front of her home earlier that day. She then knew that she must break the news that very evening, lest Townley, who was thrilled with the match, share his enthusiasm with others in the neighborhood and the news reach her mother prior to her revelation.

Jenay decided not to go into detail about her island life with her mother, but she was anxious to share news of a personal nature. As the three women talked quietly, she shared her glad tidings. Jinger was surprised, and so was Miss Paisley, when she revealed who the new love of her life was. The biggest emotional reaction came from Jinger when her daughter revealed not only the man's name but the fact that they were already married.

4

Baywater Beginnings

Surprises—some good but mostly bad—always seemed to rush into Jinger's life. An unexpected refuge had been forced upon her and Rustin when their urban home life had taken an abrupt turn, and they had been sent to the South to live with relatives. As her world collapsed, Jinger didn't know whether to count it as a blessing or as a mishap. Looking back, it seemed to her that life had a way of snatching her to safety before things got too bad. Even her name had been changed, for Jinger was first known as Jimmie. She was the oldest of three children of Olivera Mack Jackson and named after her mother's oldest brother, Jimmy. By the time "Ollie", as she was called, turned twenty-three years old, she was living as a single mother in Baywater.

Jimmie retained vague memories of a few of her mother's boyfriends visiting their tiny, dilapidated apartment in Baywater, but she never knew any of them to be her daddy. She did know that she and Rustin had the same father, whoever he was, but their little sister, Katy Marie, had a different father.

Early on, Jimmie noticed the way people made a difference between herself, her sister, and her brother. People would comment on Katy's good looks and then ask their mother, "And whose children are these?" Occasionally, older, more clever women would boldly add, "These two is cute too, though." Jimmie always interpreted such comments, referring to her and Rustin, as insincere afterthoughts and wondered about her mother's silence and long, pensive looks during such encounters.

Ollie usually answered that she was briefly married to Jimmie and Rustin's father. Having never met him, Jimmie could not recall this as a fact.

They did, however, see Katy's dad. He brought Ollie and Katy gifts and sweets. He usually told Katy to be sure to share with her brother and sister. But when he came by for buggy rides, only Ollie and Katy left with Mr. Carlyle. He stood out in Jimmie's memory because he was tall, had a moustache, and was really light-skinned for a Negro man. She remembered that he would pick Katy Marie up, twirl her in the air, and talk to her, referring to her as his "Carly". Their mother sometimes used this name to refer to their sister, as well. This confused Jimmie and Rustin because they knew their sister as Katy Marie or Lil' Katy. Jimmie felt rejected when Zoot Carlyle took her mother and sister for rides without ever inviting her and Rustin to go along. During the rides, Jimmie and Rustin stayed with Miss Ethyl Wells, who lived in an equally dilapidated apartment to the right of their own.

From as far back as she and Rustin could recall, Ollie liked to "high time"—as they called it—meaning she liked to go to clubs, parties, and consume the nightlife in uptown Baywater. When she was going to be out late or all night, Ollie arranged for their neighbor, Miss Wells to watch her children. But one day, Miss Wells abruptly moved to Gary. She said she was needed to watch her grandchildren while her daughter went to work in a factory. Afterward, Ollie occasionally asked her sister, Katie Jean, to watch them when she went out on the weekends or when Zoot picked up his two-favorite people for Sunday rides miles away from their city dwelling.

After Jimmie turned eight years old, the siblings were left home alone, at times. On such evenings, Ollie would leave her oldest child to care for the three of them while she went out for the evening. Before she left, she usually knelt and looked Jimmie in her eyes. She reminded her that she was a big girl and that she was not to open the door to anyone but Aunt Katie, Miss Vera, or Uncle Jake. She nodded yes, but she disliked it when Ollie left. Despite this, and her mother's obvious indifference, she dearly loved her anyway.

She was often at her side when she was at home, and she was always eager to help with chores. She longed to please her mother, whom she affectionately called "Mollie". If not every night, she did see Mollie every day. Although she could tell that her mother favored her half-sister, Jimmie savored the way Mollie held all three of them before she left their apartment in the evenings. She usually climbed on the bumpy sofa, that served as a bed for Rustin, to peek through the curtains of the left front-room window and watch Mollie as she walked outdoors and turned in the direction of uptown Baywater. Then she ran to the only other window in their apartment, the right front-room window, and peered down the street until she saw Mollie get into a horse-driven buggy and leave. She sometimes cried softly until she felt the tug of tiny, fat fingers on her skirt bottom. Looking into the searching eyes of her baby sister, Katy Marie, Jimmie would dry her own tears and give her sister a bottle and a wooden toy. The three of them played until they fell asleep. Jimmie was always careful to keep the curtains closed and make sure the door was locked before they began their play time for the evening and before falling to sleep.

Mollie was short for "Mother" and "Ollie". Ollie trained her children to call her Mollie, instead of Momma. Barely into her twenties, she said "Momma" made her feel old. Her three children doted on her and clung to her, having no father in the home. But Ollie found this confining. And while she loved her children, she loathed unopened and opened paper packages of oatmeal, diaper duty, and the clingy, needy look of her three offspring as they stared at her sometimes with quizzical looks, starving for her affection. She hugged her children every day, but she pampered her greater longing for adult companionship by going to the dingy clubs in the town slums to sample the limited nightlife of Baywater.

Jimmie's Mollie was a fair-skinned woman with freckles, slightly wavy, brown hair, and pretty, womanly features. She was of medium height and slimly built. Of the three of them, Katy looked the most like her mother, for she was a light bright like Mr. Carlyle, her daddy. Jimmie wished that her mother could have been as warm as she was beautiful. She was friendly enough, but she always seemed slightly uncomfortable with others, including her own children. Jimmie interpreted her mother's aloofness as shyness and longed to be lovely and elegant like her when she grew up. Her desperate wish, though, was that her mother would spend more time with the three of them and light up when she was with them like she did when she got ready to go out on the town.

Times were lean, so they often ate rice, pinto beans, and squash with ham hocks, thanks to the generosity of their neighbor, who lived in an apartment directly across from their own. Miss Vera was raising her nephew as her own son. He brought home leftover meat scraps and fruit from his job as a butcher's helper at the community grocery store. She happily shared all of this with Ollie's children as often as she could.

Miss Vera often observed how Ollie's three basked in their mother's occasional, but sparse attention. She mentioned to the younger woman that children were a blessing and urged her to spend time with them while they were young because in her words, "They won't be little long—just you watch and see!"

Afterward, Ollie would look at her children, wonder how Miss Vera would know, dismiss her neighbor's words and toss her hair. She would then look Miss Vera's way and say, "I love my children, that's a fact, but I'm young and it's time to live my life for the right time, and the right time is the nighttime!"

It pained Miss Vera to hear her speak this way, so she eventually started visiting less often. At some point, she began sending her nephew to Ollie's place with meat scraps, goodies, and fruit bags for Jimmie, Rustin, and Lil' Katy.

During Ollie and Katy Marie's infrequent trips with Mr. Carlyle, Miss Vera could be seen peering through her slightly opened curtains with a wide-eyed look. Hers was the face of concern, as if the sight of the three of them was a scary thing; a thing of jeopardy. Jimmie often spied on her neighbor's pensive looks. On a few occasions, Miss Vera surprisingly came over and ushered them into her apartment, which was slightly bigger than their place, after "Miss Lola", as she was known in the streets, had left for the evening. Jimmie remembered these events because their neighbor gave them oatmeal along with biscuits and syrup, let them listen to music on her shiny gramophone, and allowed them to play as long as they wanted. Sometimes she sang to them at bedtime.

While Jimmie had fragmented memories of her childhood with Miss Vera, she had lucid memories of Uncle Jake. He was a giant figure to Jimmie, Rustin, and Katy Marie. He was obese, walked with a limp, and had stony, piercing eyes. But Uncle Jake could be playful and seemed like a kind man. He always had extra quarters in his pockets to buy the kids ice cream; this kept them occupied while he visited with Mollie.

Jake Burns was a man with an outgoing personality, a gift for gab, and a vast knowledge of nightlife and the streets. He possessed time to spend, money to burn, and a decided way with people. Ollie's children were all familiar with his visits, as he would stop by and ask in a booming voice, "Ollie, whatcha know good?" The two would then visit for hours, sharing Baywater news. He would lend her money and warn her about certain fellows in the streets and in the clubs. It seemed like everyone who lived in the urban, run-down Uptown Apartments knew Uncle Jake. Good ole Uncle Jake, always there with a listening ear, advice, and a helping hand.

On occasion, while Ollie was out for the evening, Jake looked in on her children. He claimed he was an old friend of her father, Cecil, but she had no way of knowing this for sure, since her father died shortly after she had left the country town of Milton, Georgia, where she had been raised. He gladly took an interest in Ollie and her offspring, so they eventually started calling him "Uncle Jake", although there was no biological relation. Having no father figure in her life, Jimmie, especially, took to him. She felt guardedly comfortable by his presence. As the oldest, she had Mollie's permission to let him into the apartment when she was not there. Her fond memory of Uncle Jake came to a jolting end when she was eight years old. One Sunday evening, she heard her Aunt Katie Jean speaking in hushed tones with Mollie.

"How you gone leave yo' chil'ren with a man to look after them while you out at de club?"

"I didn't leave 'em with Jake."

"Who did you leave 'em with then?"

"Jimmie's a big girl now. She keeps her brother and sister while I am out. She musta let Jake in."

"You musta told her it was all right to let him in. Jimmie's jes' a child herself. You cain't blame her for nothin'! How she gone be responsible for three kids?"

"She did a good job in the past."

Agitated, Katie began talking in a loud and heated fashion. "A good job? You cain't leave yo chil'ren without somebody who is grown and responsible. You put yo' own children in danger! You coulda asked me; I woulda watched them my damn self!"

Although they were full sisters, Ollie was the fairer and more petite of the two. Katie was somewhat thick, big boned and slightly taller than her younger sibling. She towered over her sister's lithe frame. As Katie's voice became louder, Jimmie felt the heat in her aunt's voice. At one point, she sounded like she was holding back tears. Her next words shockingly revealed why Katy, her sister, had recently seemed so withdrawn, and tearful.

"I found that big ox with no shirt on in the kitchen on de floor with yo' little girl. I grabbed de broom handle and went afta that big joka!" Aunt Katie angrily stated.

Jimmie could not believe that all of this had happened while she and Rustin had been asleep. As her aunt's voice became louder, she described how she had yelled out into the hallway that night to attract neighbors. Miss Vera's nephew had run over first to help Katie, while Miss Vera called the police. More neighbors and the police eventually arrived at the apartment, and Jake had been taken to city jail. Katy was taken to the hospital.

While no one had explained to Jimmie why Lil' Katy had spent the night in the hospital, she sensed it was for a dark reason. Her Aunt Katie later told her and Rustin that she had been admitted for "observation", but Jimmie did not know what this meant. Ollie began to sob, which intensified Aunt Katie's anger.

"What you cryin' naah for? You livin' de life you chose. I've never seen so many trifling young women who call themselves mothers in all my life!"

"Well, at least I am a mother," Ollie spitefully responded.

"You call yo'self a mother? You won't even let these children call you Momma. What is that?" she bristled.

"But I do love my children. I'm not the problem; big, funky

Jake is the problem. And he is supposed to have religion," Ollie retorted.

"Oh, so now he funky," she said mockingly. "And religion? You don't know de Lord when yo' whole conversation is de streets!"

"Jake is wicked, and he knows betta," cried out Ollie.

"Yeah, he's wicked all right. But you need to keep yo' ass out de streets and look afta yo' own chil'ren! I don' know how many times I'm gone have to tell you that. If you don't want yo' children, you ought to give them to someone who cares about them and will give them a safe, stable place to grow up and a fightin' chance in life."

"But I do want my children," Ollie said quietly while sniffling.

"Well, you sho' got a funny way of showing it!" Katie snapped, coldly.

When the police responded, big, pitiful, repentant Jake pled with them not to take him in and said that nothing had happened. He claimed that Katie Jean had showed up just before he had come to himself. He got no sympathy from the policemen, however. Unfazed, the lead investigator's flat, detached response was, "Book him." He was arrested pending an investigation to determine if a lewd act with a child under twelve had occurred.

At the time, Jimmie never discovered what had happened to her sister, Katy, because within a few days, she and Rustin were placed on a train bound for Georgia to live with relatives of Mollie and Katie.

Jimmie knew one thing, though: her mother did not accompany them to the train station. She also remembered her Aunt Katie's tearful good-bye. She tightly embraced Jimmie and Rustin with both arms. When they asked their aunt about their sister, she said Katy Marie was at a city haven and that she would probably remain in Baywater. She told them not to worry about

Lil' Katy and that she would make sure that the three of them would see each other again one day. Their aunts tender look and good-bye stayed in Jimmie's mind, but it was how sweetly she revealed how much she loved the two of them that touched Jimmie the most. She explained that she would keep Jimmie and Rustin and raise them herself if she had a fit and proper place for them. This was not possible, given that she lived in a room atop Murdoch's Liquor Store.

"That's not enough space and no place to raise two precious chil'ren," she said to them at the train station.

Aunt Katie promised that if her circumstances ever improved and she was able to get a proper home, she would send for them to come and live with her. She said she had hopes that little Katy would follow them, but she did not think the city folks would allow her to live too far away from her daddy. She then looked each of them in the eyes and told them to be good and not give their kin, the Maxwells, any trouble.

"Remember to not be too trusting of other people. You two stick together and love one another. Outside of that, only de good Lord is your true friend, and he's a present help in de time of trouble. And if you get de chance, get you some book learning. They tell me that book learning leads to higher wages and ah easier life, but be sho' to keep de common touch," she lovingly added.

"Yessim," Jimmie and Rustin responded in unison as tears rolled down their faces.

Aunt Katie's long hug and tearful good-bye was Jimmie's warm final memory of Baywater. She cried, though, for her Mollie and wondered why she did not come to the train station and bid the two of them good-bye. Jimmie and Rustin would never see or hear from Mollie's sister, Aunt Katie, again.

On a Sunday morning in December, Katie was finishing

her graveyard-shift duties at Murdoch's Bar. A few late patrons wanted ice cream and, after making small talk and filling their orders, she went to replace the homemade ice cream in the freezer. She decided to make herself a bowl of ice cream and return to the bar to eat it as she finished her work and closed the liquor store. She bent over and reached into a low drawer beneath the icebox for a spoon. As soon as she stood up, she felt a sharp pain in her left and then right shoulders. As she stooped in pain, she felt a warm burst from her heart. She then slumped over and slid silently to the floor. The metal dipper, filled with ice cream, tumbled and landed beside her. As Katie took her last breaths, the three lingering bar guests, Della, Lee Ray, and Joe Black, laughed and told exaggerated stories. They reminisced and told half-truths, tall tales, and lies well into the wee morning hours.

"Katie dat busy she couldn't come out for a few minutes and at least make some small talk?" queried Joe Black.

"Naw, dat's not like her," said Lee Ray, shaking his head.

"Humph, that heifer can be sometimey, if ya ask me," Della snorted.

"Er'body sometimey to you. We not gone talk about how you sometimes up, sometimes down, and sometimes level to the ground ya damn self!" countered Lee Ray.

"Shut the hell up!" yelled Della.

"Joe Black!" shouted Lee Ray with a big mocking grin on his face.

"Huh?" responded Joe Black.

"Tell us a joke or two," said Lee Ray.

Joe Black, a dark-skinned, wide-eyed fellow who sat at the bar, stood up and bowed.

"Why, sho'. Allow me." He stood with his beer mug held high and engaged them in a sing-song voice, "I got this between my finger and my thumb; if I don't drink it all, I'll leave you some."

Joe Black shook his head side to side comically as he rehearsed this saying, while Della and Lee Ray laughed.

He then continued, "I think de Lawd, den blest de cook." Then he looked over his shoulder and concluded, "If you don' b'lieve it, come and look!"

He exaggerated his words and rolled his eyes during this whole drunken performance. Although these two had heard these sayings and witnessed his gestures before, they bent over laughing at Joe, instead of with him. They laughed at his appearance, his slightly tattered clothes, his yellowy eyes, and at the comical way that he presented himself. Good naturedly, and out of necessity, Joe would return to his drinking buddies and faux friends a few nights each week at Murdoch's.

As Katie lay dying in the back room, the liquor store patrons continued with their storytelling before they tired and left Murdoch's one-by-one, too inebriated to wonder why no one tended the bar or locked the door behind them as they left to face the early-morning chill.

It was several hours before daybreak when Katie was discovered by her half-brother, Eddie Bee, who always entered and left through the back door. He usually came by the liquor store around 2 a.m. for a nightcap and to keep Katie company while she closed the store. He would have been by earlier, but during the early morning hours, there had been a hold-up of a food delivery wagon at the corner of Seventh and Sycamore. He knew the delivery driver and waited with him until the police arrived and took a report. By the time he got to Murdoch's, Katie Jean's cold, rigid body had been made stiff by the coolness of the open deep freezer and the chilly visitation of death. When Eddie laid her body over on the floor, her eyes were partially open and looked as though they were fixated on a distant but welcomed destination.

Eddie Bee took Katie's death in the worst way. After locking the bar doors, he sat beside her still body, repeatedly called out her name and wailed for her. Only the silent tables, chairs, barstools, freezer, and cash register bore witness to his deafening cries. After a while, he called the Murdochs on the crank phone located on the kitchen wall.

"Come now," he said languidly to Mrs. Murdoch. "It's Katie."

He could not bring himself to utter the words that Katie Jean had gone to her reward. Sensing the unusual, understated urgency in Eddie's voice, the Murdochs hurried to the bar.

When they arrived, old man Murdoch's legs immediately betrayed him, and he fell to the floor upon seeing Katie. He sat there staring at her, remembering the good times and talks he had had with her in the past. He wept for himself; he wept for Katie; he wept for Eddie Bee because he knew her brother had lost the one person who knew him best. After his initial shock, Mr. Murdoch rose, gently closed Katie's eyes and covered her with a tablecloth. Mrs. Murdoch, sobbing like she had lost a dear sister, comforted Eddie while her husband called the undertaker.

News of Katie's passing and the way it happened swept throughout the bleak inner-city community. Many were saddened to hear of her demise, as she was known as one who vigorously stood for her convictions.

Jimmie and Rustin knew nothing about the passing of their aunt until nearly a year after they had arrived at their new home.

The train ride from Baywater was memorable for Jimmie because the traverse over the Bayside Bridge, as it crossed the river, mirrored how tenuous she felt emotionally about her destination.

She looked down and saw the willowy reflection of early sunlight on the river and thought about Katy Marie and life with Mollie in Baywater. There was something foreboding and sad to Jimmie about the river and the way she and Rustin had been hurriedly dispatched to an unknown place. There would be new people, new places, and a new life. She perked up as the view of the river gave way to a vista of long lawns and grazing farmland. Alluring shades of green grass and trees spanned for miles around. The sprawling fields of greenery were a comfort and a source of amazement to Jimmie, especially since she had only seen and experienced the littered, drab living environment and apartment complex of Uptown Manor.

Their long journey through Indiana and to their first major stop in Cincinnati, educated them about how big the country was. But as they traveled further south, Jimmie, especially, began to understand that dark people everywhere in America were probably experiencing hardships just like she and Rustin, for as they began to stop at train stations to change trains, they overheard countless stories from people who looked like them. They expressed desires and hopes about finding a better life in another place. Sometimes Jimmie thought she saw the same angst in the faces that stared at the train as it passed by. As the train proceeded further south and through Kentucky, Jimmie began to see a seemingly endless string of dark-colored workers tilling the soil of tobacco fields, not far from the tracks, from early morning until sunset.

As they rode further, they passed miles of cotton, wheat, and corn fields. Striking fields of colorful wildflowers, daisies, and bluebonnets streamed over the countryside, as well. The passing blossoms inspired hope for the young riders.

When it became too dark to see outside the train and when six-year-old Rustin was asleep, Jinger studied the tags that had been pinned on them, carrying their names and the words "Roxborough, Georgia". Reflecting on her eight years in Baywater, she now felt much older. She had been forced to grow up and bear so much of the weight of living while she was yet a child.

Nervous, stunned, and unsure, they ended up eating the two-day meal package that Aunty Katie had packed for them in one day. Before they reached Roxborough, they became hungry. An elderly couple noticed the quiet yearning on the youngsters' faces and shared their sandwiches, fruit, and water with the weary, Georgia-bound, young travelers. When they became hungry again later that evening, they slept, dreamed, and prayed.

As the train spanned its journey through Tennessee, Jimmie began to cry softly. She already missed Mollie and Lil' Katy immensely. Her emptiness and uncertainty became more palpable later, as the train began to stop at little dotty towns in Georgia. At each stop she grew more absorbed, but she was also strangely excited about what lay ahead for them as they inched onward in their trek toward the unknown and to their new life in the red hills of Georgia.

5

Aunt Tessa and Uncle Max

Jimmie and Rustin arrived in Roxborough, on a Saturday morning in early August. Aunt Tessa and Uncle Max were waiting for them at the train station. When at long last they exited the train, their new guardians inspected them thoroughly from head to toe. As the conductor removed their name tags, Uncle Max said something to him and he nodded. He hesitated for a moment, studying the tags and the children for a few seconds, before rejoining the new arrivals and Aunt Tessa. After another sweeping look at Rustin and, especially, Jimmie, Aunt Tessa looked at Uncle Max and gave him a smile that he acknowledged with a half nod.

"Hello, there you two are. I am your aunt Tessa Lee, and this is your uncle Max. You all are going to be staying with us here in Roxborough. And what is your name?" Aunt Tessa asked as she reached out to pat Jimmie on her shoulder.

"My name is Jimmie Rose, and this here is my brother, Rustin."

"Why, hello, Rustin," said Aunt Tessa.

"Pleased to meet you ma'am...and sir," Rustin said, and nodded.

"Say, yo' name Jimmie?" asked Uncle Max as he stared at her quizzically.

"Yeah, Jimmie Rose. Um named after my Momma's brother."

"Oh, I see," said Aunt Tessa cryptically. "Well, I think we'll just have to call you something daintier, like a girl's name. How about Jinger?" she asked out loud to Uncle Max.

"That's left up to you," he answered and shrugged.

"Yes. We'll call her Jinger Rose," said Aunt Tessa, pleased with herself.

Jimmie and Rustin eyeballed each other quietly with a look of befuddlement and angst. They wondered how these strangers could rename her so quickly without asking for her opinion about the changing of her own name.

Aunt Tessa then presented each of them with a small fruit bag. They were exceedingly thankful and hungry, having not eaten yet that day. They held back the temptation to tear into the fruit immediately, however, thinking it would make them look impolite and greedy. Starving, they got into Uncle Max's brown four-person carriage and headed toward their new home. Aunt Katie had instructed them to never forget that Uncle Max and Aunt Tessa were society people or, in her actual words, "High-sidity colored folks." Minding their manners, they both said thank you often and remembered Aunt Katie's admonition: "Show them that you have some class and pride about yo'self."

Neither, at their young age, knew exactly what their aunt meant by this, but they understood enough to know that they must ignore their hunger and not eat in the carriage, especially since this was the first one they had ever sat or rode in. Riding in their guardians' vehicle surprisingly drove their hunger away for a while.

Aunt Tessa was fairly tall and she struck Jinger and Rustin as a towering figure. She had light-freckles, was fair-skinned; had shoulder-length reddish-brown hair; and a medium build. What Jinger and Rustin immediately liked about Aunt Tessa was her warmth. She spoke to them by name on the way to their house and pointed out several familiar places for their future reference. She talked a lot and seemed a lot younger than Uncle Max.

Forrest Maxwell, known as Max, who was just a tad shorter

than Aunt Tessa, was a medium-brown-skinned fellow with a slightly receding hairline. He wore glasses occasionally for reading and driving. A well-dressed and proud man, he seemed constantly in motion. He didn't talk much at home, but he was what they called "plainspoken". Aunt Tessa's warmth was memorable, but it was Uncle Max's neat appearance and blatant indifference toward them that they noted most. As a Roxy—the name the townspeople of Roxborough called long time natives—he was outgoing in an orderly sort of a way. People in town respected him because he had a quaint home, a neatly trimmed yard, and a busy barbershop. A barber by day, he also played the trumpet on occasion at special gatherings. He drank a few beers on the weekends, but, for the most part, he stayed sober and focused on his hair-cutting business.

Uncle Max confounded Jinger and Rustin because he was so quiet at home yet so much more talkative away from home and when the house was filled with guests. He liked to barbecue and invite friends over, so long as they were a certain kind of people. You couldn't be too boring, too religious, too country, too dark, or a freeloader—that is a non-invitee to a Maxwell home affair. And if you were in any way too loud, you would not be invited back.

But his most peculiar characteristic surfaced twice a year. Without fail, he rode out to Eden's Prairie Rest Cemetery to lay flowers at the gravesite of his first wife, Trudy. Aunt Tessa would look distressed and disgraced when he left to go to the cemetery, but she would soon put on a happy face, her bib overalls, and later her apron to clean and then cook. Pretty soon the house would be filled with the aroma of mustard greens, candied yams, and a simmering pot roast with mushrooms, which would be served over rice with gravy. This was Uncle Max's favorite dinner.

These occasional ritual dinners were Aunt Tessa's way of

doing what she called "drawing Uncle Max's mind in." She would then put on one of her best house dresses, soft hot-comb her hair, and flutter around in an intent and frenetic manner. During such days, Aunt Tessa would invariably ask Jinger and Rustin to help her clean. They grew to expect it and were both more than willing to help their aunt Tessa, largely because of the many small kindnesses she bestowed upon them. After all was done, she would sit and wait for her husband to return from visiting the dead, greeting him at the door and letting him know that supper was ready. It appeared that she loved Uncle Max a great deal because she would brighten up and magnify her gentle, feminine ways when he would enter the house.

Jinger and Rustin usually ate their supper in a tiny room in the back of the house on such days and knew they could come to the front of the house again once they heard Aunt Tessa's soft-pitched laughter and giggles, which were elicited by Uncle Max's retelling of his funny stories about the goings-on in his shop.

When Jinger and Rustin first arrived, Tessa thought maybe their presence would help fill a void in the couple's life. Their presence gave Max a bit of purpose, since he embraced the responsibility of giving to the children and making sure they had their basic needs met, but his inner thoughts were revealed while he was getting into bed the night of their arrival, "They nice children, but they ain't no Maxwells; you can look at 'em and tell that."

Tessa dealt with this reality the best way she could. She took to Jinger Rose and Rustin right away. Although she did not view them as the most handsome, citified children, she often thought, "They are not bad to look at." They were also still young enough for her to mother and mold, which she viewed as a plus.

On New Year's Eve, several months after they arrived in

Roxborough, Jinger overheard her aunt discussing the two of them and their looks with her best friend, Bernadette.

"Those two cute chil'ren you're raisin'."

"Yeah, they are pretty nice children. That little caramel-colored Jinger is a sweet child. It's a good thing, though, that she's not any darker. I want her to be able to marry when she is of age. Because you and me both know how some of the menfolk are about lightenin' the line," responded Tessa, prompting the two women to pass knowing looks at each other.

"Rustin's kinda dark, though," opined Bernadette quietly.

"Uh-huh," was Tessa's immediate reply. "A colored boy can be dark, though," remarked Aunt Tessa after an awkward pause.

"That's the truth. People are so color struck, as if God didn't make all of these pretty shades of folks. And they 'specially hard on our girls."

"It's a shame there are so many self-hating people, but that is the way it is."

"Yeah, 'cause you sho' need somethin' to work with in this world, that's for sho'. Like you said, a girl child is alright as long as she got a pinch of color, but if she don't, Lord hep ha."

"They should both be all right and fit in. Jinger, because she has a full head of hair and a little color. Rustin, too, because although he is dark brown, he is smart in his books," replied Tessa.

"Why, sho', theya do jes' fine— 'specially Rustin. All a man or boy child got to do is wash up good; get his head cut; put on a nice suit of clothes, even if it's just a shirt and pants—then menfolk just look good. As long as he is a decent sort, he shouldn't have any problems gettin' along. Now girls and women folks, they got to be clean, smell good, keep they head done, have some sense, and they cain't be lazy. Being a light bright helps too. Yo' Jinger ain't no light bright, but she ain't no deep, dark shadow, so dat's good," said Bernadette.

Jinger grew somber as she listened. Her armpits tingled, and she felt her face turn hot with anger. Even as a newly turned nine-year-old, such talk annoyed and offended her. To her, it was born of ignorance and demeaned others. She was not in the same room as the two, but in her mind's eye, she saw her aunt Tessa nod her head in agreement with Bernadette, even though she stated that it was unfortunate that people could be that way. Jinger made a mental note about her aunt Tessa and her churchy friend and neighbor. She believed they were obsessed with skin color, and she disliked how they were always discussing others and not the good book. Her inner thoughts about her aunt's friend were particularly negative, "Ms. Bernadette is neither fair nor good looking, but she has the nerve to talk badly about the shade God gives His people. She needs to repent!"

She was equally disgusted with her aunt, whom she thought should have known better, given that she was well educated. From listening to their conversations, it seemed to Jinger that her aunt Tessa and her judgmental friend acted more like bar buddies than church pew companions. Bernadette evoked an intense visceral reaction from Jinger. Whenever her aunt's friend acted with religious fervor at church on Sundays, particularly when she "got happy" and ran at breakneck speed inside the sanctuary. Jinger would excuse herself and go to the restroom until she completed her laps along the walls inside the church.

Despite her growing misgivings about Aunt Tessa, she and Rustin learned quickly how to fit into the Maxwell family and into the Shady Grove community, the Negro section of Roxborough. They learned how to be seen and not heard, how to conduct their lives in a way that would be pleasing to their aunt, and how to deal with Uncle Max.

6

Tessa Lee Dodd Jackson

Before Tessa Lee Jackson married Forrest Maxwell at the age of twenty-seven, an age that signified old maid status to most in southern society, she taught school. She descended from a lineage that owned land, on her mother's side of the family—the Dodds. They inherited fertile land from Tessa's maternal grandmother, Lucinda, who had been a favorite slave of the Dodd slaveholding family of Richmond. Originally owning seventy-five acres of land, she eventually sold forty acres to establish funds to educate her grandchildren. Tessa Lee was one of the beneficiaries of her largess. Although she was named Odessa by her parents, when she became a teen-ager, she asked everyone to call her Tessa. She attended Howard University, which was well regarded in the Shady Grove community. Such an opportunity was viewed with awe, prompting residents to take notice. "Tessa", they thought, "is sho-nuff a Howard girl."

After graduating, she spent three years teaching affluent children of color in Hampton, and two years teaching more needy students in Mills Crossing located in the highlands. While waiting to meet the right mate, Tessa threw herself into her teaching duties. She also played the piano for Reverend and Mrs. Collins' small church on Sundays and boarded a room from them. How Tessa, a statuesque, freckle-faced beauty, ended up in West Virginia was a mystery to everyone but Tessa; an enigma that she decided to keep to herself.

A wise spinster who had befriended her can be credited with

shining the light of reason on Tessa's need to return home to Georgia to find a mate and to be with her people.

Words of kindness and prudence were offered by a red-headed old schoolmarm, Miss Greta O'Leary, who, surprisingly, became Tessa's most valuable friend during her short stay in Mills Crossing. After hearing that Tessa was seen spending late Sunday afternoons with Brit Scow, the headmaster, she cautioned Tessa one day as they watched their students play during recess.

"What a lovely pair of beads those are, Tessa…did you get them in town at Roswell's?" She asked slyly.

Tessa, surmising what Miss O'Leary's probing was all about, perked up and looked her straight in the eyes as she responded, "Oh no. They were a gift."

"Must be quite a gentleman."

"Yes…" She warily acknowledged.

"You're such a fine young lady, Miss Tessa, and you have done a beautiful job with these little ones," she returned, changing the subject.

"Why, thank you!" said Tessa.

"Where are your people from?" She asked, deftly laying her chatter trap.

"Oh, I am from Georgia, up the coast a tad from Savannah. Most of my family is still there."

"Have you been able to make many friends here at the Crossing?"

"Well…actually, just a few. There are two or three young folks at the church where I worship, but that's about it."

"You all ever go to picnics, to the town fair or the like?"

"No. Not too much. I sometimes go for coffee every now and then with a few friends from the church. Besides their company, Brit… ah… Headmaster Scow has been very generous with his time." As soon as she said it, she knew she had shared too much.

With her trap sprung, Miss O'Leary, without giving away what she was thinking, just smiled blandly. She turned her attention back to the children on the playground. After a few moments, she asked Tessa in a quiet voice, "Did Headmaster Scow give you those beads, dear?"

Tessa, uneasy, looked down, fingered the beads, and stated that he had. She clearly noticed the stark silence from her older colleague and thought she saw a pained shadow cross her face.

"Miss Tessa, please know that I admire you as a young lady and what you have done for the least of these little ones here in West Virginia, but with all due respect, please be careful," Miss O'Leary said with brevity and sincerity before revealing the fullness of her thoughts. "I wouldn't dare say anything that would lead you astray because I have my God to answer to, but just know this: sometimes menfolk show attention for the wrong reasons. I've been here in Mills County for upward of twenty years now, and I'm ashamed to say that I have seen those beads you are wearing before. They were worn by Miss Shelby Smith Heckethorn. And oh, what a beauty she was, just like you—but white, you know. I can still see those green eyes and red locks. I don't know whatever became of her. What I remember, though, is that she packed and left hastily in the night about a year after arriving here. The gossip was that her leaving had to do with the headmaster, but I didn't hear enough facts to remember, because the way I see it, only two people know what happened; the rest really don't know. I won't repeat the talk that went around in this little hick place of a town, but it wasn't anything nice, as you can well imagine. Some of the Mills people have such bad minds— vain and scandalous imaginations. I'll just say Headmaster Scow also left shortly thereafter under a cloud of suspicion. He just recently returned to the Crossing. He said he had been up North in New England country for a few years, teaching at a boy's boarding school. I don't know where he was, actually. I also don't know whatever became of Miss Heckethorn. Bless her heart. I hope she is happy. All she ever showed me was a fine Christian young lady." She paused briefly and then continued: "But I just said all that to say to you that there could not possibly be a future in this for you, dear, and I say so out of the purest heart."

Hearing all of this, Tessa felt a need to catch her breath. She looked at her counterpart intently and contemplated questions within her mind: "Could this be the babbling of an old schoolmarm whose time has come and gone? Is this the voice of a meddling spinster, passing gossip, or is this the voice of reason?"

"Maybe it would be better for you to go back home to be with your kind," she tenderly interrupted Tessa's contemplation.

At first, Tessa shot Miss O'Leary a sharp glance, but then she read her colleague's eyes, voice, and mannerism, as she dispensed with her opinions. She began to realize that her colleague was sincere and probably meant nothing in a racial way, so she listened on.

"Spry girl like you probably would have some good prospects. Try to find you a nice colored boy and go on with your life. I'm old now, but I was once young. I have yet to see a white man honor and treat a Negro woman as an equal or accord her the position of respect that can only be authenticated in marriage. Not saying it's not possible; just saying I haven't seen it done."

"Why Miss O'Leary, why ever would you think that I had designs of marrying Headmaster Scow?" Tessa bristled at her assumptions. "Besides," she thought, "I have never shown any interest in him, and he has only been friendly to me, and that's all! But is that all it means to him?" She was beginning to stumble mentally over the implications of her colleagues' words.

She did not answer the question. Instead, she paused for a

minute, turned her attention again to the running and playing children, and then asked, "He ever ask you out?"

"Yes, we have gone picnicking and even to the town square shops on occasion," answered Tessa without any hesitation or guilt, but still annoyed. "Not that it is any of your business," she thought to herself, resisting the temptation to say out loud what she was thinking.

"He ever take you to Ma Laura's house?" Miss O'Leary gently inquired, her steady, sky blue eyes peering into Tessa Lee's glimmering green eyes.

"And who might that be?" questioned Tessa.

"Why, that is his mother. Ms. Laura and Head Master Scow's brother and his sister and their families live in Pelahatchie, down by Suffolk's Way."

Now it was Tessa's turn to be silent. She distinctly remembered Headmaster Scow saying that both of his parents were dead. She did not, however, reveal this. She just looked off and listened.

"That is only a few miles from here, and if I am not mistaken, that is where he spends every other weekend. He invited the teachers to Ms. Laura's once, for a back- to- school gathering. But that was before you began teaching here. From what I saw, the Scows have a nice spread. I understand he's got an older brother who is a judge in Kentucky, but his sister and younger brother stay here to be close to Ms. Laura, which is good because she is old now. His sister Betsy has three beautiful towheads. Has he ever mentioned any of this to you or taken you to meet his family?" asked Miss O'Leary gingerly.

Noting Tessa's inability to respond to the question, she looked at the younger woman and measured her words in the only way she could: bluntly. "Miss Tessa, don't fool off your youth wishing for something that will never be. Go and make a life for yourself, because none of us are getting any younger, you know," she chuckled. "Give yourself a chance. Maybe have you some little darlings to clutch about your apron strings. I wished many a day I would have had someone to advise me before my years stacked on, but my momma died when I was just eleven, so I had no one to tell me things like I'm telling you."

Although Tessa's mind began to percolate with anger, conversely, her heart discerned good will as she saw the compassionate, pleading look in Miss O'Leary's soft eyes. This led her to believe that the older woman's unsought advice was at least animated by genuine concern.

Suddenly, a loud, rolling thunderclap interrupted their rumination. The two women looked to the sky, and then the elderly woman outpaced Tessa in gathering their children.

"We had better get the children in…looks like a storm coming up over the mountains edge," Miss O'Leary said with a raised voice as she shielded her eyes with her hands and glanced at the blinding bolts of lightning above. "Try to make it a good day, in spite of the weather." She said as she hurriedly left with her class.

Tessa rushed indoors with her class. She looked over her shoulder at Miss O'Leary as she scurried off. Part of her wanted to yell out, "You meddling old woman!" But, truthfully, she felt touched and convicted by her words. She thought for a moment and ruefully concluded that her colleague had offered her valuable, cautionary advice. She resolved to verify the details by quietly inquiring with others. As she ushered her students inside and just before the high winds crashed into the school and a deluge of rain drenched the buildings and grounds, she decided to keep her distance from Mr. Scow until she could put clothes on the truth herself.

Before long, Tessa discovered the insatiable appetites of the headmaster. She was sitting at her desk one day, grading papers for about half an hour after the end of the school day, when suddenly she looked up and saw Headmaster Scow staring at her from about ten feet away. So engrossed was she in grading her students' work that she had not heard him enter her classroom. Startled by his stealthy presence, she almost jumped out of her chair.

"Why, I see you're still here working, Miss Tessa. Be careful. All work and no play make Tessa a dull girl," he chortled, revealing a toothy grin.

His chuckle was the only sound she heard, but his presence vaporized all humor and tranquility from the classroom, which was unsettling to Tessa.

"Oh, I just wanted to finish grading these papers early, so I wouldn't have to do it later. We're having a revival at the church this evening, and I wanted to give myself a head start," she emphasized, trying hard to be calm and not show how alarmed she felt in his presence.

He just listened and peered at her. As she placed her papers in her school satchel, he placed his hand over hers.

"I'll take that for you."

Now he was too close. She could detect a faint smell of alcohol on his breath.

"I'll be going now," Tessa said as she whispered a prayer without moving her lips.

"Miss Jackson, I will walk you home."

"Oh, no…I'm sure you are busy with school matters and all. I think I can manage on my own."

Mr. Scow did not say anything, but Tessa watched him wipe his mouth with the back of his hand. She wondered silently about the meaning of this gesture.

"I said I would walk you home, Miss Jackson, and that is what I aim to do."

The firm resolve in his voice frightened Tessa, but the vision of walking over a mile to the Collins's place through a heavily wooded area with Brit Scow alarmed her even more. Pondering how she could free herself of the situation, she decided she would pretend to go along with him to at least get out of her closed-door classroom.

"Very well then," she said, displaying the most convincing smile she could manage. She carefully removed her cloak from a hook on the closet door, and the two of them walked toward the red classroom door that led outside to the school courtyard. When Tessa opened the door, she saw the glory of God. Billy Deavers, wild-eyed and all, stood outside the door staring up at her.

"Howdy, Missus Jackson. I left my jacket, and I cain't go home without it again, or I'll git a thrashing. Can I git it?"

Now, Billy was one of the most difficult and obnoxious youngsters Tessa had ever taught, but she tolerated him. She mostly did so because she liked the challenge of teaching the only white child in the school who had been kicked out of the only white school in town. After the pleadings of the black coalminers, who liked Billy's dad, the school took Billy in as a student, although state law said Negroes and whites must not be taught in the same school. His antics certainly explained his social difficulties at school.

One day she had been teaching a social studies lesson on colonialism. There was a vibrant history discussion under way, and many students raised their hands to ask and answer questions.

During the heart of the discussion, Billy had blurted out, "Missus Jackson, can you fry me some chicken? My step-momma said coloreds fry the best chicken." There was silence in the room, the students looked at each other, and a few rolled their eyes at Billy.

"No, Billy, this is not the time to discuss fried chicken," she had answered, trying to keep from laughing. "Besides everybody in Mills Crossing, including your stepmom, can fry a mean skillet of chicken."

"Well, can you clean our house every other weekend? My stepmother is looking for a cleaning woman to help her out some weekends." This was met with more somber and cross looks from Billy's classmates.

"No, Billy. I teach school for a living," was her only answer.

Insensitivity was Billy's way, but today, artless Billy became an angel. Tessa, happy at the sight of her student, addressed the most sensible request he had ever made, "Why sure, Billy. Let me get your jacket for you."

At that moment, Mr. Deavers, walking toward the class-room, yelled from outside, "Billy boy, ye come on naah, ya hear? You gonna make us late fur supper!"

When he got to the classroom door and saw Miss Jackson and the headmaster, he stepped back and took off his hat.

"Howdy do, Master Scow, Miss Jackson?" he greeted them, nodding his head. "I hope y'all doing fine. I just come after my boy."

"Why hello, Mr. Deavers. Billy is a fine boy," Tessa joyfully embellished. She gave Billy his coat and removed her school satchel from Mr. Scow's grip, while he spoke to the elder Deavers. "I was wondering if you could give me a lift today. I was just leaving school this very minute."

"Why, by all means. Yes ma'am, you needn't ask. I'm going right that direction. C'mon Billy. Mr. Scow," he said nervously, nodding at the headmaster, having never driven a Negro woman in his buggy wagon before.

Then he, Billy, and Tessa left the red-faced headmaster in the classroom doorway.

Before she climbed into the Deavers' old wagon, Mr. Deavers

told Billy to sit in the middle and ordered the horses to giddy up. Tessa, looking up at the heavens with her eyes closed, mouthed her gratitude for providing a way of escape.

From then on, she made it a point to leave her classroom just as the students left. She also made sure that she was never alone in her classroom again. When she shared the Scow incident with Pastor and Mrs. Collins, they both became alarmed and gave her suggestions about how she should be watchful at all times. Reverend Collins and his two hounds even met Tessa every day, without fail, to walk her safely back to her place of boarding.

For a long time afterward, she shuddered at the thought of what could have happened to her that day had it not been for the Deavers. She was grateful for their rescue and she even began to see little Billy as not the most obnoxious student. She also made plans to leave the West Virginia backcountry by semester's end.

7

Maxwell Living

Six weeks after Headmaster Scow revealed himself as a lecher, Tessa arrived home in Roxborough not as a stranger and not as a hero, but only as a Roxy from a prominent family who had accomplished what few in the growing town had. She had gone away to school, earned her college diploma and returned home. This brought about a mixed response from the home town people. Her family and close friends were excited and gratified to have her home. Some, who were less fortunate, envied and shunned her. Tessa made sure she was kind to everyone and tried not to dwell on the negatives that came her way. One person she hoped to impress was Superintendent Basil Scott of the Roxborough school system, who, within five days of her return, promised her a teaching position at a grade school by the spring of the next calendar year. She also needed to make an impression upon a man, a man of promise, a man of husband material.

With time on her hands, Tessa kept busy by visiting family and old friends and by reacquainting herself with Shady Grove— a place wherein she had not resided in nearly nine years. Helping her sisters, Violet and Blanche, with their fledgling laundry and baking business seemed like an ideal way for her to reintroduce herself to the community, so she jumped at this opportunity.

It was during a pie delivery downtown that Tessa was first spotted by Forrest Maxwell, known as "Max". He saw her when she walked by his window a few times on her way to make pastry and laundry deliveries.

One day Blanche asked her if she would deliver a pie and pressed shirts to Maxwell's Barbershop for a longstanding customer, Otis Kelly, because she knew this was the best place to catch the rural resident, who lived miles away in the country. When Tessa entered Maxwell's, the bells on the door jingled, and a few of the patrons looked up. Some of the menfolk took notice but made no comment.

"Hello. May I help you?" Max inquired, breaking the silence.

"I'm looking for Mr. Kelly."

"He's not quite here; 'spect him tomorrow."

"Would you be so kind as to give him his shirts and pastry? My sister, Blanche, said she usually delivers them here."

"Oh, yeah. She does once a month. I'll take the items and give them to him when he comes."

"Much obliged," said Tessa, smiling as she gave the shirts and dessert to Max. She then left unimpressed with the town's most successful barber, black or white.

His eyes followed her out of the shop, and he looked out of the window as she walked down the lane in front of the shop.

"You can look, but you cain't touch!" joked Jabbo.

"Who is she?" He asked as he placed a cape and a neck strip on his next patron.

"Oh, that's Violet and Blanche's sister. She just moved back here from West Virginey," answered Jabbo.

"What was she doing there?" asked Max, as he clipped the hair of his patron.

"They say she a schoolteacher. You know Myrtle and Fred Jackson. That's they middle daughter," replied Jabbo, surprised that he knew more than Max about the Jacksons.

"Oh, now I do recall them having three girls," said Max.

"Iz that who dat iz? I remember when she was pig-tailed and knock-kneed. She sho' made a fine lookin' mamma," chimed in

Buddy Smith, shaking his head. Buddy's folksy way of saying things brought chuckles from the fellows in the shop.

"Think I could get a date?" he continued, pantomiming with his big, brown eyes to everyone around the shop like he really wanted someone there to set him up with a date with Tessa. A few of the patrons chuckled under their breaths.

"Man, naw! That yella hammer wouldn't give no regula fellow like none of us a chance," one patron remarked.

"She ain't yella; she redbone!" yelled out another patron, causing some in the shop to laugh.

"But you must remember. Um not like the rest of you regula fellas," responded Buddy, rolling his fingers through his thick, partially straight Indian hair, getting the last laugh.

"Aahh, Buddy, sit down! You know that woman wouldn't give you the time o' day," someone shouted.

Max did not say anything, but he liked her good looks and seemingly settled personality.

Weeks afterward, he saw her walk by the shop again making deliveries, and he also saw her at church every Sunday praising the Lord, but it was not the spiritual side of Tessa that stirred the churchgoing barber's growing attraction toward her.

Max began to plan an encounter with the tall beauty. So, on the last Sunday in August, at the church's annual homecoming picnic, he made his move. First, he calculatingly offered to carry the food boxes that Tessa and her sisters had brought to the picnic. Then, later, he deliberately stepped into her path as she hurriedly helped the churchwomen prepare the food for the homecoming event. His plan worked because he got her to engage in a brief conversation with him. He found her surprisingly down to earth and easy to be around.

Throughout the fall and winter, Max continued to chat with her, whenever, and for as long as he could. Eventually, he asked her out on a date to the town fair. Tessa, not particularly struck by Max, was nonetheless, open to meeting and dating a seemingly nice man like him, so she responded positively to his advances.

Tessa was hired as a schoolteacher at the Shady Grove Grammar School in February during the spring semester. By then, they had been dating for almost six months. They went for walks by the lake, and she read him poetry in the park, under the clouds and a live oak tree, on Sunday afternoons. To Tessa's dismay, Max often fell asleep during her readings. He usually apologized afterward and assured her that it was not done purposely and explained that her voice relaxed him so, until sweet, satisfying sleep always seemed to overtake him. The two became close, and it was obvious that there was possibly a future for the couple, instigating the wagging of town tongues. However, the talk was about Max and Maxine, not Max and Tessa.

Trudy "Maxine" Maxwell had passed away on a bitter cold, windy December day. Max so adored her that he had asked everyone to call her Maxine, a nickname he had given her early in their marriage, though it was hardly close to her given Christian name. Everyone in Shady Grove knew how much he loved and doted on his wife. Although she had been sick for over three years and he knew she could die from her illness, Max had taken her death in the worst way. He had grieved for her as if she had suddenly stolen away. He mourned for weeks, disappearing from the town square and his shop for days. The community had empathized with and visited him. He received hot meals almost daily from neighbors, churchwomen, and the wives of his shop patrons. Occasionally, he received more than just food. Some days he would find a note attached to the wrapping of his sweet potato pies and roasts, disclosing the availability of a single, usually young food preparer.

Almost eight months after Trudy passed, Tessa had arrived back in Roxborough to be with her family. After a less-than-traditional courting season, Forrest Maxwell asked her to become the new Mrs. Maxwell. She agreed, and the wedding was set for summer's end. Although Max, by all accounts, had been good to Trudy, and theirs had been a strong bond full of love and mutual respect, there were some in Roxborough who marveled at how soon after her death he had decided to remarry.

"Lord, Max is marryin' so soon?" questioned the scoffers.

Nevertheless, most Roxies were happy for him. There was no doubt that he had loved Trudy. He stood by her side as she died a slow death from lupus, or what they called "that sneaky slow-killa disease". He had shown his love and devotion for her in words and in deed, so many just looked the other way at his seeming swift courtship with and engagement to Tessa and agreed with the blunt words of Ray, the town ice man: "Well hell, she ain't comin' back!"

Tessa's mother, Myrtle, and her sisters, Violet and Blanche, pointed out to her that Max was stable and churchgoing, had his own business, and was known to like redbones. Tessa asked her dad, Fred, what he thought, and he answered in his usual, cautious way: "I wouldn't rush into anything. Take time to know him." Fred's discreet response revealed his strong belief that it was unwise to be hasty in decision making. A quiet, reflective and sensitive man, he had also witnessed the chameleon nature of people in his lifetime, so he was deliberate in relationship decisions.

But Myrtle encouraged her daughter differently: "He'll make you a good husband. I'm not tryin' to hurt your feelings, Tessa, but you ain't exactly no spring chicken, so maybe you should go on and marry. You don't know if you'll get this chance again, especially at yo' age. Then too, if you're blessed with any little ones, you don't want them to come here and they are 'not right' on account of yo' age."

"Momma, Forrest seems like a good man. I know I'm in like, but I'm not so sure if I am in love."

"Ita come. Ita come. Believe that," Myrtle answered with certitude, her eyes cast downward.

She further encouraged her daughter to marry someone whom the Jackson family knew something about. Forrest "Max" Maxwell fit this description because he was a well-known barber in Roxborough, and he attended the same church as the family. Almost everyone that counted, which meant the Jackson family and their social circle, found this match agreeable—that is, all but Mildred Capers.

Mildred had never pursued Max like her feelings begged her to. Although she denied it whenever someone was bold enough to ask her, some Roxies believed and whispered that Mildred was sweet on Max and, in fact, had her sights set on him all the while she nursed Trudy during her last months of life. To some, she appeared visibly disappointed about the impending union of Max and Tessa. The word on the street was that she was a good person, not bad looking, and well-liked, but she was no match for Tessa Jackson, who had looks, learnin', and family connections. Mildred said many times while tending to Trudy that she was "just doing the Lord's work". But when the leggy and sprightly Tessa Jackson caught Max's eye, it was easier to find a $100 bill lying in the street than to find Mildred. She slowly began to be less visible in the community, and she was rarely seen at town events. This, to many, revealed her true feelings, opening her to the fodder of town gossip.

Tessa and her sisters felt sorry for Mildred, which caused them to shoot unthinking, pitying glances her way whenever they encountered her at the market. An attractive young woman, though not haughty, she was a person of reasonable pride, so she did her best to ignore sympathetic glances and outright questions about her whereabouts. If she happened to be at the market at the same time as the Jackson sisters, she pretended not to see them. Instead, she spent inordinate amounts of time at the meat counter or in the fabric section of Lily's Grocer to avoid them. Shortly before the wedding, she moved to Wichita. She put the word out that she moved to help her sister and brother-in-law care for their aging mother, but many thought she moved to mend her broken heart.

On a still, August, late afternoon, a veiled Tessa Lee Jackson, adorned in a beautiful, lacy, white wedding gown, walked amid a bright, sun-drenched setting outside the Evergreen Methodist Church and became Mrs. Forrest Maxwell. Her close friend, Naomi, along with her sisters, served as the bridal court. The bridal isle was adorned with tulle pew bows accented with pink roses and baby's breath. The bridesmaids wore lilac and carried pink and lavender daylily bouquets. The churchyard was decorated with lilies, gardenias, and roses, which led to a ribbon-laced gazebo. Guests sat in white chairs under the shade of large oaks that were planted in the grassy, church garden and side-courtyard. The bride was striking and carried a bouquet of fresh purple orchids, accented with baby's breath. Her satin and lace gown sleeves and bodice were adorned with white pearls. Her long train was carried by adorable, three-year-old, twin girls. It was the wedding of the season, and everybody who was somebody in Roxborough and the nearby towns was there for the nuptials and wedding reception.

From the moment of her return to Roxborough, her reconnection with her family, and her new life as Mrs. Maxwell, Tessa never forgot well-meaning Miss Greta O'Leary, and she cried when she heard that she had died of natural causes a few years after she had left Mills Crossing. She always fancied that if she ever had a daughter, she would name her after her dear friend Miss O'Leary. After two years of marriage, she gave birth to a tiny baby daughter. Tessa named her Greta. But she died two days later, which was disappointing to both Maxwells.

~ ~ ~

Although the ghosts of baby Greta and Trudy haunted Tessa and Max's marriage, the Maxwells had a satisfactory, if not blissful, union. They got along well, for the most part, and settled into their marriage and everyday life. The Jacksons and the Maxwells were among the few families in Roxborough who had a house with a wraparound porch, a picket fence, an expansive lawn, and two carriages. With Tessa's pay as a school teacher, although small, they lived comfortably and became established as one of the prominent families in Roxborough. Max seldom rode in his white carriage, so as not to draw the ire of some of the less fortunate Roxies. Before he married Tessa, he prospered with his barbershop and part ownership in two other businesses in town. He was proud that he, a man who worked with his hands, had landed one of the Jackson girls and bolstered his already respected status a bit.

Tessa was grateful that she had Max, and she tried not to let life's disappointments oppress her. She focused instead, on seeking ways to make their home happy, and provide proper training and schooling opportunities for Jinger and Rustin.

On a sizzling hot, late September afternoon, Tessa was waiting for Rustin in the front yard as he descended from the field wagon that carried him to work as a water boy in a cotton field.

"I have some good news for you. I was able to get you a seat at Shady Grove Grammar," revealed Tessa exuberantly.

"Really? That is good news, Aunt Tessa Lee! You mean I won't have to catch Mr. Bill's wagon anymore?" asked Rustin excitedly.

"No, you won't have to catch the wagon starting tomorrow. Uncle Max said you can help him out in the shop every day until you start school."

"I'm really glad, Auntie," Rustin said, shaking his head in disbelief. "I can't believe it. Thank you for all you did to get me that seat," he continued, his eyes filling with moisture.

"You're welcome, Rustin. You seem a little sad...and you're crying? Go on inside. Get a towel and wipe your face. I thought this news would make you glad," said a perplexed Tessa. She followed him into the house. After wiping his face with a towel in the bathroom, Rustin rejoined her in the parlor.

"I am glad, Aunt Tessa, but I was just thinking...I wish my friends who I work the fields with had this same chance. That sun is so harsh," he said with exasperation.

"Maybe they will, someday. I'm just hoping and praying that sometime soon more of our boys and girls will have better opportunities for schooling. I'm personally seeking chances to help as many as I can. Truth be told, I don't want to stop until I get every one of them off of that wagon."

"I hope so. Can I go on and go to the fields tomorrow? I want to say good-bye to some of my friends."

"Yes, if that's what you want to do," she replied.

"I met a good friend. His name is Flenney Ray. We talk and play number games in the fields to make the time go faster. He's faster than I am at figuring. I hope someday he will get to go to school," said Rustin wistfully, looking down.

"I'm not surprised about your friend Flenney. There are many capable individuals who are relegated to a life far beneath their very potential. It rends my heart if I think on it too long. I am hoping that a change will come. But we all must do more than hope. We must be alert for chances of betterment and ready to share known opportunities with others. I'll keep Flenney in mind in case another seat becomes available. Just do a good job in that seat; that's all I ask. Show them your smarts every day."

"I'll do my best. I can't wait! Do Jinger know yet?" Rustin asked with a big smile on his face.

"*Does* Jinger know?" she responded, firmly correcting him. "Yes, I told her this morning."

"I won't disappoint you, Aunt Tessa Lee," he said, tearing up again out of gratitude.

"I know you won't," she replied, watching her adopted son walk toward his bedroom, wiping the resurging tears from his eyes.

8

Rustin Stands Up

Rustin learned a lot about Uncle Max that he needed to sort out. Like most of the few men he knew, Forrest Maxwell showed very little affection. But what Uncle Max lacked in warmth, he made up for in provision. From the beginning, Rustin and his sister could count on a comfortable place to sleep, nice clothes, good food, home training, a chance to get book learning, and plenty of opportunity to socialize with their peers, which occurred mostly at church events. For Rustin, in particular, it seemed good that his uncle took an interest in him.

Uncle Max began taking Rustin to the barbershop regularly when he turned ten. He noticed his industrious work habits and the fact that he learned quickly. He began his nephew's training with allowing him to sweep the floor and get water for the customers. Rustin worked in the shop on weekends and every day, except Sunday during the summer months. On occasion, he overheard grown men's tales in the barbershop. Max tried to shield him from too much manly talk by sending him on errands, particularly when a bad-mouthed group of men came in. Rustin showed his uncle that he could take orders and did not mind performing any chore he was asked to do.

One day, Max trained him how to receive and make change at the cash register. He marveled at how quickly Rustin learned and his precision with numbers, so he gradually allowed him to accept the money and make change whenever he was at the barbershop. Rustin did this with as much skill and vigor as he did when he shined shoes or anything else that he was assigned to do. Max was pleased, and he praised Rustin for his dexterity.

Customers came from across the county to Maxwell's to get a haircut, a shave, or a shoe shine and especially for lively conversation. One Friday afternoon, Judge Seymour from the neighboring Clover County stopped by the barbershop. Judge Seymour was a tax accountant on the side, and he usually received services after reviewing the books with Max. The door to Maxwell's Place had bells on it, and everyone would inadvertently look up or take note when the bell signaled the entrance of an incoming customer. The room fell silent as the judge entered the shop, leaning on his walking stick. One of the regular customers, Jabbo, who loved to joke and talk, instinctively rose slowly, quietly took his hat from a rack, and told Max he had some errands and would return the next day for his hair trim. Whenever he did this, as he did this day, Max would ask himself, "I wonder what Jabbo has gotten himself into this time?"

Waiting patrons read the newspaper or switched their conversation to the weather, sports, or community news. A few studied their nails or looked blankly at the person whose hair was being cut.

Uncle Max acknowledged Judge Seymour right away. "Be right with ya, boss…would you like a shoe shine now or later?" Max self-effacingly asked.

"I'd like to take a look at ya books," responded the judge, flatly.

Rustin quickly retrieved the black book from a shelf in the back room and gave it to his uncle. The judge and the barber then went to a side room, emerging after twenty minutes.

"Anything special today, boss?" Uncle Max asked the judge after re-entering the front of the shop.

"My usual," he said dryly as he surveyed the shop before taking a seat in the high chair for shoeshine patrons.

Before Uncle Max could instruct him, Rustin raised the judge's feet to the shine bar, took his seat on the bench and began his normal shoe shine. Uncle Max really liked the fact that Rustin was a self-starter. The customers continued their light banter. Judge Seymour studied Rustin as he shined his shoes, changed towels, and briskly worked at his task.

"Boy, you'll make a fine shoe shiner one day; you'll make your uncle here proud," patronized the judge.

"I wish I could say that'll be all right, but I don't aim to shine shoes for long. I'd like to go up North and get some book learnin'," responded Rustin innocently as he kept shining Judge Seymour's shoes at a thorough and steady pace.

"Now, where would you get an odd-fangled notion like that?" the judge questioned.

"I reckon I just know. Miss Grady, my schoolteacher, told me that's what I ought to do and my aunt Tessa Lee, too," said Rustin confidently, as he continued to shine the jurist's shoes.

Uncle Max tuned out the small talk around him and listened nervously and intently to the judge and his adopted nephew discuss the latter's future.

"Did she tell you to look in the mirror every day, too?" quizzed Judge Seymour mockingly. "Boys like you usually work in the fields or at some task using yo' hands, nothing that gen'rally require learning out of no book. You niggras think you somethin', since we took the shackles from around yo' ankles! Just don't forget yo' place, boy," instructed Judge Seymour, raising his voice as though he was speaking to every Negro man in the barbershop.

Rustin, who had by this time finished shining the judge's shoes, looked at Uncle Max, stood up, and without thinking, defended himself. "No, sir! I don't think I'm nothing no better than nobody else, but I don't mean to be no shoe shiner for the rest of my life, I know that," said Rustin without understanding the possible consequences of his retort.

Judge Seymour immediately reached for his cane, but by this time one of the waiting regular patrons had grabbed Rustin by the arm.

"Let's take a walk, Rusty," Lester Olsen said, as Rustin looked at him with a confused look on his face.

Max quickly asked the two to go down to Mr. Ray's ice house and bring back a five-pound bag of ice and to stop by Hugo's and bring the tamales he had ordered.

"Thata be a quarter, Judge," Rustin said in his customary way as he looked the judge straight in the eyes.

Uncle Max quickly shooed him out of the shop and said the judge could pay after he received all his services. Rustin then turned and left the barbershop with Mr. Olsen, still confused, exiting in the glare of Judge Seymour's vengeful gaze.

Max gave Zack Sayles, the next customer in line, a knowing look. Zack nodded.

"Come on up, Cap'n. You're next," said Max amiably to the judge. This was his way of stroking the former barrister, while also hoping to get him out of his shop as soon as possible.

"You need to let that boy of yours know who he is and his perm'nent place."

After receiving his services, he reached inside the side pocket of his jacket and gave Max two dollars. He then reached for his briefcase and his cane, walked outside onto the street in front of the shop and spat. He wiped off his hat, placed it on his head and proceeded down Union Avenue.

By the time Rustin returned from his hastily arranged errand, Uncle Max was finishing his last customer for the day. He went to the back room and placed the ice inside the icebox and the tamales on top of it. Afterward, he returned to the front of the shop and started counting a drawer of quarters and dollar bills. Twenty minutes later, Uncle Max escorted his last customer to the door and said good-bye. He locked the door, closed the shutters, swept up the hair around his work station, and then turned and looked soberly at Rustin.

"I don't like it 'bout you talking back like you did today."

"Yes sir. But I don't see how I said anything wrong or that wasn't true, though."

"Nobody sayin' what you said wadn't true, but it jes' ain't good to answer yo' elders, particularly white folks," explained a troubled Uncle Max.

Rustin looked down, finished counting the drawer change, and kept silent—defiantly silent.

"Boy, naah, I think you betta listen to me real good," said Max, picking up his temerity. "Speaking up to white folks won't have no good end, take my word for it," he continued, sensing Rustin's demeanor becoming a tad somber.

"I was jes' saying what I want for my future. What's wrong with that?" pleaded Rustin quietly.

"What's wrong with that is that most folks don't see a future for a young colored boy. To them, yo' future is either working in the fields, as a tenant farmer, or in a serving role. I cain't blame you for wantin' a good future for yo'self, 'cause what I just named ain't no future. It's good to dream and to go after a betta life for yo'self. I'm not gone ever tell anyone not to. But you jes' have to pursue the dream and try yo' best to live the dream, 'cause people will hate you if you dare to dream. Some will make it their mission to kill you *and* yo' dream," answered Uncle Max in a fatherly way that Rustin had never experienced from his guardian before.

Rustin looked up at his uncle and listened closely.

"Next time the judge comes to the shop, you jes' let me wait on 'em. If you so much as see him comin' down the street toward you, jes' step off the sidewalk turn quietly, and go to your aunts for towels. We can always use clean towels. Jes' tell Violet or Blanche that I sent you, and I will make sho' they get paid. You may need to lay low for a while."

"Yes, sir," Rustin politely responded, but he wondered why his uncle, usually a proud man, was so relenting in this situation.

"And one more thing, Russ: never stop dreamin', and don't you get stuck in the Rox, boy, ya hear?"

"I will try not to, sir," he replied.

"Here's yo' pay for the week. Get the potatoes out of the back room and go on home. Tell Tessa Lee I'll be home direcula."

He noticed right away that his uncle Max had overpaid him.

"You paid me two dollars over my weekly wages, Uncle Max," Rustin said. He counted the dollar bills and extended them toward his uncle.

"No, son. Keep it. Go on home naah."

Rustin looked at Uncle Max quizzically. He had not only paid him double that day, but he had called him "son". He marveled to himself, "He's never fixed his mouth to say that before."

He took the money and the potatoes and jauntily headed to the door. As he neared the exit, he reflected on the satisfaction in his guardian's tone, look, and mannerism at the end of the day. It was a fleeting recall because the fear that his real uncle might show up any minute, intruded upon his thoughts, so he quickly bolted out of the door.

Later at home, Rustin thought more about what his uncle had said, and he felt sad that he had disappointed him, but he meant every word he had said to the judge. However, he decided to take his advice and began to think more than he spoke.

Rustin was grateful for the opportunity to learn at Maxwell's Place, and he did not want to give his uncle a reason to restrict him from coming to the shop. He saw this as a chance to learn more about the world and develop his interpersonal skills.

At home, Aunt Tessa had given him the rare opportunity to have study and library time. He preferred working in the barbershop, though. There he could observe patrons, hear the latest news, practice his counting, and get relief from the hot Georgia sun. By the time he turned twelve, he was working most late afternoons in the shop. He was learning the business, how to make customers feel welcome, and how to make himself useful.

~ ~ ~

Rustin experienced a major trial with his identity when he attended his first Maxwell family reunion. Multi-talented, he showed off his skills by finishing first in the instrumental and sporting competitions at the picnic. Grandpapa Willis, the patriarch of the family, rose proudly to award the family contestants. When he called on Rustin to recognize him for his first-place achievements, he asked about his specific place in the Maxwell family: "What Maxwell is this?" he asked, assuming Rustin was a direct descendant of the Maxwell clan. When Uncle Max interjected, haltingly, that Rustin was a relative of his wife's and that they had taken him and his sister in to raise, Grandpapa Willis asked gruffly, "Who yo' real folks?"

Rustin did not respond to this inquiry, having never met his father and knowing little about his family background.

The outing fell quiet as Grandpapa Willis presented Rustin his awards. Then, the patriarch cleared his throat and asked Macon Maxwell to come up to receive two second-place ribbons. Macon came forward smiling.

"Naah, that's what I mean—a pure Maxwell! This is the pride

of the family, some of the best talent in the city and this side of the Mississippi! Yes, suh, we Maxwells are a strong, proud, and talented people," exclaimed the patriarch without a hint of irony.

This proclamation was met with scattered applause and mumbling from the large Maxwell clan. Jinger looked at Rustin with abiding empathy in her eyes. Not one to show his feelings, he looked down briefly, studied his trophies, and looked around the park with resolve. Aunt Tessa gave him a long, loving hug after the family awards were given. Max started to leave the shady area where they were seated, but then turned around and shook Rustin's hand.

From then on, he refrained from participating in Maxwell family contests and rivalries, choosing instead to coach teams. In this way, he could fit in and develop friendships with family members, showing that he understood that fellowship through sideline participation, rather than talent display and competition, could shield him from the Maxwell reprisal of isolation.

Both Rustin and Jinger wanted to prove to their adoptive parents that they belonged, that they had value, and that they could learn and fit in. Although the Maxwell household felt like home, they both longed to be fully accepted by family and they trusted each other more than they did anyone else.

9

Aunt Matilda Visits

Neither Jinger nor Rustin understood how much their yearnings would intensify. Change and adversity permeated the air, and the palpable warning of trouble came on an unusual early-November morning as scurrying plump, pouting clouds rapidly darkened and blanketed the whole previously clear sky like an unexpected solar eclipse. Uncle Max was even affected by the change in the atmosphere, for he did something rare: he missed a day of work. As the wind began stirring and whistling, the door to the outside storage shed began to open and shut and beat loudly against the wooden frame. Without being asked, Rustin took a hammer and nails and went outside and nailed the door shut.

Aunt Tessa looked warily through the side picture window. As she closed the slightly ajar window, she tightened her night gown about her, complained that the wind chilled her bones, and predicted that she would get a visit from Uncle Arthur before the day was over. Uncle Arthur was the name she gave her arthritis, which flared up in her bones on chilly and stormy days. As it turned out, Uncle Arthur would not be the only visitor to the Maxwell house that day.

There was a break in the weather as the sun peeped through lighter, thinning clouds. It appeared that the storm had passed over. So, Uncle Max sent Rustin to the shop to put a "Closed Today, Open Tomorrow: Nine O'clock" sign on the door. While he was out, the skies began to darken again, and an unlikely visitor showed up on the Maxwells' steps.

Matilda, Tessa's great-aunt on her father's side, appeared to pay the Maxwell family a surprise visit. Aunt Matilda, called Aunt Pudding by the family, was a peculiar woman. Tall and contemplative, she often wore dark colors. Her persona exuded compassion despite her serious, inquisitive demeanor. She was the most mystical person Tessa and Max knew, but she also had the common touch. When she knocked on the Maxwell door, midmorning, Jinger went into the parlor and looked out of a curtained window. Without answering, she let her guardians know that someone, whom she did not know, stood outside.

"Open the door, Jinger," urged Uncle Max, who was sitting in the kitchen with Tessa.

"But I don't know who it is that stands at the door," replied Jinger.

Aunt Tessa put her coffee down, walked through the parlor room, peeked out of the window, and rushed to answer the door.

"Why, Aunt Pudding, come on in! What are you doing milling around on a day like today?" asked Tessa, hugging her aunt at the front doorway.

Aunt Pudding then entered the front room of the Maxwell home. Her tall, straight posture and luminous, copper skin tone made her look imposing as she entered the door. The broad dark-blue hat that she wore made her appear even taller than Tessa. She smiled a toothy grin that emitted warmth, wonder, and mystery. She spoke like the old country woman she was.

"Well, Lil' Tessie, I started out early for the market this blessed day just befo' the clouds showed up," reported Aunt Pudding, giving Jinger a sweeping but pleasant look and nod as she removed her dark-blue cape.

Jinger smiled politely, a gesture defining how obviously mesmerized she was with her newly discovered great aunt.

"The skies wadn't as bad early this mornin', not like it is

naah. Look like it got darker and mo' windy as I walked. I hadn't headed this way, but this is where my feet took me, so I decided to pay y'all a visit—maybe see the storm go over. Got something t'eat?" asked Aunt Pudding as she sat down and looked around the room.

"Jinger, make Auntie some coffee, tea cakes, and sausage. Child, this is your great-auntie on my daddy's side!" commanded a cheerful Aunt Tessa.

Still captivated by her new acquaintance, she scurried to retrieve their guests' cape and hat to hang them in the closet. Then she headed to the kitchen to prepare her great-aunt some comforts on their cast iron stove.

Uncle Max came in and greeted Matilda with his usual inquiry to visitors, "Aunt Puddin', whatcha know good?"

Jinger flinched, thinking, "I've heard someone else use this saying before."

"I know God is good!" she replied emphatically.

"All the time!" piped in Aunt Tessa, enjoying the moment.

"He made ways for me out ah no way," she added, growing with excitement and shaking her head back and forth.

"Whatcha say?" queried Aunt Tessa, purposely encouraging her aunt to go deeper in the spirit.

Aunt Pudding was a highly spiritual woman, and every now and then, she might emit a sudden, throaty spiritual call-out. This was exactly how she responded to Tessa's question. Speaking in tongues, as they called it, was part of who she was. Everyone accepted this as part of her persona and pretended not to notice.

Possessing the gift of gab, she made small talk with Max and Tessa. Max was good at reading people, so after a while, sensing that the two women wanted to talk, he excused himself and left the front room and retired to rest in the back room. Tessa followed him into the room to make sure he was comfortable and that he took his medication.

During this time, Aunt Pudding wandered into the kitchen to check on her newly acquainted niece. While they exchanged pleasantries, she noticed Jinger's tea cake preparations and in a kind, still voice inquired, "Is that eatin' bread or dog bread?" This question was crushing to Jinger, as she generally took pride in her cooking skills. Aunt Pudding looked around the kitchen, spotted a hanging apron and put it on. She tasted the cake mix, then she gently asked Jinger for seasonings, added them and vigorously stirred the batter. Her instructions and cooking tips were done in such an endearing way until Jinger lost track of her feelings and focused on the chance to learn. After another taste, she showed Jinger how to drop the soft batter on the hot grill. When Jinger saw the results of her fluffy, moist teacakes, instead of feeling offended, she felt nothing but gratitude to the older woman. She smiled and thanked her Aunt Pudding, who returned with a smile and a twinkle in her eye. She then removed her apron and rejoined Tessa in the parlor just as she returned from her bedroom and had gently closed the door.

Soon Uncle Max's light snoring could be heard by the ladies in the front room. Tessa felt relieved that Max was getting some rest, since he was trying to overcome a slight cold and because he was a house busybody. He would tune in to every conversation in the house if he could.

Jinger served her aunts their breakfast that morning, then went back to the kitchen and busied herself while she waited for Rustin to return from his errand in town. While she did not purposely eavesdrop on the two women, she did her work quietly and soon overheard the probable reason for the unscheduled visit.

"Well, Tessie, you didn't hear it from me, but it's two things

I wanna tell ya, just since I happened this way," warned Aunt
Pudding, pausing and looking up toward the ceiling. "Naw, with
the dream I had, that'll be three." Looking over her shoulder
first, she continued. "Ya know they say quiet talk in town is that
Max was seen walkin' from over past the railroad tracks a couple
times last month."

"Now, why would he be walking when he has a vehicle out
there?" Tessa questioned aloud.

Two years earlier, Max had bought a Model T, one of the first
persons in Roxborough to own a car. He did not drive it much
around town for the same reason he had not driven his white
carriage often, which he had traded in for the automobile.

"Cain't answer that," she replied and shrugged. "Naah, that
don't mean he got to be doing nothin' wrong, but just keep yo'
eyes and ears open to study, 'cause you know they say Leeka Jane
is back in town. She's back in on Cecilia and Buddy. That don't
mean she up to nothin' bad, but if her record perceeds her, it
don't mean she up to anything good either," she said, squinting.

"You're talking about Doletha Jenkins? The one they call
Leeka?" queried Tessa, contemptuously.

"Shhhh," she cautioned, looking toward the back room,
where Max slept.

"Just a word on the tippy side," she said quietly. "Naah,
don't you go worryin' 'bout nothin', 'cause his eyes might wander
sometimes. Mos' men's eyes do, but he ain't crazy, neither. You and
Max got a nice place here, and he got a good living and a beaut'ful
wife. That's you, my niece. Umm...jes' sayin' be watchful. You
know the word tells us to watch and to pray, don't it? Am I right
or wrong?" She asked as she looked into Tessa's confused eyes.

Not waiting to hear a response, she continued. Jinger situated
herself in the kitchen so she could hear both her aunt Tessa and
her great-auntie. She could not see into the parlor, but she was

in good earshot of the conversation. Although her guardian said very little, there was a provocative cadence to Aunt Pudding's hushed tones, and a thirst in Aunt Tessa's silence that let her know this was a serious conversation. Finally, Aunt Tessa spoke up with feigned confidence. "But Aunt Pudding, why would I be worried about Leeka Jane? My Forrest would just be fallin' for a big booty and a snagga-tooth grin."

Jinger noticed how her usually well-spoken aunt took on the dialect of the Roxies when she felt insecure but corrected her and Rustin whenever they spoke with a country accent.

"Not no mo'. You must ain't seen Leeka Jane. She ain't much bigger than 'yo niece in there. Yea, she still got back, but she got ha teef fixed. I wonder how she paid for it, and her hair is right thick and on her shoulders. And you know she always was bright-skinded," retorted Aunt Pudding.

After a brief silence, she continued. "But she ain't pretty as you though, Tessie Lee, 'cause you pretty and got sense, plus got brains. Men these days want somebody who got sompthin', like you, Tessie. You got looks, class, infloonze, and prop'ty. What Leeka Jane got? She ain't nothing, but maybe good lookin'. You gotta admit Cecilia and Buddy do have some nice-lookin' chil'ren, but they ain't got nothin' else much to speak of. They tell me 'Cille done broke, and they talk like Buddy act like he got a room for rent, sometimes. I saw him in the market last month, though, and he talked with good sense to me. Anyway, beauty's only skin deep, and it sho' ain't gone pay nary a bill."

"That's right," said Tessa, weakly.

"Anyway, that ain't the worst of it," she continued. "'Twas two dreams I had about yo' household here. The first one was right spooky." She tilted her head, looking pensively. "The dream was like a riddle or puzzle or sompthin'. You remember old Deacon Oba Drew Craney, who died two winters ago? Well, I dreamed that he peeked into one of the back rooms of yo' house. As I remember, it was late at night in the dream. I could hardly make out that it was you and Max's place. Deacon Oba Drew was bent over but movin' fast around yo' house. He had those still, large, dark eyes. His look was what you call piercin'. Well, in de dream, he just shaded his thick eyebrows with his hand and looked in yo' back window, like he wanted to come in, but he didn't. Instead, he turned and walked away," revealed an animated Aunt Pudding.

Tessa, baffled, listened attentively anyhow. She was a firm believer that dreams were sometimes the result of an overabundance of southern cuisine eaten late at night.

"I cain't seem to get the second dream I had 'bout yo' husband straight.

I dreamed he was in a great big melon patch. In de dream, Max seemed to have been reachin' for one that wadn't ripe yet. It was in a fenced-in part of the patch. There wuz melons all around, but he had his eye on a green one. He reached for this certain honeydew; then I woke up. But that dream stuck with me. You know what they say about that. I jes' hope he ain't out there doing nothin' he ain't got no bizness doing," she wished, looking prayerfully at Tessa.

There was hushed silence from Tessa, who was beginning to believe that this might not be another "pork chop" dream.

"Naah, don't look so long, Tessie. I'm not having no say to hurt you. I jes' don't want nothin' to come on you unawares, that's all. I promised my brother Benny on his dying bed that I would look after my nieces and nephews. Ev'ry since we planted him, that's jes' what I done. 'Jes' be special alert, that's all um sayin'…and pray 'cause you know as well as I do that they all do somethin'. Naah, my husband smokes cigars. I don't care how much I let him know that I don't like it and that I think it's not healthy, he jes' won't change. The smell of those cigars fare stank. He did reach a point where he goes outside with it, so that's good, but he never gave it up. He good comp'ny, though, and that's what kept us. The comp'ny keeping and the comfort, 'cause everybody gone need somebody, so I stayed and done the best I could. Don't want to be lonely if I can hep it. The good Lord helped us to raise our five children to grownups. We had a lot of ups and downs, and he still smokes those smelly cigars sometimes, but we made it."

"But you young, Tessie, and at least Max provides a good living and has been good to you and the two lil' ones that you raisin'. So, I guess you have to weigh the matter and jes' keep praying jes' like you wuz taught."

"Hmmn," responded Aunt Tessa quietly.

Jinger did not hear her aunt Tessa's response, but in her mind, she visualized the ruminative way that her aunt Tessa looked when she was worried about something.

Aunt Tessa asked Jinger to place the kettle and the pan of tea cakes and sausage back on the stove to reheat them. Still dazed, but operating on instinctive hospitality, Tessa continued talking to her great-aunt about family news. A few minutes later, Jinger brought Aunt Pudding her comfort food. After drinking her coffee and eating her tea cakes, sausage and melon, she sat awhile longer and then asked for her cape and coat.

"Look like the storm done passed ovah."

"Yes, it has cleared up some," confirmed Tessa as she peered through her curtains toward the sky. "It's still overcast, though. You don't have to be in a hurry, Auntie."

"Love to stay, but I betta start on toward the market—then homeward." Tessa thanked her great aunt for stopping by without saying she enjoyed her company, since what she revealed that day was more torrid than the storm that had just passed.

"Jinger, bring Aunt Pudding her cape and hat," requested

Aunt Tessa without raising her voice but in a way to let Jinger know that she knew she had been eavesdropping all along. She dutifully brought the older woman her coverings without realizing she had been found out.

"You know you doing a mighty fine job with these two chil'ren that was dropped on ya. The trainin' you giving them will come in handy in this world. I heard that the new mayor they got talkin' 'bout closing the colored school. Lord hep us," she sadly reported.

Jinger froze when her Aunt Pudding mentioned this because she seemed to confirm what she had heard her friends whisper. She desperately hoped this was a passing fancy, rather than the truth.

"They say he don't believe in book learnin' for future d'mestiks and field hands," she continued.

"How can he say that? Who knows what children can become after their little lamps are lit with knowledge and understanding?" Tessa asked rhetorically.

"I don' know nothin' 'bout no lamps. You see, I passed *by* the schoolhouse. One thing I do know is that some folks want to keep us in de dark. I 'spect if this notion comes to pass, you'll need to think about the two you raisin'. You done a good job raisin' somebody else's—"

Before she could finish her sentence, there was a brisk rap on the front door. It was Felix Burns from Ducks Bottom. He was shouting for Uncle Max to come quickly because Rustin was hurt.

With Aunt Pudding and Aunt Tessa enthralled in their conversation, Uncle Max enraptured in his nap, and Jinger engrossed in her eaves-dropping, no one had noticed how long Rustin had been gone. He was only supposed to place a sign on Maxwell's Place, which should have taken him just an hour at the most. It was now near noon. Rustin did have a way of "going off staying", as Tessa called it. She had often complained and corrected him about his lengthy absences, but he stayed away from home a good deal anyway. Max finally persuaded Tessa to lay off Rustin about it because "the boy has a natural and healthy wanderlust", but a nearly three-hour absence after a simple errand was not normal.

Felix, meanwhile, was physically shaken and rapidly pacing back and forth on the front porch. Aunt Tessa quickly aroused Uncle Max from his nap, and he and Felix drove down the road to where Rustin lay in a semiconscious state.

When they reached him, they grimaced. There were bite-looking marks all over his torso, and left leg, and blood on his body and clothes. It looked like a pack of dogs had attacked Rustin, who lay listless and helpless by the roadside. They hurriedly lifted him up, transported his bleeding body to the Maxwell house porch, and laid him on a blanket where his wounds could be nursed before taking him into the house. Aunt Pudding took off her cloak and sprang into action. She ordered Jinger to bring her clean water and towels. She told Tessa to put a kettle of water on the stove and to bring it outside at the boiling point. She started talking to Rustin right away as she gingerly took his shirt off and cut his left pant leg open with her pocketknife.

"Russ, do you hear me? Just hold on now," she encouraged him. Quickly, Jinger and Tessa brought her towels and water. As she cleaned his wounds, she continued to talk to him. "Go through, go through; don't give up on yo' old auntie. Talk to me, Russ—talk to me!"

"Yes, ma'am…yes, ma'am," Rustin weakly managed to say as tears streamed down his face. Jinger also began to tear up because of his condition. She had not seen her brother shed a tear since the day they had left Baywater.

"Just stay with me now, Russ; you gone be all right, ya hear?"

Rustin, in severe pain, managed to nod to his aunt.

Aunt Pudding then continued. "Hold on, hold on, hold on, let go, let go, let go."

"Poor Rustin," Jinger mused to herself. "It's a wonder if he knows whether to hold on or to let go," she thought, considering their aunt's seemingly contradictory directions. Jinger was not familiar with the praying ways of the old saints.

Jinger and Tessa continued to go back and forth into the house to bring Aunt Pudding all the healing tools she needed. She cleaned his wounds repeatedly before concocting her secret balm composed of herbs, olive oil, and liniment. She then treated his wounds with her balm and, finally, wrapped them with clean cloth bandages.

Max looked at Rustin, stared intently down the road, and then looked at Felix. He did not say anything, but he was obviously pondering in his mind what had possibly happened.

"I had taken some potatoes that I owed to Farmer Pressley, and on my way back home, I found your nephew there lying in the road hurt. Nobody around but him," Felix informed Max.

Jinger looked at her aunt Tessa, who looked frantic and pale. She looked at the pitiful state of her brother and quietly sobbed as she helped attend to him. At one point, he began to groan in pain. Aunt Pudding spoke sweetly and confidently to him. Her words seemed to salve his angst, for his groans subsided. Tessa was mortified, but her aunt assured her that Rustin was going to be alright. She did not say anything; she just focused on her aunt's instructions and calm voice, which gradually diminished her anxiety.

By now it was approaching three o'clock in the afternoon. It was decided that Aunt Pudding would stay for supper and spend the night so she could make sure Rustin was healing well.

Tessa went to change Rustin's bed linen before he would be

brought inside and placed in his bed. While she was doing this, she looked at herself in a mirror in Rustin's bedroom and saw that she, who usually did not respond well to stress, appeared relieved and assured. She had her aunt to thank for this, and she let her know how grateful she was when she went back outside.

"Auntie, the Lord sent you here for such a time as this."

"Why yes, chile. He knows what He's doing, and He never makes a mistake. He knew ahead of time what the day would bring. He know'd you whilst you wuz in the womb, and don't you forget it, Lil' Tessie. He's a present hep in a time of trouble. You know that!" proclaimed Aunt Pudding, with a twinkle in her eye as she peered at Tessa.

She then directed her attention to Rustin. "You gonna be alright, champ; you know that, don't ya?" Not waiting for a response, she continued to minister to his spirit and his bodily wounds.

"He gone be what you call tall, dark, and handsome," said Aunt Matilda as she studied her patient. She looked at Tessa with a glimmer and an assuring smile, as Uncle Max and Felix picked him up and carried him to his bedroom.

"Yes, he is that. And he has quite a mind too," thought Tessa, nodding approvingly.

Rustin, emboldened by the flattery of his great-aunt, tried to stand up in his bedroom and would have limped to his bed, but Uncle Max stopped him.

"Jes' lie still, and let us help you, Russ," instructed Uncle Max.

By sundown, Rustin was clean, bandaged up once again, and sitting up in bed. Aunt Tessa fed him some leftover stew from the icebox. After he finished eating, all five of them stared at him as he fell asleep with his chest fluctuating like tides approaching the shore.

Max and Felix went outside and talked for a while and rode by the scene of the mishap again.

Out of gratitude to her great aunt Jinger, without prompting, warmed up some pails of water, made her great-aunt a warm bath, and changed the sheets on her bed. She made herself a resting place on the wooden floor out of a pallet of thick covers, which she placed in the east corner of her room. A little while later, Aunt Pudding came into the bedroom and marveled at her place of rest for the night.

"Lord, chile, whadn't that sweet of you to make such a fresh bed for your auntie?"

"Aunt Pudding, I also made you a warm bath," informed Jinger, gleefully.

"Sho' 'nuff? My, you ah sweet child, indeed," she responded as she gave Jinger a warm pat on the shoulder.

After her bath, she slowly walked to the bed. "Well, the old lady gone lie down here and git sum rest, 'cause I got to head out jes' befo' daybreak in the morning. Yo' uncle Cab will be wonderin' where I'm at. Naah, don't you go worrying 'bout 'yo brother, ya hear, 'cause Russ is strong like that boxa Jack Johnson, so he'll pull through jes' fine. You'll see," encouraged Aunt Pudding, smiling warmly at Jinger.

"Yes, ma'am," responded Jinger, calmly.

She turned off the gas lamp, and settled on her blanketed respite on the floor. It could have been more comfortable for her, but she had given her padded goose-feather-stuffed cover to her aunt for the night. It was a worthy sacrifice, since she now understood why the Jackson family called her Aunt Pudding. She was just that sweet, even if she was quite strange.

After they said their prayers and good nights, and despite her great-aunt's reassurance, Jinger did worry about Rustin. Her thoughts soon turned to him, and she pondered what might have happened to her brother that day. She lay awake for a while, listening to her great aunt's rhythmic snoring. She remembered the time when she would have been reluctant about the prospect of sharing her space with anyone and how she was sometimes dismissive of and impatient with older people. But tonight, Aunt Pudding's age, snores, and nocturnal sounds, did not bother her at all. She was extremely grateful that she had been there for Rustin that day, and she soon fell asleep.

In a nearby room, Max was sound asleep. Tessa, however, laid thinking quietly to herself about the day's events: her aunts visit, the mysteries of her dreams and folksy sayings, and Rustin's brutal injuries and surprisingly steady recovery. Within ten minutes, she heard the full drone of her Aunt Pudding's deep sleep. She pictured her great-aunt's body heaving gently up and down in the lilt of a person at peace with herself. She pondered over the riddles and rumors that her aunt had shared and whether they meant anything. Concerns regarding the quiet talk in town about Max kept her awake for a while that night, but eventually she fitfully dozed off.

Felix, too, had stayed and ate supper with the Maxwells. He and Uncle Max had surmised that Rustin's injuries were the result of foul play. Rustin, as it turned out, had come to the same conclusion. Instantly, when he woke up the next morning, he began to plot a way out of Roxborough. He couldn't say when or how exactly, but he had a feeling that he would get a chance to leave… real soon.

10

Rustin's Chance

Rustin turned sixteen on March 7, 1915, a day that he also began to plot an escape from Shady Grove. What his Uncle Max told him the day after he was attacked simply affirmed to him that leaving Roxborough would save his life and not just his soul: "I know you jes' a youngster, but I'd rather see you runnin' for your life than swinging from a tree."

This was, for certain, an ideal time for Rustin to leave. He had experienced a growth spurt and was tall for his age—much taller than Jinger, even. His deepened voice made him seem older as well. Roxy natives called him an old soul, referring to his quiet maturity. Since the brutal event of the previous fall, he had become more of a listener. Not wanting to attract any undue attention to himself that could possibly derail his plans, he carefully chose his words and showed more deference toward the opinions of his elders. He no longer brimmed with questions as he had growing up, primarily because he had discovered answers to the questions he had posed as a youngster and held tentative answers to questions he could no longer safely ask in public. His inquisitive nature persisted, but it had to be safeguarded for a more accommodating environment.

At the end of January, the mayor successfully closed the town's school for Negroes, so Rustin had a greater incentive to leave. Besides, he was learning more away from school than he was at school, since he read every book that he could. In fact, for years he had been secretly going to a library in a larger city near

Roxborough to read after hours a few days a week when school was out. The library's janitor, who was one of Uncle Max's regular customers, gave him access while he worked the evening shift. This explained Rustin's disappearances and why he was prone to "going off staying". The librarian never learned about this; otherwise, the custodian would have surely lost his job.

As usual, he methodically completed his chores at Maxwell's, but now he went straight home after work and helped his Aunt Tessa. In the barbershop, he listened intently to the daily banter about what was happening up North, about local news, and especially stories about the lynching's in the area and other brutalities that occurred in the South. Most Shady Grove residents deserted the streets long before dark due to the tense times.

Uncle Max noticed Rustin's newfound reticence, made a mental note of it, but said nothing to him. The one long talk he had with him after the previous fall's incident was sufficient, as far as he was concerned. He hoped his young charge would heed his pointed warnings.

Aunt Tessa, pleased with Rustin's laconic transformation, was also relieved that he came home when he was not at Maxwell's Place. She grieved every time she heard stories or firsthand accounts about brutal attacks on innocent individuals in the area. Consequently, she rested better knowing Rustin was home and not at some unknown location.

Jinger, however, was bothered by the change she saw in her brother. Prior to the incident, he had been out-going and spirited, and he had displayed a deep sensitivity and distaste for injustice. To her, it seemed like Rustin's spirit had been broken.

As a family, they had never discussed the incident, so Jinger dismissed it in her mind as an accident—not because she believed it was but for the sake of her own sense of emotional stability. Uncle Max, Aunt Tessa, and their close neighbor Mr. Myles had reminded her and Rustin often that they were in the South and they had to be careful. She could still hear Aunt Tessa's warnings in her ear: "It's best not to be by yourself, if you can help it," she warned.

Jinger remembered Rustin's wounds, so she knew they had to have been either bite or knife wound marks. For many nights, before falling asleep, she tried to solve the mystery of who was responsible for the attack on Rustin. She knew of no particular enemies he had, but she recalled Uncle Max's constant refrain: "You ain't got to be nowhere actin' bad for nothin' to happen to you. Living while being colored is a crime in and of itself, in these parts."

As Jinger reflected, she thought about some possible culprits who could have instigated an attack on her brother. Rustin had confided to her once that the Jiles brothers treated him poorly and taunted him occasionally because he liked their sister, Tandy. He was smitten with the tall, high-yellow, ponytailed, and pretty Tandy Jean Jiles. She and Jinger had been friends and classmates, even though she was two years younger than Jinger, since Jinger began school for the first time as a nine-year-old after moving to Roxborough. Tandy was a year older than Rustin. While Rustin started school later than Tandy, his teachers marveled at how quickly he grasped concepts in class. Tandy was impressed with his intellect, but she initially ignored his romantic overtures. Eventually, he won her over with his fun ways, spirit, and quick wit. She had begun to allow him to walk her home after school. She was sometimes seen giggling and playing games with him in the schoolyard. By appearances, Tandy really liked Rustin. It was obvious that they had developed a mutual respect for each other and a growing friendship. That was until Tandy's father heard about it. Thomas Jiles, a blacksmith, sent word to Rustin that he should stay away from his daughter. Reportedly, he did not mince words about Rustin to his sons.

"Rustin who? You're talking about the bastard nephew of Forrest Maxwell, who ain't even real blood? No way!" he said, indignantly shaking his head after his sons shared this bit of information with him. He ignored the fact that his sons were impressed with Rustin's intellect.

"Not for my Tandy. He is too black and too ignorant, and he is not suitable in the least for my daughter."

He forbade Tandy from associating with Rustin or Jinger. At school, Tandy reacted to her father's edict with detachment and sadness, although Jinger later learned that she had tried to persuade her father to change his mind. Rustin was heartbroken, yet for a couple of months he continued to send her sweet notes and treats until their relationship tapered off, especially after the school was closed. He gradually turned his interests to other things, but Jinger sensed a lovelorn feeling of rejection in her brother. Because Mr. Jiles had gotten what he wanted, she dismissed him and his sons as suspects in the vicious attack. From one of her eavesdropping sessions she deduced that another person of interest was old Mr. Cheney.

Mr. Cheney, one of the largest landowners and richest farmers in Roxborough, heard about Rustin's ability and offered him a farm supervisor's assistant position and promised him good wages, in spite of his young age. Uncle Max and Aunt Tessa stridently opposed the idea. They saw this is as a ploy by old man Cheney to use Rustin for his own designs. Uncle Max said it would be foolish to take the bait on the offer because he saw it as just a trick to get Rustin in debt at a young age, tied to the land, and bamboozled into mistreating the field hands. He further resented the idea of a young boy being lured into working for "good wages".

"There ain't no good wages in farming, especially if it ain't your own farm. The only type of farm labor I've seen is working slave labor. I've seen other promising youngsters choose this path, only to grow old in this way of life at the expense of their own pursuit of happiness," Jinger overheard Uncle Max emphasizing to Rustin at the time.

Rustin, though, saw this as an opportunity to earn and save money to flee Roxborough. Uncle Max's response to this was, "Rustin, all money is not good money." He further cautioned him to find another way to leave Roxborough with "no weights". In finality, he told him that it was out of the question and not up for future discussion. Mr. Cheney could not get his clutches on an underage youngster without the approval of his guardian, so that was the end of that, and it eliminated Mr. Cheney from consideration as Rustin's attacker, since his real dispute was with Uncle Max. Try as she might, Jinger could not solve the mystery, but then, she had never been told about Rustin's spat with Judge Seymour.

Jinger had not been made aware of another close call. One afternoon in May, two men at the barbershop had sized her up when she made a delivery for Aunt Tessa. Rustin noticed how the two new patrons looked at his sister, who had just turned fourteen years old. He immediately felt distressed and asked for and received permission from Uncle Max to escort Jinger home that day. The two took their usual route home along the edges of a lake in a forestry area. Ever observant, Rustin heard the sound of dry leaves crackling behind them. Alarmed, he then challenged Jinger to race him home. It was a spirited race, as usual, for it was something they did on most weekends ever since they had arrived in Roxborough. Once they were within a quarter mile from home, Rustin—without Jinger noticing, since she was always faster and ahead of him—turned around and purposely looked to see if anyone was behind them. Shockingly, like a nightmare, he saw the same two men who had stared at Jinger and then at each other at the shop earlier. They were stooped over, about two hundred feet away, obviously out of breath, with one removing his faded confederate cap and slapping his knees and the other wiping his brow with his hand. Rustin never divulged this, nor the evil foreboding he had about the two men, to Jinger. Instead, he warned her to always be aware of her surroundings and not to ever take short cuts or walk long treks alone. He also made sure he mentioned the chase to his Uncle Max and Aunt Tessa that evening. Jinger never delivered lunches, or anything else, unaccompanied to Maxwell's from that day forward. As she was never told of this incident, it did not enter her mind as she tried to solve the mystery of who had attacked her brother.

Rustin, growing restless, pondered every day about how he could get out of Roxborough. Never doubting he would discover an exit strategy, he believed that the answer would merely come to him, and it did one day at his uncle's barbershop.

Business was slow that day, so Uncle Max asked Rustin to watch the shop while he went to buy a few supplies from the market.

"Be back in about an hour. I expect Cecil Blaylock. If he comes early, just tell 'em to wait. I'll be back near time to cut his hair."

"Yes, sir."

Rustin went into the back room to get a broom and dustpan. He heard the door bells jingle just as he was coming out. It was Doc, short for Doctor Hudson, who some called "Sarge".

Doc was not a medical doctor. His mother decided to give him this first name in order to elicit respect. Mrs. Hudson cringed when she heard men, including her husband, being referred to as "boy" or "Hey, boy". She wanted her son to grow up with a healthy self-esteem. Although it would be just as easy for an actual Negro doctor to be referred to as "boy", she still believed her son would escape the demeaning moniker if he had a first name that would concede respect. Part of her plan worked, since Doc grew up to become a confident and respected man. However, as a youngster, Doc was very talkative and restless. He was always in motion and touching things he shouldn't, so the folks in the Kessler household where Mrs. Hudson worked as a cook, began calling him "Rascal". To Dorothy Hudson's dismay, the name stuck with her son. So, as a youngster, he was known as Rascal. Only his family and close friends called him Doctor—or more popularly, Doc—as he grew from childhood to manhood.

Doc Hudson, down to earth and amiable, had a way with words. He served the country in uniform during the Spanish American War and came home striped. His intelligence, fair and good-natured ways endeared him to his fellow warriors, so they affectionately called him Sarge, as did many of the residents of Shady Grove after he returned home from active duty.

"Where's your uncle Max?" he inquired as he entered the shop.

"He went to get some hair supplies. Was he expecting you, Doc?"

"Just call me Sarge, son. I don't need two titles," he said, smiling. "All my life folks been giving me titles," he said amusedly as he looked around the shop.

"Yes, sir…I mean Sarge," Rustin responded.

"I don't really have an appointment with Max. I just wanted to talk a little town business, and find out what's going on in the

Grove…see if maybe he can work me in for a cut. You think you can give me a shoe shine while I wait?"

"Yes, Sarge." Rustin liked the fact that he conversed with him without calling him "boy" every few words, like many of the other patrons. Rustin offered him the daily newspaper, but he declined and said he had read it before he came to the shop.

"I'll take a glass of ice water if you have that, though."

"I have soda water…would you like a cold bottle of soda water?"

"Yeah, give me some of that red soda water."

Rustin gave his customer his requested drink and then began his shoe shine. Recognizing that he would have very little time to spend with Sarge alone, he began with small talk, hoping to steer the conversation to wartime stories and army recruitment. He was enamored with his patron because he had served as a Buffalo Soldier in the army and lived to tell about it. Rustin had heard him recount his war stories in the shop before, but he never tired of listening to them.

"You're a good shoe shiner."

"Thanks."

"Your uncle Max tells me you're good with figures, too."

"I reckon I am. Hey, Sarge, how would a young guy like me go about getting into the army?" Rustin asked, moving the armed services question along faster than he had planned.

Surprised, Sarge paused. "You think…you want to go to the army, son? What yo' Uncle Max think about that?"

"I haven't really talked with him about it. I expect he wouldn't mind, though. What he doesn't want is for me to get tied to the land and spend my life in the tenant farming way of life."

"Listen to yo' uncle, 'cause that's exactly where I was headed. And when I look around and think about my time in the army, my travels, and even my trials, I thank my great God that I got out of here when I did. Only reason I left the army is that I injured my knee, or I would still be there with the Tenth Cavalry!" confessed Sarge, pumping his fist with pride.

"How old are you, son?"

"Sixteen," answered Rustin.

"That's mighty young, but I've seen it done in my day, though...boys yo' age slip into the service. It will be tough, but it would sure beat hangin' around the Rox for a hapless life or shall I say, existence. You're smart to think in terms of giving yo'self a chance."

Sarge was quiet for a moment, and nothing could be heard but the rhythmic slap of the shoeshine rag sliding over his shoes. He studied Rustin for a few moments before saying more.

"You listen to me, son. Going to the army ain't no plaything. Especially if you serve in war time. You will see and experience things that will make you want yo' momma. It will make a man out of ya, but you must work hard in training, be willing to take orders, be humble, be a team player, and know who you are. Don't ever forget that. I can understand a smart boy like you wanting to get out of the Rox and see other parts of the states, maybe even the world, but know what you're gettin' into," he said emphatically.

Abruptly, the barbershop door opened to the sound of the bell. Max entered with his customer Cecil Blaylock and an armful of supplies.

"Whatcha know good, Doc?" queried Max.

"Nothin' up but the rent," he responded jovially.

"Be right back." Uncle Max left to retrieve another bag of supplies from the outside steps.

"I might be able to help you, Russ. Let me talk to Max, see what we can hatch out." He then reached into his pocket to pay Rustin.

"No, Sarge, this one is on me," Rustin said.

"Why, thank you, son. That's mighty generous of you," he said, smiling and slapping Rustin on the back as he took a seat in Max's chair.

When Uncle Max reentered the shop, he nodded to Cecil. He asked Sarge to take the waiter's chair until he could cut Cecil. Sarge quickly moved. The three of them soon began exchanging stories about earlier times, Shady Grove news, and current events as Max trimmed his patron's hair. They obviously enjoyed each other's company in spite of their discernable age difference. As they visited, Rustin listened quietly to their stories and laughter as he went about his work in the shop. Although he did not hear the two men discuss him, he felt confident that Sergeant Hudson would keep his word.

Max and Rustin began working shorter hours at the barbershop, as it seemed that fewer patrons were coming in. Some of the residents of Shady Grove began moving north to Chicago, Milwaukee, or New York City after racial tensions intensified in the area, especially in nearby Savannah. Aunt Tessa launched a small baking and laundry enterprise to help fill in the income gap. When Rustin delivered towels for Aunt Tessa, she would always slip him a few coins after he returned home with the day's receipt. He saved his coins for the day he would leave Roxborough. He did not know when that would be, but he had been saving his change from the day he began working at Max's place. He looked at his jar every night, which was stowed under his bed. He thought to himself that although it wasn't much, it was better than nothing. He knew he would need money when he left the borough. Although he was not sure if he would get a cash send-off from his aunt and uncle, he mused to himself that he did have "hope and cents," smiling at his own play on words.

Rustin did not hear anything from Doc Hudson for months.

He sometimes became impatient and forlorn about his future. He looked around him, and there was increasing scarcity, tension, and a contentious under-current in the Grove. He watched as some of his young peers moved north with their families; others spoke of it, and still others settled for life in Roxborough.

It was around this time that Jinger pondered her future. She thought she would make a good seamstress or maybe a schoolteacher like Aunt Tessa had once been.

One night after dinner, Rustin asked, "J. R., why do you look so sad?"

"Sometimes I'm afraid for my future. I wonder if I'll be able to get some more book learning, so when I do leave the Grove, I will have a future."

Rustin mostly listened. After the city closed Shady Grove Grammar school, which had been renamed Stony Brook, at the end of the winter session, the affected students and their parents fretted and pondered about their futures.

"It will all work out, Rosie," Rustin said, using the name he sometimes called her. "I think we will both be able to leave Shady Grove. We just have to wait for the right time."

After Mayor Gaines closed their school, he had the books shipped to Somerset in the Kingston Township, forty miles away. Somerset rejected the books, however, after they discovered where they came from. The mayor made his opinion known that book learning for Negroes served no purpose but to stir up trouble between whites and the serving class.

Maybelle Hunter, a former colleague of Aunt Tessa's at Stony Brook, had an encounter with the mayor's wife at the town grocery store. While in line, the school teacher had expressed her disappointment about the schools closing with the parents of one of her former students.

Overhearing the conversation, Mrs. Gaines had chimed,

"What a shame it is for those poor colored children not to have a school for their own kind," she had empathized. "As a woman, though, it is my place to support my husband in these things," she had said, matter-of-factly. Turning to Miss Hunter, who was now out of a job, she had offered more.

"It's sad, really, but I wouldn't imagine that a fine, smart young lassie like yourself would have any trouble finding work."

"No, ma'am, but in these parts there's not much work to be had."

Mrs. Gaines walked closer to Miss Hunter, touched her arm, and said, "Why, sure, there is work. I mean I was just looking for a housekeeper myself. You know you could keep house for me part time and tutor students, as well. All with coming-and-going privileges, after hours, of course. Why, it would work perfectly for my girls and little Jim, who could all use some tutoring on the side." Mrs. Gaines was pleased with herself for making the offer.

"Well, I was looking for something more in my field," Miss Hunter had wryly replied.

"You mean out in the fields? Out in the hot sun? Why, if you wouldn't mind my saying, I think that would be going backward," she said with a frown.

"Oh, no," Miss Hunter had reassured her. "I meant in the field of teaching school."

"Why, tutoring my three after school hours *is* in your field and right down your alley," she said.

Maybelle Hunter had already decided to return to her native Kentucky. She had family there who were seeking a teaching position for her. As soon as she knew Stony Brook would be closing for sure, she cabled her mother, sister, aunt, and cousins. She planned to leave Roxborough by month's end, but she kept this to herself.

"Thank you kindly. I will give that some thought, Mrs. Gaines."

"You jes' think about it, and let me know, dearie."

It was quite by accident that Mrs. Gaines encountered Miss Hunter again a few weeks later. She went to mail some letters at the town post office, which was located in the same building as the train depot. At first, she did not see the former teacher, who sat waiting near a window with two books neatly on her lap. When Mrs. Gaines noticed the seated woman, she rushed to her side. "Why, Miss Hunter, it's so nice to see you again."

"Likewise," Miss Hunter replied as she stood up, smiling.

"Why ever are you here? Are you mailing or receiving?" Without waiting for a response, she said quietly, "Did ya give my offer any more thought?"

"Yes, ma'am, and I made my decision. My mother said there is a schoolteacher in our hometown who is pregnant with twins and has chosen not to return to work for the spring session. I have an interview set up for the position a week from Tuesday."

Mrs. Gaines recoiled and slowly looked Miss Hunter up and then down, only then noticing how well dressed she was.

"That's if they hire ya," Mrs. Gaines blurted out.

"It's entirely possible they may not hire me. If they don't, then I have my sights set on a position at the college there."

Just as she finished her statement, the train whistled, and the conductor made a call for boarding. A porter brought Miss Hunter her suitcases and hatbox.

"They board pretty quickly, Miss Hunter," he warned. "Is there anything else I can get for ya? I 'spect you better get ready to board."

"No, Nelson. That will be all," she said as she stepped toward the train boarding area. First, she gave him a dollar bill and smiled at the old porter. He placed her bags at the point of the open train door.

"Well, here's your ticket, and Godspeed, ma'am," he said as

he held out his hand, which she took as she stepped up to the boarding platform. He then followed with her bags.

"Thank you so much, Nelson. Good-bye now, Mrs. Gaines."

Mrs. Gaines stared at her indignantly as she boarded for her destination. Miss Hunter then waved to her, but the older woman had glared, turned her head, and left the station without comment.

Stories like this were common to Shady Grove residents. Such incidents usually reached the Maxwell home by way of shop talk. Although Max was the least vocal person at home, he was careful to share such incidents with the three of them. After sharing his story about the local schoolteacher and the mayor's wife, he admonished Rustin and Jinger to learn the right lessons from these stories.

"Ya see, that's what um talking about. Perfect example of why it's good to get a good skill of your own that no one can take away. Yes, suh, get you ah education, if you can, so that you are beholden to no one. 'Cause if you hang around here long enough, you will find yourself in debt, and when ya know anything, you in so deep you'll never see yo'self out—couldn't go nowhere if you wanted to—and ya find yourself livin' and workin' for others all of your days, void of hope or promise. Colored folks think they're free, but they're not, though—not as long as Mr. Charlie sets the rules and holds all the financhel power. Remember that!"

Rustin looked at Jinger, Jinger looked at Aunt Tessa, and they all looked at Uncle Max, stunned, after never having heard him speak that many words together at home before.

~ ~ ~

Rustin grew even wearier of waiting to leave by early fall. He was quiet but was sometimes short with others and he had problems sleeping at night. He busied himself at Maxwell's Place every day and ran errands for Aunt Tessa. He longed for the day when he could leave Roxborough and Shady Grove behind. The waiting was suffocating.

Late one cold December night, he was startled abruptly from his slumber. Uncle Max was shaking him from a deep sleep.

"Get up, Russ. They're here." Though dazed, Rustin could hear voices in the next room. He threw on a shirt and pants and went into the front room. There, standing in the room, were Sarge Hudson and Chester, the letter carrier.

"Evenin', son," Sarge greeted him.

"Good evening, Sarge," he said as he wiped the glazed look and sleep from his eyes.

"Bet you thought I forgot all about ya. But I hadn't. I just needed to arrange some things. This is Mr. Chester. You know him. He's one of the letter carriers."

Rustin stifled a yawn as he greeted him.

"It's almost midnight naah, but Mr. Chester here will be leaving the Rox early in the morning. He can deliver you safely to Pelican's Peak, where an old army buddy of mine will be expecting you. His name is Samuel Crosby; he'll introduce you to some service men that will be going back to Fort Benning by week's end. Don't worry about a place to stay or any food; Sam will take care of all of that. These fellas can be trusted to deliver you safely to the army recruiters. They'll give you a good lookin' over and ask you a few questions. Nothin' that you won't be able to answer. They'll ask about the scars from your accident, so be prepared to tell 'em something. When they ask for your birth certificate, just tell 'em you wadn't quite able to locate it. Now I'm not sayin' to lie or anything, but they don't take recruits under seventeen years old, or so they say. I think you know where I'm going with this. When it comes to figurin', I want you to shine, young man. God gave you that gift, and do not put it where it cain't be seen. Make yourself useful in that area. This skill that everyone knows you have, will mor'n likely open some doors for you. Don't forget where you came from and show Max and Tessa the respect of an occasional letter or visit to let them know how you're faring. That's the least you can do after they took you in."

Rustin was wide-eyed by now, and he listened intently to his instructions. He asked a few questions and expressed his gratitude. "I sure do thank you, Sarge! I know you didn't have to do this," he said as he shook his hand.

"Think nothing of it. If we don't help one another, there ain't no help for us. The way you pay Sarge back is to help other youngsters who are coming up and pinin' for a better life. Jes' stay humble, do your best, be willing to help others, and may the light from the Lord's lighthouse shine upon you. Godspeed to you, son. Go and make Max, Tessa, and Sarge proud."

"Yes, sir!" Rustin playfully saluted.

The two men departed, one to return in a few hours. Mr. Chester would come for Rustin at 4:00 a.m. This gave him exactly four hours to pack and prepare himself to leave Roxborough for an uncertain future.

Jinger's small room was close to Rustin's, and she overheard the stirring and the conversation from her quarters. She pondered the news and instinctively went to Rustin's room to help him pack. They fluttered about packing with a sense of excitement. As they did so, Jinger's initial feelings of joy gradually turned into contrition. She began to think about how much she would miss her brother and the impact his departure might have on her own future in the Maxwell home.

Jinger grew quiet, but Rustin said, "Don't worry, J. R., things will work out for you. Just be careful and stay close to Aunt Tessa Lee. I don't think you should trust anyone else but her. And whatever you do," the two repeated at the same time, "don't get stuck in the Rox."

They both laughed. Brother and sister hugged each other and said their good-byes. Jinger cried, but Rustin had a look of anticipation in his eyes as he tucked in his shirt.

Max gave Rustin a fifty-dollar bill and instructed him to keep his eye on his money, keep it tucked away well, and to spend it sparingly. Rustin's eyes grew big. He thanked his uncle Max and reached to shake his hand. Uncle Max, instead, stared at him and gave him an awkward side hug. Aunt Tessa gave him twenty dollars. She then gave him a warm hug, exuding warmth and goodwill, just as she had on the day he and Jinger had arrived from Baywater. Rustin traded his jar of coins with Aunt Tessa in exchange for another twenty-dollar bill. He said he did not think there was twenty dollars' worth of change in the jar, but she waved him off. Not one to be left out, Jinger gave her brother nine dollars, which was the only money she had. Rustin quipped that he was a dollar short. Max then reached into his pocket and gave his nephew four quarters.

Mr. Chester arrived at four o'clock sharp. Rustin hugged his aunt again and promised to write and to return to see them. The two then left into the chilly, wet night.

When she arose the next morning, Jinger checked Rustin's room, half expecting to find him there. It then dawned on her that her brother was really gone and wouldn't be back any time soon, if at all.

She crawled back into her bed and wept.

11

Jinger Moves On

Summer waned, and a hint of fall could be felt in the crisp afternoon air. Jinger sat motionless on the front porch's two-seat rocking swing and thought about her home life. She found a happy place inside her mind, that tended toward learning about people and what it meant to be a young lady. Recognizing this, Tessa emphasized the graces of being feminine and staying near home. Rustin, it seemed, had been allowed to be away from home on occasion, while she was kept under a more watchful eye. As much as she cared for her aunt Tessa, especially, and appreciated Uncle Max, she felt slighted, at times, because she was a girl. Although this fact bothered her, she chose not to dwell on it.

She soon stood up and looked beyond a flower box of slightly wilting, pink throat daffodils, to the end of the picket fence. Looking eastward, she peered down the street. She was waiting for her friend Lacy, who was due back to Shady Grove that day. She had gone to visit her grandmother in Chicago for the month of August, as she had every summer since Jinger had known her. Upon her return, she would usually regale her friend with stories from up North about city life and a cultured way of living; a mode of life that Jinger never experienced when she and Rustin lived in the North.

Lacy said people spoke differently in Chicago, and her grandmother reminded her of where she came from by frequently correcting her southern way of speaking. She said she had resisted this new way of speaking until she overheard two girls referring to her as a "country, backwoods heifer". She had explained to Jinger how this had really hurt her feelings and prompted her to try harder to change her diction so she could fit in. After this incident, when she returned to Shady Grove after Labor Day each year, Jinger had to listen to her friends lofty and overly precise pronunciation of words and put up with her airs. A few times, she even corrected Jinger's way of speaking. She was fond of Lacy and wanted to preserve the friendship so she tolerated her and loved her the same. After all, through patience, Jinger learned that the fledgling language butterfly would usually transform back into her previous tone and fun-loving antics by winter. So, this day, like every summer's end before, she looked forward to Lacy's return. The anticipation of fun talk and gifts of sparkly trinkets and sweet candies from Chicago helped assuage her growing longings to leave the Grove permanently.

As she sat back down on the gently moving porch swing, she began to daydream about leaving on a train heading north to launch her future. Since Rustin's departure, she had stayed busy helping Aunt Tessa and her sisters with their laundry business. She sometimes accompanied her aunt on delivery errands downtown. She missed her brother immensely, but a part of her was happy that he would no longer have to look at the dusty streets of Shady Grove or walk on eggshells every day for fear of breaking southern Jim Crow rules, laws, and customs. The resident fear of offending white folks and of throwing one's life into jeopardy distressed Jinger and Rustin, as it did most Shady Grove residents.

Her reverie then turned to Uncle Max, particularly on how much less time he was spending at home and how this fact seemed to be worrisome to Aunt Tessa. Sometimes when she passed through downtown to make her deliveries, Jinger noticed how Uncle Max would eye the handful of women who visited the shop for various reasons. She thought it odd behavior for a married man to be signaling other women with his eyes, but she dared not tell Aunt Tessa. She loved her aunt and did not want to say or do anything to add to her obvious anguish. Nevertheless, she wondered if others had noticed what she saw. She thought about Violet and Blanche's recent visits to the Maxwell home to see Aunt Tessa and how the three whispered behind closed doors. Try as she might, Jinger could not hear their conversation, which was usually in the parlor. She knew something was afoot, and she was determined to find out what it was. Just as she began to ponder more deeply into the riddle of her aunts' visits and secluded conversations, her friend came barreling down the street.

Lacy was tall for her age, dark brown-skinned, and gangly, but she carried her height with a sense of elegance. Her hair was medium length, and she kept it curled under. She wore a bang to cover her forehead because she thought it was too large. She was a confident girl, and she accepted Jinger. The two greeted each other with air hugs, side to side, as they had since they were preteens. They laughed when they saw each other, at nothing in particular. Lacy then presented her friend with several small boxes. Once they were seated on the swing, Jinger opened her gifts. One contained an assortment of flavored peppermints. Inside the other small box was a pair of hooped earrings with two, ornate roses on the base.

"Oh, I love these earrings!" Lastly, she opened the brown bag that her friend presented to her. "And a record too!" Jinger said with a hint of excitement. "Let's see who it's by. Oh, my gosh!" She leaned back in the swing, feigning a faint. "Jelly Roll Morton!" Jinger thanked her friend and gave her a warm hug.

"I'm glad you like your gifts, sister girl."

"So, what's new in Chi' Town this time?"

"The people are still moving there by the droves."

"Lot of people from the South?"

"I mean a lot! They come by train and bus, whole families from Grandma and Pop to the babies."

"What's the new craze?"

"Let's see, The Swing, fashion, bright colors, proper talking, straight hair, and jazz. And they got books, art, fairs, and entertainment for *our kind* of people. They say it all started in New York, but there's excitement in Chi' Town too. I'll tell you, there's a lot going on in Chicago that we don't hear about here in Georgia."

"Wow, all of that?"

"Yes, all of that and more. Let's go in the parlor, and I can show you some moves."

The two went into the parlor; they moved the furniture to make room for dancing and played a record on the phonograph. Lacy then swung onto the floor. She began with the cakewalk but then began to loop her long legs around to a point in the front and then back. Jinger recognized this as the Charleston. She laughed as she kicked her legs high, maneuvered a backward motion, and then moved forward. Her arms, shoulders and legs swayed side to side, as she danced with high-stepping cadence.

"Come on and try it, Jin," she said between loops.

Lacy took the lead as the two girls began the hop, turning, stepping, and twirling to the music. They touched hands and strode cheek to cheek, and then one slipped the other under her arm. Then, they each flipped the other one over their backs. They laughed, danced, and performed for about half an hour.

Then Max came home from work, looked in the parlor, and frowned. He proceeded to the kitchen. When Jinger saw his countenance, she turned the music down, and the two girls gave their dance a last swirl and then collapsed on the couch. They looked at each other and laughed heartily.

Uncle Max came back into the parlor and said, "Y'all bet' not be playin' on that record player long."

He then walked deliberately across the room and opened the window, as if the room had a scent. He eyed the two girls, looked somberly around the room, and left. Jinger and Lacy looked at each other and rolled their eyes.

"We should straighten the furniture back like it was," Jinger said, her face flushed and her voice etched with slight disappointment. The two of them reconfigured the furniture and then visited for a few more minutes.

"I'd better go. Momma Sadie will be looking for me."

"Lacy, don't go. We're having so much fun and it seems like you barely got here."

"I wouldn't mind staying but it seems like your uncle Max has an attitude."

"He's just grumpy like that sometimes."

"Seems like most times, lately."

"Let's go to the picture show Saturday afternoon."

"That sounds good. Come by and pick me up from Aunt Lottie's. I have to babysit until two. I'll bring my sister's big purse, and we can hide some pickles, dry Kool-Aid packages, chips, and candy to eat at the show."

"Okay, but what about something to drink."

"You think your Aunt Tessa could give you a couple of coins for drinks."

"Yeah, I'm sure she would."

"I'll see you at two o'clock Saturday, then."

"See ya."

The two gave each other hugs on each side, and Lacy left. The gate clamped loudly behind her. Jinger stood on the porch and watched as her friend left walking down the street. Before she could turn, she felt a presence close to her. She looked up and saw her uncle Max. She walked past him on the porch and into the parlor.

"I don't want that girl hangin' round here, you hear?"

"Aunt Tessa said I could have friends over. She said it's healthy, and she's known the Paramores for a long time."

"Tessa ain't payin' no bills around here."

"She's your wife, though, and I know she has some say, doesn't she?" sassed Jinger.

"You do like I say. Anyway, it's time for you to start earnin' yo' keep," he said as they entered the house.

"Aunt Tessa has been taking me around to find a sewing or laundry job. She says we will just have to be patient, but we will find something. Then I can pay for my keep. Where is Aunt Tessa anyway—she said she would be back by now," Jinger said, fanning her face with her hand.

Max was silent. Jinger looked at him impatiently and went to her room. His eyes followed her. He did not say anything, but his expression and thoughts were dark. Jinger decided to take a short nap before starting dinner. She was anxious for her aunt to return to Shady Grove. She had joined her family on a day trip. She and her sisters and great-aunt and uncle had gone to clean the home and pay a visit to the daughter of a dear deceased friend. The sickly new mother was recovering from a difficult childbirth and needed help and support.

Feeling under the weather earlier in the day, Jinger had stayed home. She was bothered, though, by the way Uncle Max had acted while her aunt Tessa was away. She was sure she smelled alcohol on his breath, and she felt she would just rest better with her aunt at home. She thought she heard a noise at her door. She sat up. Before she lay back down, she placed a chair under her doorknob, preventing easy access to her bedroom. She lay still for a long while. Hearing nothing further, she drifted into a sound sleep.

The highway converted into an open expanse. There were grassy pastures that gave way to alluring open fields. Jinger saw leafy green plants and rows of windmills and corn crops. Fields of radiant wildflowers, lavender and pink moss coverings, along with rows of sunflowers raced past as she sat on the silver-gray bus. She yawned, looked out of the window, and smiled a half-moon smile in anticipation as she rode. She was pleased but did not know what to expect. The road seemed long, but there weren't many passengers left on the bus now, as she neared her destination. The windows were opened just enough to spread a breeze on the bus. Jinger was glad because it kept the body odors at bay earlier, when the bus was full. She was finally going up North to Shelby Falls, in the Clifton Heights enclave right outside of the big city. She clutched her papers and looked down. Her referral letter described her as a "Negro girl; five feet and seven inches tall; with a slight build, dark-brown eyes, and black hair; a good worker; willing to work weekends; requires little supervision." She hoped her letter of introduction and recommendation would land her a job with the Kendall family. She would be a nanny to their three daughters. This was not what she had planned, but it got her out of Roxborough, albeit to an uncertain future. When she arrived at the bus depot, she noted a man and his wife looking expectantly her way. They spotted her, nodded, and said something to each other. The mister introduced himself as Dr. Silas Kendall. He shook her hand and took her bags. She followed him to Mrs. Kendall, who was not as warm but friendly enough.

The Kendalls were not like regular Negroes. He looked like he had a tan, and Mrs. Kendall was of a darker hue, but had a decided air about her. When Jinger got into their automobile, she noticed three girls of different ages between three and nine years old. They may as well have been triplets; they looked so much alike. They smiled at their new governess, asked her questions, and became acquainted with her on the way to their home. Everyone was pleasant enough. They lived in a beautiful craftsman home, and Jinger's living arrangements were plainly chic. Hers was a small attic room with a slanted ceiling that had ivory laced curtains covering the window. The Kendalls seemed like nice people, so Jinger was relieved. After settling into her living quarters, she closed her bedroom door and was startled to find her uncle Max standing behind the just closed door staring at her.

Startled, she woke up from her slumber. She got out of bed, washed her face, and hands, then grabbed her apron from the door hook. She went into the kitchen, ran water into a pan, and placed it on the stove. She removed six potatoes out of the sack and began peeling them, looking down as she worked. She turned the oven on and prepared ingredients for a meatloaf. Max came into the kitchen, got a glass of water, and drank it. Jinger continued to peel the potatoes, thinking about the fun time she and Lacy had shared that afternoon. She stooped over to get the ground beef from the bottom of the refrigerator. When she stood up and turned around, Uncle Max stood in her way. He stared at her without blinking.

"Peekaboo!" Jinger said, her voice reeking with sarcasm.

"Like I said earlier, when you gone start earnin' yo' keep?" He quietly inquired.

Jinger glared at him and tried to walk around him to get back to her cooking counter. He did not move. Instead, he snatched the meat out of her hand and threw it on the counter. He penned her against the refrigerator and ran his fingers across her breast. She skirmished valiantly. He had a strong hold on her and began pressing himself upon her. As he unloosened his belt, he lost his grip. Jinger fell to the kitchen floor and sprang up, then he pushed her back to the counter and tried again to make bodily contact with her. She elbowed him, harnessed all of her strength, and kneed him as hard as she could in the stomach, causing a button to snap from his trousers. As he grabbed his stomach, she made a seamless dash for the parlor.

"You come back here!" he yelled. "You need to go to yo' room and get out of yo' clothes."

Panting and out of breath, Max pursued her into the parlor with his belt wrapped around his hand and his pants sagging.

"Get out of my clothes, for what?" She quizzed him incredulously.

"You heard what I said. You ain't twelve no mo'. Tessa ain't here. She ain't got to know nothing about it."

"I'm not doing anything like that!"

"You ah do whatever I tell you!"

He took a swipe at Jinger, his belt buckle barely missing her face. Jinger's heart and mind raced as she panicked about how she would escape. She sprinted toward the front door, hoping to get to the front porch and the safety of passing eyes, with Uncle Max steps behind her. She opened the front door, and he slammed it shut. As he tried to grab her arm and turn her toward him, they both heard a noise coming from the end of the front yard. It was the clamor of loud voices and laughter. In an instant, Max dashed into the back room, raising and straightening his disheveled pants as he moved hurriedly. Out of breath, Jinger was relieved as she opened the front door again and stepped onto the front porch. She discovered her aunt Tessa, her great aunt Pudding and her husband, Cab, coming through the front gate. Although he was short and walked stooped over, Uncle Cab was laden down with three bags. Jinger halted in relief as she saw the three of them.

A smile disappeared from Tessa's face and she asked, "What's wrong, Jinger?"

"I—I just needed to get some air," she lied, once all faces were turned to her.

Aunt Pudding soberly asked, "Is everything alright, Sugar?"

"Yes. Let me help you, Uncle Cab," she quickly stated, as the wild beat of her heart became fainter and steadier. She hoped her relatives did not notice the quiver in her hands.

"There are a few more bags in the carriage, Jinger," her aunt said, in a distracted voice as she pondered her demeanor. "Could you get them out for us?"

Aunt Pudding didn't say anything, but she glanced at her great niece, and then peered at the Maxwell house, as if in deep thought.

"Yes, ma'am," Jinger said dutifully. She used this task as an opportunity to steady her hands and regain her composure.

She helped unpack the groceries in the kitchen. She did so in silence as the adults spoke of their day trip and caught up on family news. Normally at her aunt's side, helping in the kitchen, Jinger slipped into her bedroom and took a bath instead.

Aunt Tessa came to her bedroom to check on her after the space of an hour.

"Jinger, what's wrong?"

"Nothing. Really. It's nothing."

"I don't believe you."

As she flushed, fast, hot tears began to roll down her face under her aunt's compassionate stare. Tessa gave her a handkerchief and sat on the bed's edge for a few moments. They sat in silence. Jinger chose not to make an issue of the incident with family present, as there would surely have been a scene, particularly with her aunt Pudding, who kept a loose shoe and did not mince words. On occasion, she spoke unapologetically about those she had "dug out" in her lifetime. Although a kind woman of discretion, she disliked injustice and was not one to stand idly by if her loved ones were being threatened or mistreated.

"Just relax, and we will talk about it tomorrow. I want to know what happened and what is troubling you."

Jinger did not answer but felt a cool breeze of relief and comfort as her aunt adjusted her bedclothes and left the room.

The Maxwell's' company stayed until the late hours of the night visiting. To Jinger's chagrin, she heard Uncle Max join in the conversation, sharing funny stories and making himself generally agreeable. She frowned as she listened to her hypocritical uncle. As far as she was concerned, the person she had known affectionately as Uncle Max was nothing more than a villainous, dark-hearted, evil old man.

"Old dirty bastard," she thought out loud and turned her back to the bedroom door.

As the evening laughter and visitation grew dim, Jinger placed a wooden plank in her bedroom windowsill and checked to make sure the window could not be opened from the outside. She then dragged her dresser partially in front of her bedroom door, blocking the entrance. As she lay and listened, she did not lay idly. She pondered an exit far away from the Maxwells and Roxborough. It was difficult for her to fall asleep, and her slumber was fitful. As she drifted in and out of sleep, she knew she had to share the ugly incident with her aunt Tessa the next morning. Though she was not sure how she would broach the subject, she was sure of one thing: her time in Max and Tessa's house was drawing to an end. Though she cried softly with trepidation about the uncertainty of her future and sure exit, she shuddered to think what would happen if she stayed.

Max left for the shop before nine the next morning, as he usually did. By midmorning, Jinger had related the previous day's incident to Aunt Tessa. To her surprise, her aunt seemed only mildly surprised but visibly angry. She listened somberly and intently. She did not say much during her niece's recounting, but as soon as Jinger finished talking, Tessa sprang into action. The two of them packed up Jinger's clothes and personal items. Aunt Tessa said they would have to move quickly because sometimes Max came home for lunch unannounced. After packing her belongings, a tearful, yet eager, Jinger turned to look at her bedroom. She looked sadly around the room and at her bed and dresser. She was leaving the surroundings where she had slept, dreamed, played, talked to Rustin, and entertained her girlfriends. She took one long, last look around. It was a bittersweet moment. Her time to leave the Maxwell home had come abruptly and sooner than she expected. She was filled at once with sadness, relief, anticipation, and certainty. She was convinced that staying one more day in the Maxwell home with her surly host could be ruinous to her future and to her very being.

She studied her aunt Tessa as they hurriedly packed and she thought about how fortunate she was to have an aunt who believed her when she shared her plight. She looked at the slightly graying, yet proud woman whom she had come to know as mother and aunt. She contrasted this visual with the day that she and Rustin had arrived in Roxborough. Her warmth and strength had endured the test of time.

Aunt Tessa paused for a moment and said, "You made a fine young lady, Jinger. You weren't mine in the beginning, but you're mine now, and I am proud of the young woman that you have become." She paused and then stated in a firm tone with a frown, "And I'll be damned if I let Forrest Maxwell have his way with you. We're going over to Blanche and Violet's. You will be safe there until I figure out what to do. You won't be there long; I have a few thoughts. I just need to make some arrangements."

"I love you, Aunt T," Jinger said spontaneously, "and I appreciate all that you have done for me." She walked over and gave her aunt a long hug. Aunt Tessa melted, and a breached dam of tears flowed. Jinger cried softly too, seeing her aunt in such anguish. The two stood for a moment, the younger holding up the older woman. After a few moments in silence, they dabbed their eyes with dainty, handy handkerchiefs, and finished packing.

12

Jinger and Ole 'Gin

It was a windy and hollow day when Jinger arrived in Highland Springs. She was on her way to Virginia Common College to resume her education. After she moved from the Maxwell home, she lived with her Aunt Tessa's sisters. Since Stony Brook closed right before she earned her high school diploma, she had to score well on an alternate college aptitude exam in order to be admitted. Under Aunt Tessa's tutelage, she studied for the test and subsequently, earned a passing score. She won the approval of the interview panel, was admitted, and had begun her campus studies a few years earlier, mid-year.

As the dusty train chugged along, a loud horn blew, and the train came to a crawling stop at the depot. Jinger awakened to the train steward's loud and boisterous, "Highland Sprangs! Y'all git up back here before you miss yer stop!"

She wiped her eyes, gathered her two duffel bags and suitcase, and dragged herself toward the train platform with the rest of the weary travelers. The first thing she noticed on her descent was a neatly printed sign that read, "Highland Springs—Food and Cold Drinks." The words "Coloreds go to the back" were scrawled in as an afterthought in different-sized letters. As she stepped down to the wooden platform, Jinger's eyes followed some of the tired train riders to the back of the depot. When no one was looking, she daringly used the indoor restroom and freshened up. Inside the dimly lit room, she quickly used the latrine, washed her hands thoroughly and hurriedly, and splashed her face with cold water.

She returned to the side lobby, dried her face and then bought herself a cool drink from the rusty soda machine in the back room of the waiting area. Not seeing her ride, she got in line and inquired about transportation to the college.

The ticket taker did not look her in the eyes, but stated, "Don't know nothin' 'bout no school for coloreds in this area."

Jinger protested, "But of course there is—I was here last spring, and Virginia Common is—"

The ticket taker abruptly stated, "Said I don't know nothin' 'bout no school for coloreds. Step aside ma'am," he huffed and called, "Next!" A man with a wife and two small children brushed by her and approached the ticket window.

After sitting for the space of about an hour, pondering how she would get from the outlying train depot to Virginia Common, she looked around and began to worry.

Shortly, an older gentleman who was working inside the train station noticed Jinger but kept sweeping. When he saw that no one would help her, he walked closely by her as he swept and stated, "My wife ah be here direcula. We can hep you git to the college, if you would like. Be here in just a little bit."

Jinger, not sure if the sweeper was addressing her, asked in a quiet tone, "Are you speaking to me?"

The porter responded, "I only speak when um spoken to, that's all and that's it. I jes' thought I'd try to hep you, 'cause I have a niece who attends Virginia Common. I know the chil'ren need young folks like you to hep them in their learnin'."

All this he said as he swept the area near the window where she sat, not once raising his eyes from the broom or the floor. Jinger looked at the tired floor sweeper, looked around the train station, and reluctantly stated that she would be much obliged to him and his wife if they would help her get to school.

The porter responded, "Okay, be witcha soon as my wife

git here." He then began dusting the seats and windowsills and cleaning the ticket windows, working his way toward the latrine. The crowd at the depot grew sparse as he emptied the wastepaper baskets and cleaned the rest rooms.

Jinger had expected Aunt Tessa's kin, Lennox and Audrey, to pick her up at the depot as they had in times past. Aunt Violet had accompanied her on the trip a year earlier, but this year she was alone on her return to Ole 'Gin, as she had affectionately come to call the college. She took in her tenuous situation and decided to follow her intuition, but she knew she would have to be careful. She sat, waited, and looked about the train depot, noticing the people, their drawled language, the remoteness of the area, and the hot, stale air. Periodically, she walked to the train stoop, placed her hand over her eyes, and looked as far east as she could, but she saw no approaching vehicle.

As she waited, she made a fan out of the thin snack shop menu. She checked her timepiece, turned it to the photo side, and stared pensively. There, inside the locket, was a picture of her and Rustin when they were children. The picture had been taken the day they had arrived in Roxborough. She reflected upon the times, good and bad, they had experienced growing up with the Maxwells. While she had not heard from Rustin, there was a quietness within her and an assurance that he was alright and that she would see him again.

Within half an hour, the porter's wife arrived in a rumbling, noisy, faded blue truck. She was riding with one good tire and one tire that was slightly dwindling to the rim, which gave the truck a slanted look. She entered through the back door and beckoned the busy gentleman.

"Come on, Walta. We got to go."

He put away his cleaning supplies, went into a back room in the train depot, and returned with a wrinkled sack left over from his lunch. He went outside to speak to his wife and came back a few minutes later and motioned to Jinger.

"We fixin' ta go. You comin'? Or did you decide to wait on for yo' ride?" He looked around the station, as if with a bad omen on his mind. "It's whatever you decide, but I wouldn't recommend you staying here tho', miss, if you don't mind my sayin'. You're welcome, if you would like to get a ride nearer to school. You ain't the first one we ever give a ride to. Nothin' to worry about."

After checking out the old gentleman, the truck, and the wife, Jinger tentatively consented to leave with the couple.

"What else am I going to do?" she thought to herself as she looked toward the diminishing sun. She did not want to be left alone at night at the train depot. All of the trains had come in for the day, leaving the area isolated. She decided to take her chances with the seemingly kind porter and his wife. Walter took her bags, placed them in the back of the truck, and opened the door for her. One of the ticket takers looked at the situation from behind the enclosed glass and watched Jinger leave the depot with the couple. He stared at the three of them through an ashy window, in thinly-veiled disgust, shook his head, went back to the counter, and busied himself counting money.

Walter's wife looked at Jinger suspiciously when she came out of the depot but moved to the middle of the spring-exposed seat, uncrossed her arms, and greeted her with a "How de do?"

Jinger returned a warm hello and a smile. Her seatmate looked somewhat younger than Walter, but tired. She kept her eyes on the dusty road ahead.

As Jinger rode along with Walter and his wife, Gracie, she felt the contrasting emotions of fear and peace, trust and skepticism, relief and uncertainty. They rode for the space of twenty minutes, making small talk. She discovered that their last name was Moore. Their children were all grown, and all but one daughter had moved North. They explained that they had finished raising his niece after they found out "she didn't have nobody". She soon discovered from their conversation that Walter's niece, Lia, attended Virginia Common and that she would be leaving the next day for the fall session. The Moores assured her that she could take the bus to school along with their niece.

After a short stretch, to Jinger's surprise, they came to a quaint suburb. It wasn't the most modern little town, but it was dotted with well-kept, attractive picket-fenced-enclosed homes. A wishing well surrounded by peach and mango punch- colored daffodils was located in the center of a roundabout. They drove past a stretch of refined homes to houses that were much plainer in appearance but still somewhat appealing.

Walter Moore stopped the truck in front of a brick, detached home. Rows of marigolds, strawberry tulips and daisies lined the front porch. He then announced, "This is it." He parked the truck on the side of a plain dwelling with a neatly manicured front yard, which lead to a small, neat-looking home. The front porch was somewhat dusty but presentable. Jinger noticed that the humble couple displayed a quiet pride regarding their home.

While Walter parked the truck, Jinger went inside with Mrs. Moore. By this time, she knew she had made the right decision to abandon her wait for her relatives and leave the train depot before dark.

Jinger felt slight trepidation upon entering the home of people she did not know and with whom she had only shared a ride. She suppressed these feelings as she walked onto the porch and into the house. She was struck by the stark neatness of the Moore's' home.

"Come on in, and make yo'self at home," Mrs. Moore stated without glancing her way. "It ain't much, but it belongs to us," she said with satisfaction. She grabbed a broom and swept the front porch. Jinger noticed a difference in the stout woman, as she reentered the house. She was calmer and even began looking at her guest more directly.

Walter then came in through the open front door. He sat Jinger's bags down and went outside again and returned with a few boxes of produce, which he took into the kitchen. Jinger paused and looked at the family photos on the small fireplace mantle.

"Sit down, chile," Mrs. Moore offered. "Have you some cool lemonade. I know you must be thirsty from yo' travels."

"Yes, ma'am. Thank you."

"Lia will be here shortly. Just rest off yo' feet."

"How long have you been a student at the college?"

"I've been there for the last few years. I hope to finish this year and secure a teaching position by the fall. My aunt Tessa, who raised me, taught also, so I'll be following in her footsteps."

"Well, that's good. It's always good to have somebody to pattern yourself after. That's so nice they have colleges and book learnin' where our people can go and get ah education. You can place your suitcase and bags in here." She directed Jinger to a small room next to the kitchen. When she returned, the two women talked further, and the conversation turned to Lia.

Mrs. Moore put on a slightly wrinkled apron and busied herself preparing food. "Naah, Lia is Walta's niece. It wadn't nice how she got in dis world, but she's made a pretty nice young lady so far. At least she is tryin'. We helped to raise her and all. She ain't got momma or daddy to depend on, you know." Mrs. Moore paused reflectively and then continued, "You two should hit it off just right. Uh-oh, here she is naah," she said as Lia passed by the paned glass window.

The front door opened. Lia walked back to the kitchen, and Jinger stood to greet her.

"Hello, I'm Jinger. Nice to meet you." She extended her hand. "Hi, I'm Ophelia." She sighed and shook Jinger's hand. Out of the side of her eye, Jinger saw Lia wipe her hand on her skirt after the handshake. Jinger then sat and visited briefly with Mrs. Moore and her niece. Although she was polite, Lia's physical presence bespoke a preoccupation with other thoughts.

She hoped her face did not show it, but she was somewhat surprised by Lia's appearance. She did not remotely favor the Moores or any of their framed offspring. She was medium height and had hazel eyes and light-tan skin. Her hair fell just above her shoulders. Her carriage was regal, and she had an aloofness about her that evoked sympathy. She was plainly dressed and spoke very little, but Jinger did manage to find out that she had skipped the previous year at Virginia Common but had attended the year before that. Lia did not explain the interruption in her studies, and Jinger did not ask. To Jinger's delight, Lia planned to take the short bus ride to Ole 'Gin the next morning.

Jinger imagined they would share college-girl chatter along the way—maybe exchange stories and have a few laughs. Because the campus had a small student population, it occurred to Jinger that, in fact, she had not seen Lia on campus the year before. She thought she would surely have remembered her. Now she knew Lia had skipped a year and was returning to finish school.

After a simple dinner of baked chicken, cabbage, beans, rice, and cornbread, the household shared pleasantries while they sipped their sweet tea before retiring for the evening. Jinger slept on the floor that night in the corner of the room where she had laid her bags. Mrs. Moore made her a pallet of blankets on the floor, which was not the most comfortable, but she was thankful to have a safe place to lay her head.

After attempting to converse with Lia and receiving one-word responses, Jinger closed her eyes, meditated and drifted off to sleep. She woke up the next morning to the smell of bacon, country biscuits, grits, and eggs. As she washed and prepared for breakfast, she noticed Lia looking her way.

She smiled at Lia and said, "Good morning."

"Good morning. How did you sleep?"

"Real well, thanks."

"Oh, that's good to know, because you were snoring and thrashing about some, so I didn't get much sleep," Lia said matter-of-factly.

"Oh, I'm sorry, I'll need to correct that so I won't keep my roommate awake at night." Jinger replied good naturedly.

"No, it was no problem. I can make up for it on the bus." Lia shrugged without smiling. Jinger felt badly that she had caused her hostess to lose sleep.

After a large breakfast, the two gathered their belongings. They hugged and thanked Mrs. Moore while Walter got the truck.

"Y'all be good, and study hard. Once you git yo' learning, be sho' to come out 'umble, 'cause you know you're mighty blessed to go to that school, and it won't be uncommon for folks to dislike you, on account of they cain't go. 'Cause if you ain't 'umble, some people already hatin', then they takes offense. Next thing you know, you lonely and ain't got no friends to socialize with. And who wants that? Friends is de spice of life. Whatever you do, just come out of school, go to work, be a blessing to somebody else, and be nice. You know it's just nice to be nice."

Lia scowled and rolled her eyes when her aunt turned her back. "Aunt Gracie, do you mean humble?" she asked.

"Yeah, that's the word I was reaching for, humble," she nodded her head pleasantly.

Jinger listened to what she said, and thanked her for her words. Mrs. Moore then gave the two young women care packages as they boarded the bus, for which Jinger expressed her gratitude, and Lia gave her aunt a brief hug.

Jinger was relaxed and relieved as she sat down for the hour-long ride to school. She got on the bus first and selected a seat, leaving the vacant seat beside her for Lia. Lia, however, selected a window seat across the aisle. When she caught Jinger's eye in her peripheral vision, she promptly placed her duffle bag in the seat, as if to disinvite Jinger from moving to the seat next to her. She then stared out of the window beside her seat.

So, the two young women rode to school separated spatially by seats, thoughts, and distance herself. They may as well have been total strangers. Jinger's face and armpits stung because of Lia's decided unfriendliness. She looked down and then looked across the aisle at Lia, who looked out of the window. The aisle filled as other passengers passed by en route to their seats.

Jinger then reclined in her seat. The words of one of Uncle Max's faithful patrons rang in her ears: "Everybody's got a story," Jinger thought to herself, "Well, I guess, it's true."

Refusing to ruminate further, she dismissed her aloof, sunshine-colored, cloudy acquaintance. She sighed and turned her thoughts toward Ole 'Gin.

13

Catering and Courting

Jinger woke up as the slow, stuffy bus turned onto the campus. Her eyes were drawn to the cool college greens, the colonial-style buildings, the flower gardens, and the large, billowy spruce and sycamore trees that lined the campus' main corridor. She saw a few young sisters already milling about the campus, lounging beneath shade trees or standing on the stoop of the staid, dated dormitory steps. She had been struck, from the beginning of her first year, with the beauty of the campus. She soon learned of the riveting cultural aspects of the school: the diverse faculty; the bookstore offering cultural, Greek, and college gear, along with course materials; and the comely student center. This would become a familiar meeting and relaxation place. It was here that she discovered camaraderie. These were life-changing times that she would never have experienced in Roxborough or Shady Grove, and she knew it. The southern hospitality; verdant, soothing scenery; and campus atmosphere evoked a sense of excitement that seemed new every morning.

She looked around the campus and was relieved to be back in the insular setting. As she got off the bus, she thought the polite thing to do would be to offer well wishes for the new school year to Ophelia, which she did. This gesture was met with a brief "you too" and a closed- lip smile. Jinger did not fret or respond to Ophelia's unfriendliness. She dismissively thought of her as strange and diverted her attention to getting off of the bus and settling in for another year. She retrieved her belongings and headed toward her dorm room in Magnolia Hall.

Jinger was concerned about her finances for the school year. Aunt Tessa and her kin had barely scraped together enough money for her to get to college. Even Uncle Max had pitched in toward getting her to freshman status the first year. She thanked her former guardian, but this did not diminish her thoughts of him as sinister and not to be trusted. Each year thereafter, she worked with her aunts in Shady Grove during the summer months, and saved for school expenses. Because of limited funds, she knew she would have to live frugally and work each semester. She sought work right away and found a job in the student center café in exchange for room and board. Her plan was to serve at parties in order to supplement her finances.

Jinger enjoyed her classes at Common, particularly educational foundations and teaching methods, along with home economics. While she enjoyed the academic side of college, her social life was stifled. She wished for carefree weekends. She saw other girls from affluent family's frolic around the campus, go away for long weekends with their kin and wear the latest fashions. The same was not her lot, though, and she accepted it. She was just grateful to be at Ole 'Gin. She knew she would have to balance her classes and café work in order to reach her goals. Her Aunt Tessa often encouraged her to "just stay focused, and things will work out in due season."

As Jinger approached her room with travel bags in hand, she noticed that the door was slightly ajar. Puzzled, she stood in the hallway and called out her roommate's name.

"Jo Eddy?" she called. Presently, a plump, attractive, cheerful Jo Eddy Burton showed up at the door and greeted Jinger with a huge smile and a hug.

"I just walked in and sat my bags down. I can't believe we got here at the same time. How was home?" she inquired of Jinger.

"It was alright, but I tell you, I'm glad to be back at Ole 'Gin." Jinger smiled at her roommate and sat her suitcase and bags down. "I never thought I would say that."

"Yeah, me too. I spent most of the summer tending to Mama Kassie, but I didn't mind much because it is on her account that I got a chance to come to Ole 'Gin."

"How is she doing?"

"Fair to middling. I don't know if she'll be there by the time I return home for the Harvest holiday in November, but I'm not worried, because I was good to my grand momma, and she was good to me, my momma, my daddy, and my sisters and brother. I'ma miss her, though, if she goes. I hope she beats her sickness and lives to be one hundred years old. It won't be long now. She turned ninety-nine on Juneteenth. Hopefully, I will get to see her before she goes to her long home. How is your Aunt Tessa Lee and Uncle Max?"

"Pretty good. They're still going through some changes, though, on account of his behavior. I spent almost all of my time with Aunt Violet. We had a ball. It seems like she thinks she's still in her twenties." Jinger laughed. "You know she's wearing light-brown, almost blond hair now."

"Girl, stop!" Jo Eddy laughed.

"Yes, and Grandma Myrtle says her skirts are worn way too short. She told her that a real lady knows when to call it quits," Jinger mused with Jo Eddy, and they both laughed.

"Did she listen?"

"You know she didn't. She says she still has some razzle in her tazzle and that she plans to flaunt it while she's still got it," Jinger said with a chuckle. "I must admit she does look good for almost forty."

"Well, as they say"—Jo Eddy stepped into some purple high-heeled pumps, threw a scarf around her neck, playfully gave a look of supreme sophistication, and spoke with a French accent— "If you've got it, flaunt it!" She held her head high and strutted in an exaggerated, crisp stride around the dorm room. She promptly stumbled on a box and tumbled onto her bed. The two roommates rolled over with laughter at this gaffe.

"Shake it, but don't break it," Jinger chimed in playfully.

"It's really good to be back, Jin," Jo Eddy said as she lay in her bed.

"Yeah, it is. We'll see what Ole 'Gin will be like this year."

"Let's put our things away and then walk toward the café. I think I saw the Holloway sisters out on the yard. They can catch us up on the scene and the heard."

"That sounds really good."

Jinger settled into her classes and daily routine. Between school and work, she managed to attend church and enjoy a few of the social activities of the season. Several weekends a month, however, she helped cater events at Nightingale's, a club near the school, or at galas at the president's campus mansion.

On the second weekend in September, Jinger worked a small dinner party for visiting dignitaries to the college. Her supervisor, Miss Hannah, introduced her to her counterpart for the evening, a young man by the name of Louis Morgan. Dressed in crisp black-and-white serving attire, the two of them served food and drinks to the college president, his family, members of his cabinet and special guests.

Among them were two visiting scholars from prominent southern universities. Jinger had served at the mansion before, but there seemed to be quite a bit of excitement and anticipation in the air on this particular occasion, and she guessed that it may have something to do with the invited guests. A Caucasian gentleman and his wife joined the elite group about halfway through the evening. By this time, Jinger and Louis, joined by Miss Hannah, were serving dessert and hot and cold drinks. The group lounged in the great room and participated in polite conversation.

After everyone was served, President Bannister raised his voice and tapped his glass lightly with a spoon. After getting his guests' attention, he asked a rhetorical question. The minute he did so, the room became starkly quiet. The question brought up the much-debated contemporary issue and topic of whether southern colleges should educate students of color for trade and domestic positions in society versus more intellectual professions.

The first respondent answered emphatically. He made a case for why the Negro must aspire to excel in all rungs of society, including entrance into law, medicine, finance, business, the sciences, and entrepreneurship, along with teaching. His eloquence was met with light applause and bobbing heads.

Dr. Bannister then pointedly asked a visiting professor from a nearby state to provide his point of view for their hearing. This professor began by agreeing with the former, that Negroes must indeed expand their preparation, particularly in the sciences. He pointedly stated that such knowledge could be useful in finding better ways to harvest staple crops in the fields. He also pointed out the merits of educating students toward home economics and the need for proficiency in the skilled trades. He said he felt that much could be done to advance the race in society through hard work and discipline. He finished his statement by saying that the Negro must know their place, learn to work with their hands, and gradually move toward loftier intellectual pursuits. He maintained, however, that the time was not yet at hand. While he fully supported a great need for varied educational choices for students of color, he emphasized deliberate speed and cooperation with the dominant class.

Ever observant, Jinger thought she saw the tardy gentleman smile. He notably seemed to exhale and began to smoke a cigar. His wife listened attentively.

The latter opening statement was met with stronger applause and was followed by a spirited debate between the two. The elder debater said he envisioned seeing a Negro serve as president of the United States one day and live in the White House with his family. This prospect was met with murmuring, skeptical looks, outright chuckles, and frowning disbelief from some individuals seated in the room. A few nodded their heads in contemplation. Jinger and Louis listened intently to the debate, and both had to be reminded by Miss Hannah to collect the dessert dishes. As they cleared small plates, cups, napkins, glasses, and silverware, they both tuned in to the discussion.

"Do you have children?" The question was posed by one of the debaters to the other.

As this question seemed irrelevant, the agricultural college professor replied, "Yes sir, I do. They are in their teens, but I do not see how this is germane to the conversation."

"Fine man like you would undoubtedly make sure that his offspring are well-educated and trained for their future endeavors. I just have one question for you," the debater inquired, as he leaned forward. "Now, tell me, and tell us: Are they attending a southern agricultural college or a northern school of academe?"

All eyes rested on the professor being questioned. He paused and stated in a flustered voice, "Why, my daughter is but a high school student, but my son began this fall at Bates College in Maine." This response was met with instant murmurs from those in attendance, as his actions appeared to contradict his philosophy. The Caucasian gentleman and his wife shifted their weight in their seats.

"I rest my case," said the seasoned professor.

Louis then dropped a glass on the floor, which seemed almost like a punctuation. Miss Hannah was mortified and rolled her eyes at him. He promptly cleaned up the mess with Jinger's help. Professor Bannister then acknowledged the visitor and his wife, who presented a check to the southern agricultural college professor. He explained that it was a donation to the professor's home school. This was met with polite applause, nodding heads, pensive looks, loud thoughts, and a few murmurs.

As the evening guests prepared to leave the mansion, Jinger and Louis cleared the tables and washed dishes in the back room. Jinger just looked at him and smiled. He winked at her and smiled back, but his grin disappeared when Miss Hannah came into the kitchen and gave him a tongue lashing for dropping the glass. Jinger's head dropped as she delved into the suds and dishes before her in the deep sink. But she secretly admired her bold companion.

After their work shift, Louis noticed Jinger walking back to her dormitory room.

"Are you walkin' back to your dorm room alone?"

"Yes. I have no other choice, really; there are no guys allowed on campus after dark."

"Well, at least let me walk you to the gate."

"Okay," Jinger demurred. "You know you were wrong for dropping that glass on purpose like that," she joshed her companion with a chuckle.

"Well, I figure a brother sometimes has to give an amen the best way he can." He, too, smiled at the afterthought.

"I don't think Miss Hannah took too kindly to that caper."

"Miss Hannah and everybody there knows that it is wrong

to restrict a class—or shall I say a people —in their educational and life prospects. It is such a personal matter. Sometimes I don't know what some people are thinking."

"Well, I am an education major with a minor in home economics myself. This is the field that I chose, but I think everyone should have the same opportunity to select a field of interest and work in it."

Louis nodded and added, "And there should be no constraint on how high anyone can excel in their chosen vocation, as long as they are excellent in their work. To me, it is a part of their pursuit of happiness."

"Well said, Louis," Jinger nodded. "Are you in school right now?"

"No, I started at Livingston, but I soon had to stop going, because I was needed to work and help bring money home, being the oldest."

"You ever thought about going back?"

"Yeah, but it won't be any time soon. I'm interested in business management. My dream is to open my own restaurant someday. Besides my day job, I sometimes take on gigs like this in order to learn about the food and service industry."

He then looked at Jinger and made a friendly inquiry. "What about you? What's a nice girl like you doing serving on the weekends?"

"Just trying to make ends meet so I can stay in school and not disappoint my Aunt Tessa, who sent me here."

"You ever take weekends off?"

"Yes. I will have every other weekend off until semester's end."

They had reached the gate near her dormitory. "I overheard Miss Hannah say we would probably be working together again at the Simpson girl's wedding reception at the end of next month. I was thinking, if you have time, maybe I can see you again before then, since that's four weeks from now."

"Sometimes I go over to some of the football games at Summerhill with my girlfriends. Maybe we can meet there."

"I think I can arrange to meet you there next Friday night, if you would like."

"I would like," Jinger said and smiled as she looked down.

"Well, then, see you on the Hill," he said.

"All right, see you then," she said awkwardly, smiling and looking down at the crisp green grass, under the campus lights.

"Goodnight," they both said at once.

Jinger then turned and scampered toward her dorm room. She wasn't sure why she was nearly running shortly after the gate clasped as she headed to her room. She caught herself and walked the rest of the way to Magnolia Hall nonchalantly. For some reason, she was conscious of her loud heartbeat that night. When she reached her room, a hair-rollered Jo Eddy was coming back to the room from using the quad-level facilities.

"You just getting in from the mansion? How was it? Lot of snooty people, I bet."

"Not really. Some of the cabinet members can be down to earth...and Dr. Bannister is easy to be around. They had some highbrow visitors, though. I mean these two guys could really speak and express their points of view. Their debate was kind of interesting, really."

"Is that why you're glowing so? For it to be midnight, you sho' looking like high noon. You're shining kinda bright there. Anything I should know about?" Jo Eddy gave Jinger a sly look.

"Umm, no. It was one of the easier nights, and Miss Hannah was in a good mood," Jinger lied.

"Well, that's something to write home about," Jo Eddy teased as they turned in for the evening.

Jinger was not ready to talk about Louis with anyone. She first wanted to sort through her feelings and decide what it was about him that made her heart skip.

As she fell asleep, she tried to place her finger on it. Was it his confidence? His sense of humor? His efficiency in his work? His ambition? His natural intelligence? His gentlemanly behavior? His social consciousness? Or was it those unusual ash gray eyes? She was tired and dozed off to sleep. When she awakened the next morning trying to find herself, she thought of Louis and stretched.

As time passed, Jinger applied herself in her studies, worked, and made some time to see Louis. She worked with him once a month and they dated when they could.

They took long walks and shared their upbringing, dreams, hopes, and dish duty. Toward the end of the first semester, things became serious between the two of them. After a late November homecoming game, Jinger tipped into her room and was met by Jo Eddy, who lounged on her bed, and their classmate Millie. Her dorm room was on the same floor as theirs, and she was counted as a friend by both young women. Millie pulled a chair out from the desk for Jinger and invited her to sit.

As her dorm mates exchanged knowing looks, Millie coaxed, "Do tell everything," with a demure smile and raised eyebrows. Trapped by two pairs of gazing, unrelenting eyes, Jinger sat down good naturedly after putting away her umbrella and taking off her coat.

"What?" Jinger looked around and feigned ignorance.

"What else? You have been seen in the company of a certain young man lately," coaxed Millie, who looked at Jo Eddy playfully.

"Oh, that's Louis. We work together at Hannah's Catering."

"And."

"And...we sometimes see each other at football games," she shrugged.

"And you take long walks together," said Millie.

"Ye-ah," Jinger felt her way, with an innocent, inquisitive retort.

"Girl, quit beating around the bush, and holler at your girls. Are you two going together, as in, is he your boyfriend?" Millie asked nosily.

"Well, he never formally asked," she shrugged. "But I guess you could say that."

"So, he's a good guy and all?" asked Millie.

"Louis seems to be a nice guy. It sounds like he is from a good family, although I haven't met them yet. He is fun, spontaneous, smart, and confident. He has a lot of the qualities that I like in a man," Jinger replied.

"Does he go to Summerhill?" asked Jo Eddy.

"No. He used to attend Livingston, but he dropped out in order to work and help out at home."

"Sounds like he's pretty smart, though," said Millie.

"Very—and cares a lot about the plight of our people."

Jo Eddy lay quietly, lounging on her bed. She listened intently to the conversation. Finally, unable to contain herself any longer, she sat up and burst out, "Your boyfriend is fine!" in an exaggerated, admiring voice.

This broke the ice, and the three laughed jovially. Then, they talked girl talk into the wee hours of the morning. Each heartily shared her hopes, ideas, relationships, times at Virginia Common, their classes, and campus gossip. Jinger reveled in the sisterhood as she shared with her dormitory mates, but was careful not to mention that this may be her last semester at Ole 'Gin.

14

Phases

By the time the butterflies made their flower hopscotch in the new year, Jinger and Louis's mutual admiration had blossomed into a love known only to springtime. Their chance encounter working at the president's mansion was life changing for the young couple. She was taken by his perceptiveness, confidence, and courage. He admired her intelligence, beauty, and personality. The ties that bound them were an affection for each other, a satirical sense of humor, and a similar outlook on life. While the pair knew each other passionately—and both young hearts blazed only for one another—they both thought it best for Jinger to finish her year at Ole 'Gin before marrying.

Happy well-wishers descended on the campus rose garden on a clear, sunny, second Sunday in May, 1920. The garden was sprinkled with large decorative plants, which accented the florid rose bushes. White lawn chairs, set in neat rows on each side of the isle, graced the graduate seating area. Obviously well-to-do guests, some laden with gifts and flowers, strode to their seats with a sense of entitlement. Mixed in the audience with the fine and fancy were the inconspicuous. This group of plain folks had a humble and unassuming demeanor. The men were dressed plainly. Their womenfolk and children were attired in their casual best, though they appeared shabby chic to their more affluent seat neighbors. They moved eagerly to their seats, looked on with anticipation, and willingly gave the gift of their presence.

Aunt Tessa, her friend, Bernadette, Aunt Violet, Aunt

Blanche, Ma Myrtle, and Papa Fred came to see Jinger graduate from Virginia Common College. Seated in the audience was her soon-to-be husband, Lemuel Louis Morgan; his mother; and his sister. An air of excitement filled the rose-scented graduation arena. A violinist played a classical prelude as they waited for the program opening. On this fine day, fifty young women, radiant in white, lined up in two lines of twenty-five along opposing sides of the dais. They patiently awaited their signal to proceed to their seats. A quiet energy prevailed, as the graduates tried desperately to hide their giddiness on the long-awaited day. As they stood in even lines, they strained to see loved ones; some whispered and pointed into the audience, and all were full of smiles.

As a soft, uplifting tune was played on the piano, the graduates began their procession crisply at the strike of ten o'clock. The first to take their seats, on the elevated stage, were the college president, Dr. Andrew Bannister; his administration; and invited commencement speakers, followed by the college professors.

The audience stood in pride and solemnity as the young graduates took their seats in neat rows facing their decorated professors and invited dignitaries. The graduates beheld the faces of those who had taught them both their core subjects, electives, and priceless life skills.

As they looked up at their campus leader, Dr. Bannister, some thought of the treasures he had shared at their weekly Wednesday-morning mass meetings. No Virginia Common student missed mass, if she could help it. This was partly because of the eagle eye of the campus president, who would sometimes mention students by name who missed the previous weeks mass, before his always timely and relevant homily. His messages about personal responsibility, the times and struggles of a people, success strategies, and volunteerism were a campus staple. He often shared how he foresaw a time in which all races would have access to societal opportunities. He then lectured his young audience on how to prepare themselves for life beyond Virginia Common and stressed being a blessing to others. They remembered and pondered their coming of age as they took their seats as proud members of the thirty-seventh graduating class of Virginia Common College.

The graduates, the college president and his cabinet, visiting dignitaries, faculty, performing artists, family and friends of the honorees all sat in captive anticipation.

"Where she at? I don't see ha," Violet queried.

"Let's see." Tessa scanned the graduating class. "There, I see her," she said.

She looked through her handy binoculars, adjusted her lens, then haltingly looked through the lens twice again and grew quiet.

"Oh, I see her naah. She looks a little stout to me. Wonder what they feeding these girls up here?" asked Violet.

Blanche looked about her and commented on the beautiful morning and occasion.

Papa Fred looked on in silent interest with his hat on his knee as Ma Myrtle looked around and declared, "Everything is just lovely!" The Jackson's cousins, Lennox and Audrey Mayweather slipped in right before the commencement and sat with the family.

Seat conversations was interrupted when Dr. Bannister went to the stage and asked everyone to stand. An opening prayer was rendered by the chaplain and the pledge of allegiance recited. One of the graduates, Marjorie Starks, sang "America the Beautiful". A tall, slender young man then took the stage and introduced himself. He shared the background and origin of the next selection and asked everyone to continue standing. He presented a local boys' choir to sing a few stanzas of an eloquent tribute which had been set to music:

Lift every voice and sing
Till earth and heaven ring,
Ring with the harmonies of Liberty;
Let our rejoicing rise
High as the listening skies,
Let it resound loud as the rolling sea.
Sing a song full of the faith that the dark past has
taught us,
Sing a song full of the hope that the present has
brought us.
Facing the rising sun of our new day begun,
Let us march on till victory is won [2]

This song was met with lasting applause. The boys choir then sang "Fare Thee Well". This was followed by a solitary classical dance rendition by an undergraduate student.

The commencement speakers were then introduced. The first orator spoke on women's suffrage. She highlighted the struggles of the feminine sex and the hard-fought battle of the times for women to receive the right to vote. She mentioned the imminent ratification of the legislation and encouraged the graduates to exercise their right to vote in the near future. Her speech was met with quiet attention and polite applause.

This message was supplanted by the next speaker. Her rousing message called for an end to Jim Crow, a demand for full citizenship and voting rights, without suppression, for all men and women. Her thesis was met with round applause from those in attendance. She stressed that men and women of color had suffered together and desired simultaneous full enfranchisement. She expressively espoused a desire for respect and opportunity for all Americans regardless of color or gender.

She had a sober message for the young graduates. She spoke

of their unusual opportunity and newfound responsibility of helping others. The old stalwart paused and took a sweeping, stern look at the graduates. She then admonished them to "think not that you will escape the crooked finger of discrimination on account of you got yourself a piece of paper. You will face obstacles, but you must persevere through the dark seasons and think of others, as well as yourself. Find a way to act on the behalf of the less fortunate. Someone helped you learn how to read and figure. So now you must extend yourself to someone else by helping them in their learnin'. It must be a priority and a life goal of each one of you seated before me to help uplift someone else. The advancement of our communities depends on it."

The graduates were told not to forget those who helped them get to their present place of distinction nor to ever forget where they came from.

Each young woman crossed the stage and received her diploma and a red rose. After turning their tassels in unison, the graduates let out celebratory claps and verbal expressions of joy. The graduation event ended with an acknowledgment of the graduates' loved ones by the schools' president, Dr. Bannister. He commended the parents and the gathered families for their great sacrifices on behalf of those who were seated before him. The graduates then stood in ovation, turned to the audience and showed their gratitude through hand claps, tears, and windblown hand kisses directed to the attendees. President Bannister blessed and released the thirty- seventh graduating class of Virginia Common College. He charged them to "go forward and do good works."

As the graduates recessed to Pomp and Circumstance, the audience applauded. Hugs were exchanged before the young women joined their doting families. Jinger, while it was only ever-so-slightly noticeable, was with child. She made her way to her waiting and future family, after exchanging long hugs and tearful good-byes with Jo Eddy, Millie, the Holloway sisters, and a few of her other classmates. Upon frontal eye range of the graduate, her family, at first, looked on in complete silence.

Ma Myrtle broke the silence. "There's my grand girl! Congratulations, baby," she said in a strained, high-pitched tone. She then gave Jinger a warm hug.

"Thank you, Ma Myrtle," Jinger said and smiled, coyly. She was still wiping away her farewell tears.

Papa Fred then gathered her into his arms and said, "You gained some weight, but you looks good!" Myrtle shot Fred an ornery look, and he said, "No, I'm just sayin'." He then backed away shyly, squeezed his hat, and looked as if a certain reality had dawned upon him.

"Well, naah!" Bernadette exclaimed with crossed arms. "Humph. I see your knowin' reached beyond your schoolbooks," she said disapprovingly. Jinger patently ignored Ms. Bernadette, who then looked sympathetically at her wounded friend Tessa, shook her head, and ceased talking.

Violet then blurted out a sweeping congratulatory: "Look at ya, college graduate. Gone, girl!" She nudged her niece, squeezed her good-naturedly, and whispered, "Girl, when was you gone tell yo' young auntie that you had a bun in the oven?"

Jinger did not respond to her question.

"Come here, baby. Congratulations—you did it!" said Aunt Blanche with a sweeping hug. "You just precious, you know it?" She stared lovingly at her niece. Blanche then flinched mildly, looked at Tessa, and stepped aside. All eyes were on the graduate.

Jinger awkwardly looked down and past her aunt. Tessa stared at her in silence; her face was hot with disapproval. "Hello, Jinger Rose," she said without smiling.

The sting and absence of congratulatory warmth were

apparent and reflected in Jinger's downward glance. Chastened, she felt badly that she had disappointed her aunt. To break the pregnant pause, Blanche passed a fresh bouquet of raspberry peonies, lilac orchids, and yellow daffodils to Tessa, who gave them to the graduate with a vague smile. Jinger's invited guests, who now formed a semicircle, watched in captive silence, some with surface cheerfulness, others veiling unspoken condemnation.

At this point, Louis stepped forward and asked Tessa for Jinger's hand in marriage. Taken aback, she peered at the young man and looked at Jinger, back at Louis, and then at her family.

"This is Louis Morgan, Aunt Tessa, my fiancée. I meant to tell you that we are planning to be married," she humbly offered.

"Hello, Mrs. Maxwell. Pleased to meet you. This is my mother, Dorothea, and my sister, Inez," he said, nudging the two forward. Tessa, her eyes glazed, spun around and stared at the two of them. She quickly composed herself and whispered a cordial greeting to the Morgans. Louis then stood by Jinger and placed his arm around her shoulder.

"Of course, we would like to be married with your blessing," said Louis.

Noticing her daughter's disappointment and faint posture, Myrtle rescued Tessa by taking her by her arm. They walked several yards away. She led her obviously scorned daughter to a shady spot under a large, spreading bay tree. They were joined by the rest of the Jacksons and Tessa's friend, Bernadette.

The clan huddled under the tree and deliberated on the matter.

"What is it really to talk about?" asked Violet glancing back at the small group. "She's grown, and he's fine. She should da told us she was seeing a white man, though."

"Violet!" Ma Myrtle shot her daughter a glance and a rebuke with one word.

"He's not white. He's Creole," said Blanche dismissively to her sister.

"Is?" responded Violet as she turned and stared at Louis. "He got eyes like a cat; I know dat."

"The only thing I say is that sometimes those light-bright brothers won't treat you right," said Blanche.

"Don't I know it." Violet frowned in agreement.

"Now stop, 'cause my cousin Tootie married a chocolate man and he wadn't nothing but a rolling stone. He left her with two little ones to raise all by herself. So, you cain't judge a book by its cover. Good and bad come in all flavors and colors," chastised Ma Myrtle.

"I can't believe this…" Tessa shook her head. "I gave her my best, and this is how she has repaid me," she said in cross tones, fighting back tears of anger and disappointment.

"You take in somebody else's chil'ren, and you don't know what you gettin'!" said Bernadette emphatically, shaking her head.

"Well…I'll tell ya about that: some you birth in this world, and ya *still* don't know what you gettin'," deadpanned Myrtle.

Fred didn't say anything but nodded his head vigorously at his wife's statement.

Mrs. Jackson then took Tessa's arm and said, "In life, honey, you just have to take the bitter along with the sweet. I know you're disappointed but look at it this way: she came to school, finished and received her diploma. That's what counts. You did a good job with her, Tessa Lee. Just remember what's important in life." She glanced at Jinger and added, "Sure, we would all have liked for her to have done things differently, but it does not always happen that way. This is one of the best times in her life; let's let her enjoy it without being judgmental," she softly pleaded.

Tessa then looked at Papa Fred. "Well, that's left up to you," he shrugged. "I think ita be nice if she gone and marry her baby daddy. You see"—he gestured with his hands, as he always did when he was about to make a point— "they became one when they decided they was gone do what married folks do..." He tilted his head. "Anytime you decide you gone start layin' up..."

The women shot him strained looks of disgust. "I think we get the picture, Daddy," said Blanche.

"No, I...I'm just sayin'. They're already one." He hunched his shoulders, relaxed them, stepped back, threw his arms forward, and gave a look of surrender.

"What you are sayin' is right, Daddy. Hell, what you gone do? Tell a grown-ass woman she cain't get married? Then what? If she knew like I know, she would take 'em and run," said Violet.

"You will watch your mouth, Violet!" Ma Myrtle looked disapprovingly at her youngest daughter.

Turning her attention to her middle daughter, Ma Myrtle said, "Tessa, we don't want to appear to be rude, honey. It is up to you how you will respond, but we need to rejoin Jinger and the Morgans."

Tessa sighed, pulled on the bottom of her ruffled blouse at the waist, looked around, and squared her shoulders. She peered at Jinger and the Morgans and pensively stated, "I think a decision has been made."

She dried her eyes with her lace trimmed handkerchief, and her mother hugged her warmly. Her father rubbed her back. Without further discussion, the Jacksons and Bernadette rejoined the Morgans.

"Congratulations, Jinger. You have my blessing," announced Tessa cryptically. She then paused and added, "And from now on young man, Louis, to you, I am Aunt Tessa Lee."

Louis exhaled, gave Aunt Tessa a brief, warm hug, and then turned and looked adoringly at his bride-to-be. "Tomorrow, at half-past five, we will become husband and wife," Louis happily announced to the family. This was met with happy claps from those who lingered.

"Where?" asked Tessa.

"Y'all done made arrangements already?" asked Violet.

"Right here in the rose garden. Since we both worked in catering, we were able to make plans for an arch, a few decorations, and a reception, right here on the greens. With such beauty here in the garden, it won't take much in décor. Miss Hannah, our former boss, said not to worry about the food; she would lay out everything as a gift to Louis and me," Jinger said and looked at Tessa. "Of course, all was dependent upon your blessing."

"Well, you have that now," Tessa said quietly.

Louis looked around the crowd. "She's standing with the Burtons now. Excuse me, but I'd better let her know everything is a go." Louis left to speak to Miss Hannah.

The Jacksons and the Morgans exchanged pleasantries, in spite of the fact that Bernadette Winters overtly sized up Inez, by staring at her down and then up, as they visited. The Jackson sisters observed Tessa's friend, prompting Violet to whisper, "Maybe next time, she can keep her tail at home." Blanche nodded her approval.

When Louis returned, they headed to Lizzie's Café for a celebratory lunch for the graduate.

The next day, the bride and mother-to-be wore an eggshell, tea length taffeta dress. She carried a bouquet of peach orchids. Papa Fred walked her down the aisle. JoEddy Burton stayed a day past commencement in order to stand with Jinger as her maid of honor. The rose garden was tastefully decorated with a stark-white-ribboned lattice arch, decorated in pastel flowers and summer greens. Two little girls from the audience were recruited, and they dropped colorful rose petals down the bridal aisle. The ceremony was simple but strewn with color.

Several of Jinger's classmates, acquaintances of the groom, the Morgans, the Jacksons, the Mayweathers, the Burtons, the Moores and several on-lookers sat in the lawn-chaired garden area. Ophelia held a sandy-haired boy of almost two years old on her lap.

The happy couple was all smiles as they walked down the aisle after the ceremony, with well-wishers on both sides. They greeted each guest, had dinner and socialized with their friends and family until eventide. Then, they left the rose garden under a hail of rice and well wishes at the first hint of sundown.

Miss Hannah covered the reception with plenty of finger food, a main course, cake, and punch for the guests. She said it was her way of thanking Jinger and Louis for their hard work and loyalty in helping to make her catering business a campus and a commercial success. Tessa was quietly pleasant but reflective. She thought it all would have been so much more complete if Max had been there. Her friend, Bernadette, quietly took it all in, trying desperately and failing to not show her silent disapproval.

The Morgans planned to work for the summer at a bed and breakfast at a Galena resort in North Carolina and then move to Troutdale by winter to be close to Louis' family and to begin their lives anew, as heirs together in the grace of life. But first, they headed to the blue mountains of Carolina.

15

Blue Mountains, Apricot Skies

Tall white birches, and towering forest pine trees lined each side of the winding road. Firs and spruce trees declared the magnificence of the Blue Mountain Ridge area, which was seen for miles around. The huge green trees and thick, lush, grassy-side slopes wound themselves into the destination of a snug French-style chalet resort. Flowing brooks, steady streams, and flowering blossoms, set against the dark mountains, gave the retreat a refreshing, magical aura. The insular, cozy atmosphere of the vacation spot offered the comforts of home, along with fishing, day trips to the beach, scenic walking trails, and plentiful indoor and outdoor games for tourists and vacationers.

The Morgans arrived at their work destination on the first day of summer. Their plan was to spend the summer and early fall of their new life at the scenic Galena resort enclave. The destination was nestled between several lake resort hotels. Louis thought accepting this job would be a good way to give his new bride a honeymoon and make a few extra dollars on the side. He found favor with the owners, and the Morgans worked days and returned to comfortable quarters in the evening. Though in a delicate condition, Jinger insisted on working alongside her husband. It was a new resort, and she was handy with the décor and furnishing selections of the home away from home. Mr. and Mrs. Penniston, an early-graying, middle-aged couple, had spent their life's savings to open Ri' Chalet, a French country bed and breakfast. Lenora Penniston, a tall, proud woman of elegance, style, and grace, especially praised Jinger's eye for color and her homemaking skills.

The Pennistons welcomed Louis and Jinger to help with their new enterprise. Louis was in charge of the lawn and garden crew and was an occasional chauffeur for Mr. Penniston. He and Jinger served guests one evening during the week for bridge games and at special social cotillions. Jinger did light housekeeping, kept the housekeepers' carts stocked, sometimes directed the household staff, and helped Mrs. Penniston select furnishings for the chalet. The Horace Pennistons were fond of the young couple, treated them well and doted upon the expectant mother. The pay was reasonable and having free housing, the Morgans were able to save a fair amount of their earnings. While they worked weekdays, they managed to enjoy the splendor of the surrounding area on the weekends.

They took day trips on the bus as often as they could. From their seats on the bus, they drank in the beauty of the mountains, lakes, prairies, and countryside. On occasion, they prepared lunch, and picnicked in the park. Louis, especially, wanted to show his new wife the natural splendor of the area.

Often during their outings, they would see signs that stated, "No coloreds or dogs allowed." They learned to revise their plans at such times and managed to see the beautiful Carolina countryside, visit museums, enjoy scenic tours and observe genteel living. Louis was sometimes mistaken for a white man and invited to sit near the front of the bus. A proud man, he tried hard to hide his disappointment and quietly sat with his wife; but his countenance, sometimes for miles, would display his angst because of obvious colorism. Jinger fared better, having faced similar affronts all of her life and because she and Rustin had been educated daily in Roxborough about the perils and tribulations they would face. Louis, however, was from a family whose members routinely passed for white and experienced the dichotomy of light-skin tone privilege.

As a young child, accompanying his mother and sister, he frequently sat in the front of the bus and enjoyed favorable accommodations wherever he went. After the death of his father, things changed for the Morgans. Following the lead of his mother, Dorothea, Louis learned to embrace his maternal heritage.

The couple's original intention to work at Ri' Chalet for the summer and then make their home in Troutdale by years end was tenuous. Jinger's condition and the forecast of an unseasonably cold and snowy winter threatened to alter the young couple's plans.

"It's really beautiful here. Maybe we can stay here for the year and then head to Troutdale next summer," Jinger thought aloud one evening.

"I was thinking that we need to be near family when the baby gets here."

"Yeah, you're probably right. The Pennistons have been really nice, though."

"Um-hum," Louis responded.

Jinger looked away from the mirror where she was combing her hair. Her new husband seemed unusually quiet in his responses of late.

"So, tell me what you are really thinking, Lemuel," she jauntily inquired, addressing him by his first name.

"I wonder sometimes how long we will be here."

"Well, we agreed to stay until winter, I thought."

"Yeah, that was the plan, but somehow I have my doubts now."

"Is everything going alright with the landscape crew?"

"Pretty much."

"And how are things between you and Mr. Penniston?"

"No complaints there, either."

"Well, my fair husband, why have you been so deep thinking of late? You haven't been your usual cheery self. Pray tell what the matter could be," she questioned in a coy, falsetto voice.

"Just a few things I have noticed lately."

"Noticed or overheard?"

They both chuckled because when Louis chauffeured his boss, he usually listened in on his conversations.

"I overheard Horace talking to one of his guest executives about the state of the economy."

"But the resort has been at near capacity on most days since our arrival."

"Pretty much, but there has been somewhat of a drop in the number of lodgers in the last few weeks, if you notice. It also seems that Horace is having problems getting the wines and liquor that he is accustomed to providing. I think these situations weigh heavily on him at times."

"But it's not just the chalet. I thought the hard stuff and the wines were scarce all over on account of the Prohibition."

"That's true. But try telling that to Horace. He gets red-faced and irritable. He said this hiatus is costing him plenty. He thinks the whole thing is a ridiculous ruse. Apparently, the guests keep asking for it."

"Well, they can't get wine out of a turnip," Jinger intoned.

"Yeah, I know. Somehow, though, I think it is more than just that. I can't put my finger on it, but something is brewing." They both looked at each other and laughed at the pun.

"Lenora does not seem bothered in the least. It seems like she has slowed some of her lavish spending on the resort, though. It looks lovely and wonderful."

"That could be part of Horace's angst. He seems more fiscally prudent than his wife. I understand the year began with a hint of a depression across the States. And you know how that goes. You never know how deeply it may cut into business, but you know for sure that it will change things, and usually for the worse."

"We have had a few abrupt vacancies, but I just chalked it up to business. It seems to go in a cycle, that way. Miss Lenora does not mention it. She just charges along optimistically."

"That's a good contrast, I guess—an optimist and a realist. But somehow, I think Horace does well to be concerned. I understand that his father lost a fortune twice, and I overheard him in the car tell one of his partners that he wanted to be shrewd in business and not have himself and Lenora suffer as he did when he was a boy."

"It does not seem that the guests are too overly concerned about tomorrow. They are living it up in high style. Lots of flapper-girl types and genteel fellows, long on money, cigars, and cars. Both the men and the women smoke in this crowd. It's really different to see a woman smoke."

"Yeah, that is different. I even saw a woman in long, flowing pants at the last chalet evening social. The times are a-changing, money-wise and socially. My, what a day can bring."

"I wonder if Horace knows more than what he is saying about the state of Ri' Chalet."

"Probably. He says he usually has a good sense—almost a foreboding about things, sometimes. Said he wants to make his money in a few years and get out. Maybe it is just a passing sense of caution. But if this enterprise falters and a depression sets in, we don't want to be around here."

"That might not be good," Jinger returned solemnly.

"No. It wouldn't be good by any means because you know as well as I do that if they start laying people off, that means you and I could be the new maid and butler of Ri' Chalet, and I am not about to let that happen."

Jinger's eyes widened and then narrowed. "Well, now, to even the good white folks, 'We's the servin' class'," she said in an exaggerated and mocking tone.

Louis did not laugh. "But, Jinger, you finished college, and I attended Livingston. That should count for something."

"But my uncle Max drilled into us that sometimes book learning doesn't make a lick of difference, where prejudice and discrimination rule."

"But we can never accept that. We have to strive for education and knowledge even when it looks grim. We must keep the attitude that it will pay off at some point."

"I'm with you there."

"Anyway, enough of our trials. How is my beautiful wife?" He reached for her, and, standing over her seated husband, she coyly slipped into his embrace. He placed his ear to her belly and hugged his wife and child.

"She is fabulously blessed to be with the love of her life and with child," she said as she hugged him tightly. "One day soon we will be in a home of our own and bringing up baby."

"Yeah, it's going to be nice." Louis closed his eyes and luxuriated at the thought.

Louis kept his eyes and ears open in the coming weeks in order to determine a direction for his family. At his request, Jinger was alert to the trends inside of the inn, as well. Through closer observation, she discovered that Louis was right. Ri' Chalet was booking fewer rooms. There was a Labor Day resurgence, however, which yielded a busy weekend. The bed and breakfast saw a steady stream of new arrivals and few departures, and it was near capacity.

What happened a month later, after Columbus Day, confirmed Horace Penniston's premonition. The 1920 Depression had spread to the Galena resort.

Arriving just a few minutes early, on a golden mid-October morning, Jinger walked into the side lobby of the Ri' Chalet. The first thing she noticed was the movement of the occupants and the clutter. The valet and the baggage handlers were in constant motion: collecting money and giving change, moving luggage, and arranging transportation for departing guests. She noticed a furrow in Mrs. Penniston's brow that she had never seen. A recently hired young assistant was working busily at the counter when Jinger inquired about her schedule for the day. Mrs. Penniston asked her to work with the housekeepers, as she continued looking over paperwork at the front desk. She had acted the gracious hostess to guests since the opening of the chalet, and Jinger found it odd to see the owner attending to front desk details.

Upon checking in with Sumatra, a thin Indian woman with a huge work ethic, Jinger noticed the checkered housekeeping checkout board. A number of afternoon check-ins were scheduled, but almost a fourth of the board was clearly pinpointed with a sea of red marks, indicating impending departures.

"Mornin', Ms. Jin."

"Good morning, Sumatra. It looks like it will be a busy day today."

"Yes, ma'am. We have way more checkouts than usual. One of the girls didn't come in today, so we must work fast to make sure all the rooms are clean."

Recognizing that there were fewer than usual impending check-ins, Jinger responded, "That sounds fine, but it looks like there will be ample time for checkout cleaning today and tomorrow."

"But, Shrimati, Missus Penniston herself asked us to clean the rooms as quickly as possible because she was not sure how many arrivals may come in today."

"Well, of course, Sumatra You do exactly as Mrs. Penniston has directed you to do."

Jinger wondered to herself about the hurry of it all, because it seemed to her, that judging by recent trend, Ri' Chalet was going to be barely three-fourths full by week's end.

"I will give you all a hand and help out."

"But no, miss, I cannot let you do that, for you are with child."

"Oh, I'm fine, I can still help out with the light stuff. We'll get it all done."

"Oh, thank you Shrimati."

Jinger busied herself throughout the day assisting with the room supply carts and light cleaning. At the end of the day, she carried the time sheets to the front desk, as she usually did. When she entered from the side entrance, she noticed that Lenora and her assistant looked exhausted and were focused on what appeared to be account paperwork. It seemed to Jinger that the two stopped speaking when she approached. She took it in stride, as she had noticed a change in Lenora since she had hired Mindy Li, a slight Asian woman, as a front-desk clerk and bookkeeper. The two seemed to have bonded in a way that excluded others, almost as if the accountant had been hired partly as a confidante.

"Good night," she said as she handed Mrs. Penniston the time sheets.

"Good night, Jin," said Lenora. Jinger detected a faux cheerfulness in her boss's voice. Ms. Li said nothing but kept her head bent as she focused on her paperwork. Her face belied concern, in spite of her calm demeanor.

A supper of sandwiches and soup awaited Louis that evening, as Jinger found herself becoming increasingly tired each day. She relaxed and waited to share the news of her day, but there was no Louis. She became concerned and looked out of the window. It was close to sundown when she saw the Penniston car wind toward the chalet. She watched as her husband dropped the owner off at the inn's main entry before parking. Then, peering through the curtains of their small cottage, her eyes followed Louis up the path toward their front door. His gait was one of weariness. She opened the door for him as he approached.

"Good day, monsieur," Jinger said playfully in a French tone.

Louis responded to her with an uncustomary weary look and a cheek peck. He sat down and removed his shoes. "Sit down, Jinger."

Her husband rarely called her by her first name, so she knew something was wrong.

"How far along are you exactly?"

"Just past seven months. Why do you ask?"

"You feel up to traveling this week?"

"This week? Why, what's wrong?"

"The ship is sinking, Jinger, and I need to get you and the baby to a safe haven before your due date. I need to know how you are feeling, wifey, because we may be leaving the chalet by month's end," he said as they both sat, and he took both of her hands.

"By month's end? I'm growing more tired as the days go by, but I'm not having any other discomfort right now. I feel well enough to travel, I guess. How soon would we be leaving?"

"I still need to arrange a few things, but my plan is to have us on the road by daybreak on the last Friday of October, if not before."

"Does Horace know about this?"

"No. But he will, as soon as we are on our way out."

Jinger grew quiet and stared at her husband. "Do you think it's right to let him know at the last minute like that? I mean, they've been decent to us, and I think we should do right by them."

"Did Lenora ever have any open conversations with you about the business trends at the chalet?"

"Well, no. But she doesn't really owe that to the help, you know."

Jinger regretted what she said as soon as she said it. Louis, somehow, had fashioned in his mind that he and his wife were more than mere employees at the inn. It was evident in their young marriage that he had severe misgivings over the societal inequities between the races. Jinger had learned not to bring it up.

"Is she still charging around like everything is alright?"

Jinger left her seat and began to pace and run her fingers through her hair. "She was pretty upbeat this past week, but with so many checkouts today…I mean, it's obvious that business has taken a turn for the worse," she sighed.

"I just think they should be a lot more forthcoming to us about the fiscal condition of the chalet."

"Really, to two coloreds?"

Louis reddened at this comment, as he detested the idea that he and his wife were seen first as colored, second as the help, and third for their intelligence.

"Yeah, that's right. We're not supposed to be able to figure it out," he said cynically.

Jinger did not comment. She knew this was a sore spot with her husband, so she just remained quiet and listened.

"I made a connection with a driver to take us up the coast past Suffolk Way and into Troutdale in the next few weeks. It should be about a nine-hour drive. The car leaves early every Friday morning before day. Here lately, he hasn't had as many passengers going out. He said he was sure he could make room for us. I think we ought to take it. I'll let Horace know, but I would prefer if you did not say anything to Lenora yet. Do I have your word?"

"You have my word. I'll just listen in at the inn and see what I can find out. Since Mindy started, I have not had nearly as much conversation with Lenora as when we opened the chalet. I know we are doing the decent thing by letting Horace know before time. That's all I care about is that we treat people the way we want to be treated."

"I am equally concerned with getting you to Troutdale before much more time passes, so you can have our baby under the right conditions."

"Yeah." Jinger sat down and wiped her forehead.

"Are you alright?"

"Yeah, it's just that my stamina is not what it used to be."

Louis asked his wife to lie down, and he propped her feet up. "Well, you know you are living for two now. I understand there is an early cold front coming this way. We need to make our move. Are you okay with that?" He looked at his wife.

"Yes. It's a long ride, but we'll be fine."

"Just making sure. I'll feel better once we are on the road. The driver said we would be making several rest stops."

"Are you hungry?"

"I can eat."

"There's not much there but some soup and sandwiches. I wasn't feeling the best. I just…"

"It's fine. I will eat what's there. Just lie down, and we can visit for a while. Have you eaten anything?"

"Yeah, baby was getting hungry, so I had a bite earlier."

The couple ate, relaxed, and finalized their plans to leave the Blue Ridge Mountains.

Louis told Horace the next day that he and his family would be leaving the chalet soon, due to his wife's condition and their desire to beat the cold front. He was visibly disappointed but said he understood. Lenora was a bit more silent about their departure, questioning why they would leave the Pennistons during an obvious pinch. Louis, in turn, questioned why she would put the chalet above their child. Horace apologized to the couple and told them that Lenora's focus was wholly on the affairs of the chalet and that she meant no harm. Jinger also smoothed things over, apologizing for her husband's retort—an apology that Louis felt was unwarranted.

Two weeks went by quickly, and business at Ri' Chalet continued to falter. The obvious was never mentioned or discussed between the two couples, and they managed an amiable separation. The Pennistons and the Morgans said their good-byes on the last Thursday evening in October. The young couple planned to leave by 5:00 a.m. the next morning. Louis thanked the Pennistons for the opportunities the couple had given them.

Early the next morning, the Morgans left their small cottage to catch their ride to Troutdale. There were more passengers waiting for the car than expected, but they managed seats near the back window of the long dark car. Although it was misty outside, Jinger instinctively turned for a last peek at the charming Ri' Chalet in the hazy lamplit glow. Louis looked straight ahead, squeezed his wife's hand, and cautioned her to never look back.

16

Troutdale Times

Thunderous sky claps resounded just as thick, pouring rain pelted Troutdale just as the Morgans arrived. The driver took them to Louis' mother's home. She was excited to see her son and daughter and extended to them the comfort of her home. The couple planned to move into a tiny apartment before the first frost, but Dorothea would not hear of it. She insisted that they stay with her at least until her first grandchild was born.

Jinger's pains came sudden and early. After a brief but painful delivery, she gave birth to a baby girl on Thanksgiving Day. Jinger and Louis' daughter was christened Louisa Jenay Morgan at the Travelers Rest Baptist Church on New Year's Day, 1921, by Pastor Calvin Brewster. Louis' sister, Janie Inez, became her godmother, to the family's delight. This was one of the few occasions that Louis attended church.

Easily finding favor with the local townspeople, Louis found work in a nearby township at a grocery store, where he worked weekdays and a few evenings every month. Theirs was a happy marriage, and they looked forward to a home for themselves and their daughter. By the time Jenay, as she was called, was two years old, the couple had their eye on a home near Mulberry Park, a few blocks from Dorothea. This lovely home was being vacated by the McIntosh family, who had abruptly decided to join the growing northern migration. Their decision was hastened when a cousin of their family was nearly lynched when he was accused of stealing. One of the leading town residents' pig had run away and found refuge in their relative's backyard, underneath his house. Despite his pleading and disavowal of stealing, he had been dragged from his home. His life was saved because the pig owner's eleven-year-old son insisted that he saw the pig run, on his own, under the house which was hoisted by bricks on four corners. After this incident, the McIntosh's made quiet plans to flee from the South.

They and their three sons, Tenor, Alto, and Sax, who had a performing group, left the Carolinas to escape southern oppression, in search of opportunity in the North, and to seek their fortune. Their seven-room, picket fenced home was perfect for the young Morgan family. Around the time they moved in, there was an undercurrent of fear in the Troutdale streets.

Louis, particularly, had a difficult time with the restraints of the Jim Crow laws. His stocking job at the grocery store involved him traveling half an hour each way on the bus. Although he was offered seating in the front of the bus, he sat in the back, on most occasions. There were times when, after a long day at the grocery store, he chose to sit in the midsection. He noted that he was never asked to move to the back of the bus. And although conflicted, he chose this section more often. On one of those rides home, he was the last one left on the bus with the driver.

"Been noticin' how you choose to sit in the back of the bus."

Not wanting to antagonize the driver, he said, "Yes, sometimes I sit in the back."

"You ain't one of them fancy lawyers from up North, takin' notes and testin' how it is to live colored, are ya?"

"No, that wouldn't be me," Louis responded and looked out of the window.

"I don't see how ya can stand it back there. Hurts my eyes and nostrils jes' to see 'em comin'."

"I never smelled anything any different in the back. The

whole bus is hot and stuffy, if ya ask me." Louis tried to keep the anger out of his voice.

The driver looked in the rearview mirror at his contrary rider. After a few miles, he asked him, "What's yo' angle, mister? T'ain't natural to mix with them that ain't your own kind."

"All people with red blood running through their veins are my kind of people," Louis responded.

"Now don't go puttin' everyone in the same basket."

"Like I said, people are just people to me."

"If that ain't the oddest thing I ever heard. Never heard of such."

"You make it sound like a bad thing to accept all people."

"I think it is. They wadn't made to enjoy what we enjoy. Most of 'em that I met is slow and lazy and got no right to be nothing but in their natural place."

"And what place is that?" Louis's face reddened.

"In the back or at least out of the sight of decent folks, that's for sure."

Louis was so angry now that he had to contain himself. The thought of the long walk home, however, deterred him from speaking angrily to the driver.

"As I see it, a man's decency comes from how he treats other people and how he lives his life. Wouldn't you say?"

The driver paused. "You ask foolish questions, ya know it? You must not be from these parts."

"I've been around here long enough to know that Jim Crow is alive and well."

"Jim Crow? Who is that? Is he black or white?"

"He's see through. You know. He's the color of hate. A hatred that breeds evil and makes people separate themselves from each other."

"I wouldn't have it any other way. It's the natural order of the

way things 'sposed to be. I never want to be seen eating with —
not even mingling with— none of 'em. Bad enough to have to
be on the same bus with 'em."

"It's not so bad. I love sharing a meal with and loving my
wife."

"Well, I'll be." The driver stared at him in his rearview mirror.
"You know there's a law against that, don't ya?"

"Against what?"

"You know, miscegenation."

"I do, but I'm not breaking any laws."

The driver looked at Louis again. "If you ain't a peculiar
one," he said.

Louis pointedly stated, "What is peculiar to me is how one
group of people can think themselves superior to another race of
people. We all bleed the same color, we all take a dump when we
need to, and we all have similar needs, dreams, and desires. Yes,
sir, prejudice is beyond me. It's right peculiar."

The driver drove the next five minutes without speaking any
further to his outspoken passenger.

He soon delivered Louis to his stop. Neither man spoke as
Louis got off of the bus. The bus door had barely closed when
the driver sped off, the force of speed sending a gust to Louis'
backside.

"Crazy cracker!" Louis spat as the driver sped away.

Such incidents took a toll on Louis, and he sometimes went
home from work irritable. He never spoke about his skin color,
and whenever he was asked about it, he simply stated that he was
Creole.

It was hard to make ends meet, so Jinger suggested that
she pick up a few days a week working for one of the affluent
Carolina families.

"Louis, I've been taking in laundry for a nice woman, a Mrs.

Wright. She just lives about ten minutes away, and I was thinking of doing day work for her two days a week. We could use the money."

"Is there a Mr. Wright, and do they have sons?"

"Yes, but their sons are mere boys."

"Still out of the question," Louis said without looking up. "Heard too many horror stories of the abuse of Negro women while doing private housework."

"Like what?"

Louis put his paper aside and looked sternly at his wife. "Like men forcing themselves on unaccompanied women. Not only that, but you've heard of the River Bridge Pass? I heard them speak of it on the bus. When some women finish a day's maid work, Lord help them if they have no ride home. If they must walk across the river bridge underpass, they are pounced upon and taken advantage of in the worst way. This is not storybook stuff, Jinger. It's real. Just content yourself with what I bring home for you and Lil' Jen and with what you take in from the laundry. Even then, make sure whoever delivers or accepts the clothes is a woman, girl, or small boy. You can't be too careful in these Carolinas or anyplace else, for that matter, North or South."

"I know you're right, Louis. I was just trying to think of ways to help make ends meet."

"Come here."

Louis took his wife's left hand in both of his hands.

"Jinger, you just don't know how badly it hurts. It is painful to see our people take the time and effort to get learning but still cannot find respectable work. That's how it is so much of the time. And then I see those white girls, sometimes with barely any skills, and they get prime positions downtown. They're typing, filing, or whatever else the hell they do in those offices. They hire on with so few skills and sometimes move up in no time. It's tough for me to see, Jinger. I mean really tough."

"I'm hurt too. But what can we do? One thing our pastor in Shady Grove used to say, is that anger rests in the bosom of fools. We'll just have to stay positive and work the hand we have been dealt."

Louis sighed and shook his head soberly.

~ ~ ~

One Sunday afternoon, Louis told Jinger he had a surprise for her and that he would show it to her on the next Saturday morning. Jinger looked forward all week to her husband's surprise. She guessed that it must be very special because he twinkled each time he mentioned it. All week she tried to guess what the surprise might be. Saturday morning when she awakened, Louis was not in bed. He had apparently gone on an errand. Jinger thought this odd because her husband always slept in on Saturdays.

"Guess it has something to do with my surprise," she mused. After looking in on Jenay, who slept soundly, Jinger soaked some clothes and began cooking breakfast. She went to the backyard and hung up freshly cleaned clothes in the crisp morning air.

Louis came home about an hour later. He sneaked up behind her in the backyard and gave her a peck on the cheek. He had something behind his back.

"All right now. You know it can be dangerous sneaking up on a sister," she said, her voice smiling.

"Here—brought you some flowers for the breakfast table. It smells good in there."

"What a nice surprise," she said and smiled at the bouquet of daisies. "Let me hang these few pieces up, and I'll be in to give you your breakfast."

Louis went back into the house, and Jinger finished her laundry. She wiped her hands on her apron as she entered in through the back door.

"I'll have to put these flowers in a vase to keep them fr—"

She stopped in her tracks when she saw Louis and a gentleman seated at the table.

"Oh, I forgot to tell you, we are having company for breakfast."

Jinger barely glanced at the person seated at the table with her husband. She immediately stepped back, placed her hands to her somewhat untidy mane, and straightened her clothes.

"Aren't you gonna say hello to your brother?"

Jinger's mouth flew open, and she stared as tears welled up instantly in her eyes. She rushed to her brother, Rustin, who had stood beside the kitchen table. She could not speak at first; instead, she just beheld him. He seemed taller than before and his cropped hair made him look mature. She looked at him admiringly and hugged him, rocking him in her arms.

"Hello, J.R." He grabbed her into his strong embrace.

"It's so good to see you again," she said between tears. "I'm sorry, I just couldn't help…"

She narrowed her eyes, looked mockingly at Louis, and said, "The next time you bring me a surprise, let me know ahead of time so I can at least comb my hair," she mused.

"Nothing wrong with your hair, J.R. You look beautiful," interjected her brother.

Louis beamed at brother and sister and smiled broadly.

"You look so handsome, brother."

"Go on and sit down, Jinger, and I'll serve the breakfast today," Louis said.

"Thanks, sweetheart."

She sat and looked at Rustin again, through teary eyes.

He offered her his handkerchief, which she took.

"Are you just passing through? How did you find us?" Jinger was full of questions as she listened to her brother and to the sound of her racing heart.

"Me and my family settled north of here about a year ago in a seaport town by the name of Cedars Bluff. I was passing through downtown on the bus, and I overheard Louis talking to one of the passengers. He talked about his wife, who had graduated from Virginia Common, and was showing pictures of his little girl. I thought Aunt Tessa had mentioned that that was where you went to school, so I wanted to check with her first. I saw your husband here several times on the bus but did not introduce myself until I wrote and heard back. She wrote and told me that you and your family had settled here. I then made it a point to speak to Louis the next time I saw him on the bus. I introduced myself, and we have been planning this reunion for a few weeks now. We wanted to surprise you."

Jinger marveled through tears that he, whom she had thought of so often, even dreamed of—the one whom she had last seen as a gangly sixteen-year-old who had left in the icy chill of a dark Roxborough morning with the mailman—now sat before her.

"I'll let the two of you talk while me and Jonas ride to the store to get some bait and tackle for our fishing trip," Louis said after serving breakfast. Brother and sister reminisced and shared accounts of their recent lives. Rustin stayed for an afternoon supper, then left the Morgans headed for his home in Cedars Bluff, hoping to arrive by dusk.

17

Piney Woods

Five woolly green oak trees led up to the reedy complex cloaked in a forested field. There on the grassy plateau ahead stood three buildings. On the opposite side of the lane stood another, taller brick structure that dwarfed the other three.

"That must be the office complex and auditorium," Jinger thought aloud. Fragrant gardenias, forget-me-nots, purple and blue black-eyed pansies, harvest-golden daffodils, and cream-colored yellow button daisies dotted the primrose path that led to an inviting brick school.

The tall brick structure looked newer than the freshly painted, adjacent, dull clapboard buildings. The scent of wet paint greeted Jinger as she arose from the tree stump where she had rested for a few minutes from her forestry walk. As she walked toward the elevated building, she focused on the central bright green door and reminisced about how she had arrived there.

The Fitzpughs had driven her as far as they could, before driving onto Highway 21. They had dropped Jinger off beside the wooden sign that pointed to the direction of Piney Woods Academy and wished her well. They were leaving Carolina behind with high hopes for a future in the northern city of Milwaukee.

"Thank God for the good white folks," she thought as their dusty blue Ford looped slowly into traffic on the highway above.

Mr. Fitzpugh was a milk delivery man. His father had passed away the previous spring and left him an inheritance. Northern England transplants, the Fitzpughs didn't particularly like the

South, so Ed Fitzpugh, known as "Fitz", chose to use the money to relocate his family. He joined a marketing team that was expanding dairy subsidiaries northward. He set his sights on working in the Wisconsin dairy land. He would no longer deliver milk but had been promised a job with supervisory duties in the industry. The Fitzpughs were leaving the South behind to seek their milky fortune in the North, and Jinger was glad for them. Along with doing the family laundry, she worked soirees and card games for Nelda Fitzpugh's women's circle. It was at a bridge party that she overheard her patron and her bridge friend Minnie discussing the school in the "shrubs," as they called it, and their need for teachers.

"Why ever would they open and conduct school in such a woodsy area?" asked Minnie Poole.

"It's actually not that far into the pines. Just about three or four minutes off Highway 21," said Lessy Warren.

"Humph!" enjoined Naomi Strong.

"Well, I guess that matters little to the townspeople. They just want a school for their young ones to attend. It is somewhat centrally located here in the county, when you think about how spread out Troutdale is getting to be now," said Nelda.

"I heard there might be a fall opening delay because they're having trouble attracting teachers. They had a schoolmarm, but they said she got married and left these parts," said Naomi.

"Well, that's good for her, because it makes no sense to miss out on all of the little joys of life," was Lurlene Cooper's sly reply.

"Well, maybe she married in time to have at least one little one," said Minnie hopefully.

"Yeah, let's just hope it doesn't come here with one ear on account of her age," said Lurlene.

This statement was met with silence.

"Why, thirty-year-olds have children, you know," said Nelda.

More silence.

As the card game continued, Jinger served the bridge ladies fruit, cheese, finger sandwiches, sweets and beverages before assembling two bags of dirty laundry to take home. Nelda stared intently at her cards and then lifted her head and turned her right shoulder from her card hand. "Jinger, didn't you graduate from college?" she asked, as she cleared the cucumber-and-tuna-sandwich platter.

"Yes, ma'am."

"Hmmm…book learning for darkies," Lurlene quietly mocked under her breath.

"Well, why don't you apply for that teaching job in the Pines?" asked Nelda.

The hostess' card cronies sat silently, looked on uncomfortably, or shifted in their seats.

"You think they would consider a person of color?" Jinger responded quietly.

"It's your turn, Minnie," coaxed Nelda.

Minnie reddened and distractedly plunked down a card.

Lessy, seated on Nelda's new divan, sat out the game and observed quietly.

"Why, sure. Learning is learning. I watched you with my Abner and Flora. It's not everyone who can tutor young people, actually engage them, and explain subjects in a clear way like you do," answered Nelda.

Only the sound of the ticking grandfather clock could be heard, as the women studied their game. Lurlene and Naomi exchanged looks as they silently looked at their card hands. Lessy cleared her throat.

"I wonder how the parents and grandparents would feel about that?" queried Naomi, expressionless, staring at the cards before her.

"Why, I should think they would be grateful to have anyone with the knowledge and skills to teach their little ones," said Nelda.

"I heard it's an all-white school," offered Minnie in a whispery tone.

"Most of 'em are in these parts. Seeing as they have few takers, I think you should go for it, Jinger. Why are you looking so glum?" returned Nelda.

Her bridge mates and Lessy sat stoically.

"Frankly, I don't know if I would even be considered, but I can try," returned Jinger.

Unable to contain herself any longer, Naomi looked up from the game and pointedly asked, "Really? A Negra teaching in a white school?" she questioned before bluntly dropping her hand of cards on the table and staring incredulously.

"Oh look! There's a whitetail!" Lessy buoyantly pointed out of the window, causing the card players to abandon their game and scramble from the table to the large picture window. They had heard about the young deer and hoped to spot her. Gawking out of the window, they marveled at the rarely seen, elusive albino doe. She stood in suspended animation for a few seconds, flashing powder pink-looking eyes. Her milky mane looked like a coat of snow. Turning her head slightly, the women got a good view of her upright, pink, padded ears and mauve-colored nose. She looked nervously about her, as if she knew she was being watched, and then dashed into the woods, evading the awe of her admirers.

Mrs. Fitzpugh turned from the window in time to see Jinger move toward the side door, hoping to slip out in the excitement of the moment. While her guests marveled at the fawn sighting, Nelda followed Jinger to the door and sized up her preoccupied laundress and day worker.

She then flatly stated, "I think you should go for it. Nothing beats a failure but a try."

"I'll give it some thought," Jinger quietly responded.

"Remember what I said, dear." She spoke to her as if to a close friend as she opened the door.

"Good day, Mrs. Fitz. I'll have these clothes back to you in a few days."

~ ~ ~

After her day of caring for Jenay in the Morgan home, Dorothea accepted her daughter-in-law's invitation to stay for dinner that evening. Afterward, she offered to give Jenay her bath and put her to bed. Jinger gave her daughter a tight squeeze and wished her 'hugs and bubbles' before she released her to her grandmother. Louis, still seated at the dinner table, stretched, looked dotingly at his family, poured a cup of coffee, and looked on contentedly. It had been a good day at work for him, and he inquired, as he did daily, about Jinger's day. When she broached the subject about Mrs. Fitzpugh's suggestion, she began at a soft pace, but her voice began to skip at the possibility of teaching at Piney Woods. Her eyes pled for his approval as she told him of her plan to visit the school the coming week. Louis sat silently and listened as she eagerly told him about the opportunity. At first, he seemed pleased, but then she noticed a sobriety in his listening, as he did when he thought deeply about what was being said.

"Where's the school located?"

"Right off of Highway 21. The bus line rides close by, and I can walk to the clearing. It's just a few minutes' walk from there to the school, really," answered Jinger. "I'm sure others will be taking the path at the same time as I do."

"That's a woody area, so that's good to know. Just so long as it's safe," was his quiet answer. "You think you would fit the bill of who they are looking for?" he asked after a few minutes.

"And just who would that be, Louis?" Jinger asked in an annoyed voice.

He did not answer.

Jinger got up from the table and began to pace. She ran her fingers through her hair and asked, "Louis, can you just be happy at the prospect of it all? Just once not size up and overthink the situation?"

"The truth be told; I'm actually pleased about the possibility. I just don't want you to get your hopes up, that's all," he answered.

"But if we never venture out, take risks, and hope for the best, we will never progress as individuals or as a people."

Louis sat for a moment and pondered. He then said tenderly, "Jinger, you must know how proud I am that a door of opportunity may open to you. It's just that I don't want you to be disappointed if it is slammed in your face, that's all. Of course, you are qualified—overqualified, I'm sure—but most of the time, that does not mean a damned thing. Whether we are skilled, talented, educated, or not, to the powers that be we all came to America on different ships, but, henceforth, we are in the same boat."

"So, we should just mark time, just because of the prejudice and limited thinking of others?"

He then walked over to her. She had moved into the dining room doorway. He placed his arms around her shoulders, drew her to him, and looked down at her.

"Jinger, can't you see that this is what I've always wanted for you…a chance to walk through doors that await your special God-given skills and talent, with no apologies. For once, not to have to worry about how you will be received based solely on the color of your skin." This time Louis' eyes pled with his wife. "You are my heart, and I support you on this, but you must promise me that you will be strong. Just know that you will have to prove yourself to everyone at Piney Woods, including your students. If you think you can do that, then I'm with you," he said gently.

"I'll take that as a blessing," she said, quietly as she embraced her husband.

~ ~ ~

Jinger chose to make her husband's decided skepticism and the bridge ladies' obvious doubts a blur, as she straightened her dress and belt and squared her shoulders. She walked the short distance to the gates of the Piney Woods Academy with purpose, drowning the voices of reservation.

Tiny bells, attached to the school door's inner handles, jingled a cheery welcome as the three occupants of the room looked up. Seeming startled, the strawberry-blond-haired woman, along with two gentlemen in suits, stared at her in silence. Jinger noticed how deeply the woman reddened as she rose from her desk.

"May I help you?" she deadpanned. Before Jinger could respond, she said, "We've had all of the furniture polished already for the fall session."

The two men sat back in their seats and looked on. Jinger then presented the woman, who turned out to be the school clerk, a newspaper ad seeking a K–8 schoolteacher.

"I would like to apply for your teaching position that is advertised here," she said as she showed the clerk the ad.

"Oh, I see. Well, the position is closed. The interviews were completed yesterday." She handed the paper back to Jinger.

"I see...well, I hope you hired a good one." Jinger mustered up a smile.

"He...ah...she will do a splendid job, I'm sure," the clerk stammered and looked toward the two seated men.

The grayer of the two men stood and spoke up. "I'd like to see a copy of your credentials, if I may," he drawled in a steady southern tone.

"Of course." Jinger smiled and handed him a copy of her Virginia Common College diploma and transcript.

The men looked over her credentials and exchanged looks.

"Marva, get Miss..."

"Morgan," Jinger returned, with a smile.

"Miss or Mrs.?" he queried

"Mrs."

"Get Mrs. Morgan here a big ole glass of ice water, tea, or a cup of coffee, her choice."

"I'll take water with lemon on the side," Jinger enjoined.

The clerk gave the older gentleman a dubious look but complied with his request.

"Sit down," the younger man offered, pulling out a chair.

The clerk soon brought in Jinger's drink request, which she covertly examined before taking a sip. The two men invited her into an inner office, and she was seated at a round table facing them. They drilled her for over half an hour on arithmetic, grammar, spelling, reading concepts, geography, and the writing process. They further questioned her regarding her background, training and experience. They did not introduce themselves, but Jinger noticed that the elder gentleman seemed to take satisfaction in the propriety and precision of her answers, while the younger was quieter and asked more pointed questions. Following the oral exam, they finally introduced themselves.

The white-haired gentleman shook her hand and said, "I'm

Superintendent Warren Kratky. I'm in charge of human resources for the new and expanding school's division in the county school district. And this is Mr. Marshall Denby, the headmaster here at Piney Woods." The latter shook her hand and smiled at Jinger for the first time.

The two men exchanged looks, and the superintendent said, "Well, the truth is we could use someone like you…of your certain skill level, I mean. There're a few ways you get into teaching in our schools: through the Pillsbury Schools Human Resources Division application process, or by proxy. We're still finalizing our licensing and hiring procedures for new teachers, but it looks like you answered the questions to our satisfaction. So, by the power vested in me, I'd like to offer you a teaching contract for this academic year. Now, I see home economics is one of your areas of study, but we really need you to teach the intermediate grade levels. The job is yours if you want it. Isn't that right, Denby?"

Jinger noticed a veiled slyness in this gentle coax. Superintendent Kratky gave the headmaster a slap on the shoulder and a direct look of satisfaction.

"I reckon so," Mr. Denby answered, sounding less confident, with downcast eyes. "I'll get my wife started on your contract. She may need some information from you, though," he said.

"That is, if you decide you want to accept the position," said the superintendent.

Jinger pondered about the school staff members' body language, the unnecessary literacy and math drill, the office ambiance, and the location of the school. Yet she announced, "I would be much obliged."

"Yes, ma'am. My wife will need to see you for your signing. All learning materials will be supplied. It might be a good idea for you to bring a sack lunch and something to drink each day," he said, diverting his eyes.

Jinger was directed back to the front office. She took a seat across from Mrs. Denby, who continued to type and then looked up and said haltingly, "I will be right with you." She typed ten minutes longer. Jinger thought to herself that she may as well have been in the office alone, with the plants, furniture, and the walls. The clerk seemed a planet removed from Piney Woods and her dark presence. She occupied her mind by admiring the student art work on the walls that had been so tastefully done. There was an innocence and a vitality in the paintings that was particularly endearing.

Finally, Mrs. Denby acknowledged her by asking her to sign her name to a document. Jinger accepted the contract, returned to her seat, and began to read it, silently.

"Well, all it is, is an agreement to teach here from eight to three Monday through Friday," she said flatly.

"Yes, I see, and I earn fifty dollars per week, two paid sick leave days, plus medical benefits," read Jinger aloud, nodding her head. "Are there any retirement benefits? Do you know?" Jinger asked.

"You will have to see Mr. Denby about that," she replied, slightly reddening.

Jinger silently read the rest of the contract and decided to sign it before speaking to the headmaster. The secretary then kept the original and gave her the signed carbon copy.

"School begins at eight o'clock sharp, Tuesday morning, September 4. You might want to come a few minutes early to receive your room assignment," she said as she gave Jinger a copy of her enveloped contract, scarcely looking up from her desk.

"Very well," Jinger responded to the solemn secretary.

On the walk back to the main road, Jinger contemplated

if she would go through with the teaching assignment. It was obvious that she had demonstrated her competence, but she was relieved that the district was moving toward printed licenses. She felt this would alleviate future applicant 'knowledge drills', and qualms about discrimination and the school district's seeming degrees of acceptance.

Jinger had almost cleared the grassy plateau, when she turned and looked at Piney Woods. Its lovely, luscious façade belied the tenuous aura of skepticism that she had just experienced. It would have been easy for her to have kept walking and blocked out the obvious competency examination and decidedly cool office reception and never looked back.

"Somehow, that would be too easy," thought Jinger. She could hear her husband's rationale ringing in her ears. "If you walk away when things get tough, you'll soon get holes in your soles, because you'll always be walking or running away. And that is not good for the sole or the soul." Louis said his father had instilled this in him. Recalling this, flight did not appeal to her, so she resolved to show up in ten days to test her fate.

When she saw Louis that evening, he listened closely to her account of her interview and asked, "What was your impression of the headmaster, since that's who you will be interacting with every day?"

"A reluctant supervisor but open to working with me," answered Jinger.

"Open on his own accord or in order to please the Supe?" he asked, peering at her.

Jinger paused and looked down. She knew it would be this way. Louis' precise mode of inquiry was all too familiar.

"On both accords," she said looking up, as if trying to convince herself.

"And the wife? She seemed contrary?" he asked.

"More of a quiet defiance. But she will be in the office most of the time, and I may not encounter her that often," she bargained.

"You can never tell what is being said nightly, though. You know what they say about pillow talk. I just hope the headmaster is professional enough to be even-handed. Remember, a twice-bound cord is not easily broken."

Jinger remained silent.

Louis then gave his wife a wide smile and a pleased look. "Congratulations!" he exclaimed. This is a proud moment. Look at ya!" He embraced his wife tightly and rocked her in his arms.

Relieved, she closed her eyes and felt the love. What she did not see was his slightly uncertain look. "Stay strong, Jinger," he said to himself silently. "Stay strong," he intoned again, aloud this time.

~ ~ ~

They showed up gradually. It was September 4, 1923, the first day of school at Piney Woods. The first to arrive was Adler. He was tall for his age and strode into the classroom looking around expectantly. In a boisterous voice, he inquired, "Where is the teacher? Guess she hadn't made it here yet."

"Oh, I've been here since seven-thirty this morning."

"Well, I'll be!" he said, leaning back. "Where should I sit, ma'am?" His inquiry seemed to question more than his seat assignment.

"You can call me Mrs. Morgan." Jinger then pointed out his assigned seat.

"Be all right if I look over the book rack, ma'am?" he inquired as he tossed his satchel into the chair.

"Please call me Mrs. Morgan."

"Yes ma'am—I mean, Mrs. Morgan."

"If you would be so kind as to remove your satchel and place it on the rack underneath the desk, we will be off to a good start."

"Oh, certainly," he said.

Next, the Cottonwood sisters entered the classroom. They wore similar but not matching plaid. When they beheld their new teacher, they froze and looked at each other. The shorter, plainer of the two spoke up. "It says here that our teacher is Mrs. Morgan."

"Good morning. You must be Rachel and Adele. I'm Mrs. Morgan."

Instinctively, the two girls looked at each other again, turned and rushed from the room, half-amused and half-stunned, looking over their shoulders.

Adler looked up, chuckled under his breath, looked at Mrs. Morgan, and then quickly erased the laughter from his lips as he delved into the book he held.

The two girls returned to the classroom with their mother, a stout, blue-eyed brunette, who walked in the middle of the girls and held a hand of each. She demanded, "Why are you here? Where is Agnes Scott, my daughters' presumed teacher from last spring's Open House?"

Before Jinger could answer, Headmaster Denby appeared at the door and announced that everyone was gathering in the circle by the flagpole for the school year opening and prayer. Mrs. Cottonwood and her daughters rushed from the room after the headmaster. Adler grabbed his satchel and followed. Jinger trailed the group, wondering why no mention of the opening assembly had been shared with her. On the circle were two other teachers standing in front of their lined-up students. A line of eleven students awaited Jinger, along with a thinly-veiled hush, side looks, and some blatant stares as she walked to her place on the circle.

The first girl in line, a freckled-faced redhead, appeared somewhat smaller than the others. She looked up at her new teacher and smiled broadly. Before the opening prayer began, she kneeled, rummaged through her bag, stood back up, and presented her teacher with a grin and a bright-red apple, which Jinger accepted with an appreciative smile. The rest of her students, some wearing tattered clothing, looked on expressionless. All of the students were white, except one. The last student was of a darker hue and appeared to hide behind the person in front of him. He was a dark-skinned Negro with curly hair.

After the headmaster's prayer and school opening, the students recited the Pledge of Allegiance, then proceeded to their classes. Jinger walked her motley crew to class, where she introduced herself. She was met with mostly solemn looks; the most abject look was that of the Negro pupil. He avoided eye contact with Jinger. The most pleased and buoyant reception was from the sparkly redhead. The Cottonwood girls were missing, but Jinger proceeded with the class roll call.

By nine o'clock, she had received the reluctant, the repulsed, the patronizing, and the respectful. Her students had dispositions as mixed as their ability levels.

Halfway through her lesson on writing, the Cottonwood sisters showed up and took their seats. Jinger assigned her students an essay regarding their summer vacation. This gave her an opportunity to walk around the class and get an early idea of her students' ability levels. She was surprised to see that Adele's and Rachel's skills only approached standards.

The morning went by swiftly, and right before lunch, Zander, the most able of the students, inquired, "Mrs. Morgan, do you know any math?"

"Yes, Zander. I couldn't have graduated from college if I didn't know any math."

"I need help on my decimals and order of operations."

"I can help you with that," stated the teacher.

Jinger handily assisted her pupil but was taken aback that he had questioned her competence. Her armpits twitched, and her face was flushed.

At noon, she walked her pupils to the cafeteria for lunch. Afterwards, she escorted them past the outside benches to the playground near the oaks. The two other Piney Woods teachers were there when she arrived. She looked at them to make eye contact, but at the same time, they both diverted their eyes upward and outward to the towering pine trees. About this time, the headmaster came out and signaled to the teachers that he would watch the children so they could eat their lunch. The two teachers brushed past her on their way inside. One offered a stoic hello, and the other one gave a brittle smile, as they chattily continued their insular conversation, making plans to dine together during their lunch break. Jinger returned to her classroom and ate alone.

"How do you like your teaching job?"

"I like it really well."

"I noticed you leaving out a little earlier every day."

"I hope it doesn't put you out too much to watch Jenay?"

"No. Not at all. She usually doesn't wake up until after you've been gone for a few hours. Around midmorning, shea start stirring."

Jinger listened closely with a sad heart, because she wanted to be there when her Jenay woke up each morning. "Does she look around for me?"

"Yeah, her little eyes search the room every day for you. Then, most times, shea start crying."

"I'm sorry that you have to pick up the slack because I'm not here."

"No, watching Jenay is a cakewalk compared to me worryin' about you, my daughter, walkin' to and from work. In rural Carolina, at that."

Jinger could hear the strain in her mother- in- laws voice.

"I catch the bus for most of the way. This cuts down on the distance I have to walk. I go in a little early to set up the classroom each day."

"If you don't mind my sayin' even that distance is not a good thing. I've been in Troutdale now the better part of thirty years, and I have heard horror stories about crimes against our people. It's not safe, I tell ya."

Jinger was quiet. Since she rode most of the way, she felt relatively safe walking into the shrubs.

"Does Louis know about this?"

"You mean about me working? Yes, he knows. He's really excited for me."

"Does he know how far you have to go, and how early you leave, daughter?" Dorothea's quiet voice faded.

"Not exactly."

"You think you ought to tell him?"

"Yes, ma'am. I aim to tell him this weekend."

Dorothea studied her son's wife. Little Jenay had recited her alphabet, and sang a complete song to her grandmother the previous afternoon. She decided not to mention it, being sensitive to her daughter-in-law's long looks at the mention of any new developments concerning Jenay.

"You be careful, daughter," she said soberly.

In the new calendar year, word reached Piney Woods that Superintendent Kratky had retired. By March, at the beginning of the last trimester, the headmaster verbally released Jinger from her teaching position. At first, she was given no clear reason. Later, he said she was being dismissed because she had a husband and a child. He said her work was good but that "the law is the law". He claimed that once a young woman married and had children, she was expected to stay at home and raise her children. When Jinger protested that she had never read that law, he said it was an unwritten law and an expectation in the southern way of life. When she produced a copy of her teaching contract, he acquiesced and agreed to allow her to remain for the rest of the school term. He made it clear, though, that her contract would not be renewed.

Although angry, skeptical, and sorely disappointed, Jinger rationalized that she could now look after her Jenay every day, herself. She felt proud of the progress that her thirteen students made during the brief time she had been their schoolteacher.

Shortly after her last day, Jinger heard that Headmaster Denby had hired his daughter-in-law to fill the vacant position for the subsequent school year. Although this stung, and she felt angry for weeks, she hid this fact from Louis, who may have acted unwisely. Eventually, she accepted it as a relief that she was no longer in harm's way, walking the lonely half mile, alone. It was a bitter pill to swallow, but she grudgingly accepted it as part of Negro southern living.

Jinger tried not to dwell on this unjust treatment but found herself being verbally short with her family sometimes. This disappointed her, and she made a deliberate effort to focus on the present. She drew upon her past experience and returned to her work as a laundress. She took in laundry and tutored students when she could, in order to help make ends meet. She busied herself raising her daughter, working at home, and being a wife to Louis. She also accompanied her mother-in-law to Travelers Rest Baptist Church regularly and decided to join. Louis visited, on occasion, but refrained from joining the church.

18

It Happened on the Lake One Night

The Morgans had lived in their home for three years and had plans to relocate to New York City in the spring of 1925. Louis had kept in touch with Bud McIntosh, who told him about an upcoming opening as a Pullman porter. Louis was reluctant at first, as this line of work did not particularly interest him. He had heard about the low pay, long hours and condescension that the porters routinely endured. Bud said they had recently unionized and it appeared the workers might begin receiving better treatment, compensation, and hours. He said the union would be in need of negotiators and that they could use someone of Louis' intellect and natural skill set. He mentioned that he had a connection in the front office and the prospect of moving into such a position was good. This incentive, a chance to use his mind, appealed to Louis. Pullman porters were respected within many communities of color, and he reasoned that he could use the opportunity as a stepping stone to get his family to "warmer suns" in the North.

Lemuel Louis Morgan went fishing late one Friday morning with his close friend, Jonas. When they had not returned after sunrise the next day, Jinger was concerned. She sent her neighbors' twins, Lyle and Lizinell, to get a message to her brother, Rustin, in Cedars Bluff. Simon Fields, at the town depot, gave the message right away to Chester, the mailman, who knew how to deliver speedy messages long distance.

It took Rustin a few hours to receive his sister's urgent

summon to come to her home in Troutdale. He knew something was wrong as soon as he saw her. She was nervous looking and obviously distressed. He had never seen that frown and deep worry in her eyes. When he reached her, she sat rocking on the porch, with an anxious, distant look in her eyes and a faint tremble in her hands, which she kept raising to her eyebrows in doubtful anticipation. When she began to stoop in her rocker, Rustin raised her by the shoulders and led her to a couch in her front room to lie down. He tried his best to console her, saying everything was going to be alright. He made her a tall glass of iced tea, arranged her pillows, and left her in the hands of her faithful neighbor, Flossie, while he resumed the porch vigil.

Jinger then took a short, restless nap, snapped awake, and went quickly to the porch.

"I'm really worried about Louis, brother," she said quietly.

"I expect everything will be fine. There must be a reason for their delay." Rustin responded. "Is there anything I can get you, anything at all? I told Chérisse not to expect me home today. No worries. I'll just sleep on the couch." He looked at her sadly. "I can make lunch for you and bring you some juice, if you'd like?"

As she shook her head no, she cast her glance toward the street.

"I'm here for you, J. R. You know that. I'm here for as long as you need me to be."

"I know, brother, and I sure appreciate it," Jinger whispered, exhausted from worry.

"Let me at least get you some juice," he said as he left the porch.

Rustin was the one person in the world, besides her longtime friends, Flossie and Miss Paisley, whom she knew she could count on, but that day, somehow, even that did not seem to be enough. They sat for about an hour, not saying much.

Then, shortly before sundown, brother and sister spotted Jonas "Jay Jon" Poteet walking through the neighborhood, past Miss Paisley's house, toward them. Jinger jumped up hopefully, her weary eyes searching for relief, but Rustin noticed Jonas' gait right away. He had joined the two close friends in times past on fishing outings and was somewhat familiar with his body language, which was telling more often than not. As a matter of fact, Rustin and Louis had teased Jonas not to ever play poker because he wore his emotions. So, Rustin's skeptical eyes greeted Jonas in a studied way before he stood to greet the tardy fellow.

On her feet already with hopeful gaze cast, Jinger placed her trembling left hand above her eyebrow and her right hand over her heart in shelter of her eyes and her emotions. She descended the porch steps to meet Jonas. It was then that she noticed his red eyes and sad, slow, stilted gait. Instantly a dream she had three weeks earlier flashed before her, and she faltered. Before Jonas could open his mouth, or before either man could stifle her fall, Jinger fell to a dusty patch on the front lawn. Both men rushed to lift her from the ground. They took her up the porch steps, into the house and laid her on a couch in the front room.

At the point of her awakening, she had not heard Jay Jon's account of what had occurred. But as she stared into the faces of her neighbors standing over the couch, she beheld people praying and others looking silent and pensive—but there was no Louis. She looked expectantly into her brother's eyes and Rustin shook his head morosely. The reality dawned on her then, that she would not see her husband again and Jinger could not reconcile herself to his absence. She began to cry uncontrollably, shouting, "Lord, no! Lord, have mercy! No, Lord."

Her head jerked back and forth, and she looked to Rustin. "You promised me! You promised me!" Tears rushed to Rustin's eyes at the stark news that defied his optimism. He embraced his sister tightly, as tear after tear streamed down her face and rolled down her neck. After a few frenzied, struggling moments, she lay limply in his arms and cried bitter tears into his chest. As others stood around with wet eyelids, pitying hearts, and faraway gazes, Reverend Brewster arrived to comfort his short-term, but loyal member, Jinger Rose Morgan.

Jonas told Rustin the complete story of Louis' rendezvous with death. He said the two of them went fishing that Friday morning. By late afternoon, all was quiet. As there was little movement in the water, they decided to abandon their small boat and rent a larger one from fisherman Bates and launch out further.

Cappy Bates had been a seafarer all of his life. Before retiring, he had been a merchant ship captain. In his later years, the old man had settled on the calm banks of Lake Manasseh and lived in a houseboat, where he planned to live the rest of his life. He took his fortune and bought several water vessels and rented them to the townspeople who wanted to fish on the lake.

When the two inquired about the boat, Cappy had instinctively looked up at the sky. "Jay Jon, Louis." He nodded as he greeted them. "You all sure you want to take her out this afternoon? The weatherman said there is a strong chance of rain and a high tide this evening," he said soberly.

The two had followed the captain's upward glance but decided they would take the boat out but would not stay as late as they had planned. "We'll go on and take her out for a few hours, Cap," Louis had answered. "We won't be gone for long. We'll return before the tempest rolls in. Be home by then."

Being a natural follower, Jonas had nodded and shrugged his agreement.

"If that's what you want to do, *Kasey*'s available; you can take her out. You can just pay me when you dock."

Captain Bates had unhooked the water vessel and watched the two men launch out. His eyes followed Louis and Jay Jon. He then took another quiet glance at the sky and returned to his houseboat.

After they took the boat three miles out from the dock, they cast their bait and then talked while they waited for the fish to bite. As they shared stories and fished, they lost track of time until the wind began a quiet stir and the clouds began a slow stealthy dance. Jay Jon had been the first to notice it.

"Well, Lou, you think we betta haul her in?" His statement had come after a thunderclap from the increasingly overhung sky.

After standing up and looking at the clouds and water below, Louis had stated, "Yeah, but let's wait just a few minutes longer and see if the fish are jumping any better and go in for a final catch. Then we'll launch her inland."

The few minutes turned into almost twenty minutes as the two buddies continued to reminisce and drink on the waves. Their catch had improved. They had red snapper, striped bass and catfish to show for their efforts. As Jay Jon unhooked his final catch, the boat began to sway in the increasing wind. Without speaking, the two men had instinctively drawn in their poles and prepared to return to shore.

As Jay Jon started the Voyager's motor, he noticed a wind gust and large wave swipe at the boat on the end where Louis stood and then sat. Seeking to regain his balance, Louis had swayed with the boat and tried to stand again. As the boat rocked, it began to drizzle lightly. Louis threw a plastic shield over their catch. Jay Jon said the motor had purred softly, started and then faltered. As he worked to get the engine started, he unwound the boat anchor.

As he did so, he turned and saw Louis rise to his feet. He staggered as he tried to reach Jay Jon's side of the boat. He recounted that each time Louis had stood to try to come to him, thick waves on each side struck him. He tripped on the rope from the anchor but did not fall. He charged forward like a drunken sailor, and then fell back, working to keep his footing. Jay Jon sadly recalled how the fierce waves drenched Louis from both sides of the boat. Unable to get his balance, he had appeared to play possum, lying down in the hull of the boat in hopes that the winds, waves, and rain would cease. Jay Jon tried to anchor the boat, but it did not catch.

For a several minutes, Louis laid still in the careening, unsteady boat. He stood and made a final attempt to leave his side of the boat. By then his eyes were bloodshot, and his walk became an unsteady lunge. He was then spun around in a tempest and knocked overboard by a gigantic wave. Jay Jon said he had seen Louis swimming for his life. He began to duck under water, then reappear, gasping for air; swimming vigorously, he went under the water again. He said he had jumped into the water and tried to help Louis, but his bobbing up and down in the water and the rain made it hard to reach him. He clutched Louis's arm once to try to rescue him but lost his grip. He then grabbed him around the waist, but he felt a strong drag on his legs trying to tug him under. In his striving to free himself from the suction on his body, he lost his grasp of his friend. Unable to see clearly because of the rainstorm, Jay Jon swam back to the boat with all of his might.

After reentering the boat, he grabbed a towel and wiped his water-blinded eyes. Shivering, he looked about for his friend. He was worried and began to shake and cry out but did not see Louis rise. It was then that it dawned on him that he may have lost his close friend and dear buddy forever to the dark lake. As he continued to wait, call out, and then wail for his lost friend, the winds and rain decreased.

He tried several more times and was finally successful in getting the motor running. He drove around the area, refusing to leave his overboard friend. He said he began to sob and call Louis' name. After about ten minutes, he spotted Louis' body floating in the water and had nearly capsized the boat bringing his now-heavy friend aboard.

He said he prayed and cried for his friend. He checked his breathing and moved him side to side, trying in vain to "bring him back this way", through mouth to mouth resuscitation. But Louis never regained consciousness. He said he had never seen anything like it in all of his days. After recounting the incident, he shook his head sadly, and pensively declared, "Supanatchel. It was jes' plain supanatchel the way the waves was ragin', and the sudden calm on the lake after Louis' death." This was his last word on the subject, and he spoke of it no more after he relayed the details of the episode to Jinger's brother, Rustin.

Jinger walked through the next days of her life in a daze but kept her door open to neighbors, family, and fellow parishioners. They came; they cooked for her, sang hymns, listened to her, and consoled her. It was their prayers and vigilance that carried Jinger through this "night train" experience.

Dorothea and Inez moved in for a few weeks to clean the house and comfort Jinger, while Flossie and her daughters took good, mindful care of active, bright-eyed Jenay. She was right at home with her grandmother, aunt, and neighbors. Her wide eyes looked speculatively, though, when she was not playing. She asked for her daddy. After receiving only hugs and food in return, she began to cry quietly. During these times Jinger held her daughter closely, and they both cried.

Mother Milner was there. It was she who had suggested the name Jenay instead of Jimmie. Jinger had first planned to name her baby Jimmie in honor of her mother's late brother and to restore her own christened name. When Mother Milner found out she was naming her new daughter after her uncle, she suggested to Jinger, "That pretty thing don't want no mannish name. Why don't you name her something soft?" Jinger had agreed, and noting her newborn's resemblance to her husband, Louis, she named her baby Louisa Jenay Morgan.

Louis's funeral was a brief and somber occasion. Aunt Tessa, Violet, and Blanche came to Troutdale to console and support their kin. The church was full of flowers and plants; church members, family, friends, and spectators. Pastor Brewster chronicled Louis' life, preached a message of hope and spoke words of comfort to the Morgan family. He cautioned those present and reminded them of the ephemeral nature of time in his sermon "Life is but a Vapor." Some who came to pay their last respects could be seen nodding their heads as the eulogy was delivered. Jinger managed to sit through the entire service, until they opened the casket for a final viewing of her husband. The Travelers Rest choir then rose and began a medley of songs. Grover Bousley led the first song in a strong, upbeat tenor voice - "One glad morning when this life is over, I'll fly away..." The chorus accompanied him, and they followed with several spirituals. Jinger fainted and was taken out of the church when they launched their final hymn:

> Swing low, sweet chariot,
> Comin' for to carry me home;
> Swing low, sweet chariot,
> Comin' for to carry me home.
>
> I looked over Jordan, and what did I see,
> Comin' for to carry me home,
> A band of angels comin' after me,
> Comin' for to carry me home.[3]

The songs of yonder life did little to stem the flow of tears from the family of the deceased. The eyes of sympathetic friends were moist with tears upon Louis' demise. Most were saddened to see Jinger so distraught. Some of the attendees fanned and looked on pitifully.

After Rustin and the ushers took Jinger into the vestibule, the parishioners filed by the casket for a parting view. Few seemed to notice the several young, attractive weeping women who paused, looked down at Louis and cried as they passed by the casket to show their last respects. These women were not readily known in the close-knit Creek community. They went unnoticed except by the eagle eyes of Pastor Brewster, Jay Jon, and Bessie Nell. Pastor Brewster stood by silently and looked straight ahead. Jonas looked down, and Bessie's eyes stared and followed each one as they paused by the coffin, beheld the deceased, and then tearfully left the church. She then glanced cynically at the casket and shook her head in judgment.

Except for a short-lived marriage to Nathaniel Keys when Jenay was ten years old, Jinger focused mostly on raising her daughter. She clung to her, nurtured her, and stood by her. Her daughter was her life after she lost Louis.

"It hasn't always been easy. Matter of fact it's been mostly hard," Jinger sometimes reflected, but she said it had been worth it. "Besides, life is just a mountain railroad; none of us know what twists and turns lie right around the bend, but as sure as we live, we will face some type of difficulty and suffering before we shut our eyes, but nothing that He won't see us through. 'Man that is born of a woman is of a few days and full of trouble'," she said, quoting Job 14:1 KJV. "We all weather the tempest, but God sees us through every time."

That was Jinger's testimony, a conviction she was gently reminded of, as her Jenay grew up and came of age in Troutdale by the Chickasaw Creek.

19

Bessie's Labyrinth

The large billowy oaks, poplars and colorful Red Maples gave cool shade to the travelers. Even under the big top, a few of the women fanned themselves. It was the middle of the annual Founder's Day picnic on a July day. The deacons had arrived at daybreak to cordon off a picnic space, set up nets, fire the barbecue grill and begin cooking. The deaconesses delivered their home-baked, pickled and fried food, meat trays, salads and desserts to Mulberry Park by sunrise. Children ran and swam; teens and young adults played card games, volleyball and baseball; and the older set played croquet, fished, walked around the park, or sat and visited. A few mostly ate. Some gossiped. Planted in the middle of the deaconess circle, near a huge weeping willow tree, Bessie Nell Slack sipped from a tall, slender ice-filled glass of grape soda. She drank and looked about her.

Jinger walked down the street from her home toward the park crowd. She was accompanied by her in- laws, and her daughter. It had been exactly nine months prior that she had lost the love of her life. A small group of women walked across the greens to greet them. A few picnickers and deaconesses looked on and bantered lightly. Rachel Satterfield and Bessie Slack did most of the talking.

"Glad to see Jinger out and about," Rachel observed.

"Yeah, it is. It must have been mighty awful to lose a husband in his prime like that," said Bessie.

"Wadn't in his prime yet, really. He was barely thirty-two, they say."

"Looks like she and her little girl doing pretty good, though. So dat's good."

"Well, he's gone to his reward now, but she can rest in the fond memories of him."

"Yeah, 'cause she had him whilst he was here."

"I know she miss him. They sho' seemed to have enjoyed one another. They always seemed so cheerful."

Humph," said Bessie dismissively. "Y'all know dees little women wadn't gone let her have dat man all to herself."

"She seemed pretty happy with him to me."

"Happy sharin', maybe," Bessie returned as she drank a swig of grape soda water.

"Now, why would you say a thing like that?'

"I jes' be thinkin'. Jes' lookin' and thinkin' sometimes. I see mor'n a lot of people."

"Are you saying you think Dorothea's son wasn't faithful to his wife?"

"No, not saying what I think. Saying what I know," said Bessie confidently.

"You know, they say believe half ah what you see and none ah what ya hear. I wouldn't go spreading anything I don't know for sure, and then sometimes if you do know, best to jes' keep quiet and watch."

"Yeah, um just prayin' for Jinger, 'cause it just wadn't right how de deceased ran those little women."

"And how would you know that?"

"Well, it was as clear as day for anybody that wanted to see. It was any number of young women who we ain't seen around here at the funeral, you know, and did they cry some tears over Lemuel Louis."

"Bessie Nell, hush yo' mouth! That don't mean he was messing around with 'em, just because they shed a few tears at the funeral."

"Naw, it doesn't. But you would have had to have been there to see it for yo'self. Um tellin' you, it wadn't natural the way those women was mourning over Louis. That wadn't they husband to be so distraught ovah. That's what let me know it must have been somethin' going on. Naah, he could have still been here. Some people just don't want to do right, and they shortens they days, I tell ya. Had a good wife and pretty little baby, but these men naah—it just wadn't enough," she said as she shook her head.

Bessie had not noticed Miss Paisley's presence near the dessert table as she continued to disparage the deceased. The elder woman listened and then took a seat near the talking sisters. She quietly inquired of Bessie whether she had any proof of the rumors that she was spreading.

"Well, I was always told that where there's smoke, there must be a fire," she said assuredly.

"Sometimes a mist can look like smoke," said Miss Paisley.

Bessie looked up from her soda at Miss Paisley. "Call it anything you want to, but the truth is the light."

"Whose truth?"

"The word's truth."

"Does it say anything about bearing false witness?"

"Why, sho'. That's why I can say for sho', 'cause I know what I saw."

"And what did you see?"

"Skinny, wispy-like, pretty women weeping over a man that wadn't theirs."

"So, then you know for a fact that they were romantically linked to Louis Morgan?"

"Well, it doesn't take book learnin' to put that together."

"No, it doesn't, but it takes a person with a good heart to speak of things that are true and of a good report."

"Well, that's the word. I think like that sometime."

"But that is not what we hear from you."

"And who made you so suchy much to judge what I say? Maybe you haven't been hearin' what I've been sayin'," said Bessie indignantly.

"Oh, I heard what you said. I've been listening, watching, and takin' it all in, and I am not alone," was Miss Paisley's bold retort.

"Speak plainly, if you got something to say to me."

"Well, some have been noticing how Deacon Punch takes a special interest in your little girl. Seems there is nothing she asks him for that he won't give to her."

"That's 'cause he's her god daddy," she stated emphatically. She also loudly thought, "Not that it's any business of yours."

"To some of the saints, it just doesn't seem natural."

Stunned, Bessie sat her soda aside and glared at Miss Paisley. "Jes' what are you suggestin'?"

"Why, I'm not suggestin' anything, but you know what they say: 'Where there is smoke, there must be a fire.'" Miss Paisley shrugged her shoulders. She then lifted her slice of chocolate cake and walked off coolly.

"Or a mist!" Bessie returned, by this time speaking to the church mother's back.

Bessie swallowed, threw the rest of her food and soda in the trash receptacle, rose, and called for her daughter.

"We better be going naah. Y'all enjoy the rest of the picnic," she said to those seated nearby. She excused herself as she called to her daughter.

"But I'm not ready to go. We just started kickball," she complained.

"Come on. It's time to go naah."

"But I don't wanna go."

"You don't have no wants! Bring your little narrow behind on."

The two left the picnic, the seven-year-old looking back quizzically and the mother looking straight ahead.

Some shot sympathetic looks toward Bessie's daughter.

One senior deaconess who had silently overheard the conversation between Bessie and Miss Paisley deadpanned, "I always wondered why she called that child Misty.'"

20

Young Hearts Run Free

"I know you're grievin' your husband. It's a hard thing, and I know how it feels. I was a young widow too. Louis was my firstborn, and he wasn't more than thirteen when I lost my Donald. So, I can truly say I know *just* how you feel," Dorothea said to her daughter-in-law. Jinger listened, but the teardrops flooded down her face. She sat motionless while the tears dropped. The elder woman silently looked on. She then moved next to Jinger, placed her arm around her shoulder, and gave her a handkerchief.

"What you have to look at is that all is not lost. You and Jenay have each other. Your baby has my son's features, so he will live on in her. The best part is that you are not left in this world alone."

"He was so young, though, Mother. He was cut off in his prime."

"Yes, chile, I know. All I can say to that is- some go early. I know it's no comfort to you now, but the good Lord giveth, and he taketh away. Sometimes he plucks one in their prime for himself."

"I would give anything to just behold his face, hold him again, and listen to his logic and laughter."

"I know you would, darlin'. We all loved him and will miss him dearly. But we must go on—for your sake and for your little starlet, who is my granddaughter. I'm hurt too. But we will make it through this season."

Time did her best to soften the blow of Louis' demise, but

nothing could replace the memory of him. When she hurt, Jinger cried. As the days and months went by, although she still missed him immensely, she gradually cried less and began to revel in her daughter, who looked so much like her lost love.

"I may not have him anymore, but I had him and I still have him here in my heart." She nodded and consoled herself.

She looked at her Jenay and thought, "I see him every day in the sparkle and light of her eyes and in her jubilant spirit," she thought.

Jinger brushed off others' preoccupation with her daughter's looks, surmising that beauty could be a curse as well. She chose to emphasize her inner beauty and character.

"That's the most important thing," she thought. "Because good looks alone will not get her through this life. It will take a proper raising and the help of the good Lord."

So Jinger set about making sure that her daughter had a wholesome upbringing. At three years old, she started singing songs at the altar with the Little Sunbeams. She stayed busy in youth organizations as a pre-teen. As a child, she was called Jenny. As a teenager, she chose to be called Jenay.

~ ~ ~

In her later years, Jinger remembered her daughter's coming of age.

> *She was seventeen then, and what a beauty she was. A rare beauty, some said. Pure, beautiful, leggy, Louisa Jenay Morgan. From a toddler Sunbeam through the Young Ladies' Culture Club and formal introduction to society as a debutante, Jenay was a Landing belle and her mother's*

delight. Fair skinned, with shoulder length, thick coal-black hair; striking eyelashes, hazel eyes; subtle features; tall, thin, and graceful, she came of age in Troutdale, a glistening summer rose. Her melodic singing voice, good nature, looks, and connections made her a Creek favorite, and she enjoyed her youth. A mutual attraction with a schoolmate, Wyatt Fleming, brought her young love; a kind that is new every morning. They could be seen biking, studying, and coupled at church and community events. The town approved of these high school sweethearts and expected a sure summer wedding once Jenay graduated from high school. Wyatt, a year older, already had plans to attend college in their home state. The plan was that she would join him a year later, after summer nuptials. Life was full and good for Jenay. She was doted upon by her mother, grandmothers, and aunts. It was smooth sailing until the Juneteenth picnic at Barley's Fairground. It was the summer after her junior year in high school.

Jenay saw her first. She was a newcomer to Carolina, Miss Ari Sue Saxton, Professor Miles Saxton's only child. A dark beauty, she was brown-skinned with silky long hair, good looks, and charm.

Already a student at Creighton College, hers was an air of a travelled sophisticate, but with a common touch.

"Hello. You must be new to Troutdale," was Jenay's friendly introduction to Ari, as they stood in line awaiting barbecue ribs at the grill.

"Actually, I've been here before. My father and I came through for one of his university conferences when we were headed to Raleigh."

"My name is Jenay Morgan, but some call me Jen."

"Ari Sue Saxton. You can call me Ari or Sue."

"I'll introduce you to a few people."

"I would like that," Ari said, smiling.

Jenay introduced her to the teenaged picnickers, including Wyatt, who soon found himself in a conversation with the newcomer. When she decided to go for more punch, her aunt Inez grabbed her by the arm and steered her the long way to the punch bowl. She then cheerfully said, "Let me walk with my favorite niece." Once they were out of ear range to the others, she pulled her goddaughter close to her and firmly stated, "You keep those young whipper-snappers away from Wyatt." This was said as she stole side looks at Jenay's boyfriend and Ari.

"Oh, Wyatt is just being Wyatt. I don't think he ever met a stranger."

"Just keep your eyes and ears open, niecy. You know some girls smile and steal at the same time. That's all I'm sayin'," stated Inez soberly.

"Yes, ma'am," returned Jenay, politely.

Sure of his love for her, and taking little heed to her aunt's observance, she shrugged when she learned that Wyatt would be attending college at Creighton, in a nearby state, instead of Raleigh, as he had long planned. They said their tearful good-byes during the churches annual August homecoming weekend and promised to write to each other.

The two wrote to each other during his first semester away, but she did not hear from him as often as she would have liked to. She pondered this in her heart but did not make an issue of it.

He broke the news to her at the end of winter break during his first visit home as a college man. She remembered noticing a quietness about him during his vacation from school. He seemed preoccupied, and she decided that he was

*a different Wyatt than the one who had left Troutdale.
She soon found out the reason for his reticence and why she
had heard from him so sparingly during his first semester
away at school.*

*Right before his return to college and during what
would be their last date, he broke it to her softly. With
feeling and heart, he told Jenay that he wanted to be free
to date others and said he thought it would be a good idea
if she did the same.*

*She would like to have said the news came to her as
an icepick injury; keen, quick, and sharp. Instead, it
came like the slow-motion pain of a fragile windowpane
being tossed high above a skyscraper and then abandoned
to let the pieces shatter on the ground below. Upon sudden
impact, her heart splintered into pieces—too many pieces
to count. When she asked if it was Ari, he did not answer
at first. He looked at her lovingly, with tears in his eyes,
and nodded. The tears formed, swelled instantly and rolled
down her face. She remembered feeling as if she would faint,
but her salty teardrops kept her alert. His earnest attempts
to console her by assuring her that she was a beautiful girl
and that she was sure to meet another guy did nothing to
soothe her crestfallen state. In the days and months to come,
she just hurt, and they all knew it.*

*News of the breakup circulated quickly. The saga set
off a debate within the town and church. Some said Wyatt
was right to go with his heart, that he was a young man
and had a right to shop around, live a little, and get his
education before settling. Others declared that all men were
dogs. The color struck openly opined, "Jenay looks better
than that girl any day of de week. It must be book learnin'
that done messed with his mind. Anytime he falls for a*

dark chocolate ovah a light bright, you know somethin' is wrong there." The rational among them returned, "Naah, wait a minute. We all know Jenay is a beauty, that's without a doubt, but Dr. Saxton's daughter is pretty on pretty; she looks like a living doll, so let's just keep it one hundred!"

When Bousley, the choir director, with a huge heart and a girth to match it, made a sympathetic marriage proposal to Jenay, she dropped out of sight for a time. News of this drew vexation and scorn from some of the Creek congregants and townsfolk. Bessie commented, "Naah, big Bousley know he outta bounds; the girl is just heartbroken, not broke down, desperate, and crazy. Naah what he needs to do is push away from dat table, cut his head, and get a steady job, then somebody might notice 'em. He know don't nobody want nobody big, shapeless, and crusty like him." Ignoring their stares and awkward silences, Jenay threw herself into her studies and graduated from high school that May with honors, nostalgic at times, pondering her future.

Jinger felt badly for her only child. She consoled her, supported, and encouraged her the best way that she could. Miss Paisley's only quiet repose was, "It's coming up again."

Jinger had hoped that her daughter would carry on the family tradition and attend college after high school graduation. But she had other plans. After working as a cashier for a year, Jenay left Troutdale to seek island living, to her mother's dismay and to the town's buzz.

On a Friday afternoon, after work, she said good-bye to her mother and let her know she was going to Florida and from there to the Virgin Islands. With her belongings in three suitcases, she caught the night train to Miami. She noted the slightly wilted, fading mustard daffodils, purple pansies, and marsh grass under the street lights, along the lake next to the depot. The withering grass and blossoms bade her a leery adieu in the dark night as the train began a slow trek, then picked up speed on its journey south.

21

At the Seashell

Townley took a sip of his martini and looked intently at the pianist. He slid down slightly in his seat, cocked his head to the side, and looked around the room.

"Love the crowd," he mused to himself.

"What was that?" asked his tablemate.

"Nothin', man; just surveyin' the crowd, that's all. Scoping the hotsy-totsies."

"My cousin Townley," the patron remarked with a twinkle in his tone and left eye. He shook his head and smiled. "Always the player."

"That's playa, man, playa. Oh, I forgot, you college boys like to round off all of your words." He playfully took a swipe at his cousin. "And what's this Townley stuff? I haven't been called that since I was four years old. I'm with the cool set now, so it's just 'T'," he informed his cousin in a jovial voice.

The pianist continued with his quiet jazz reverie as patrons streamed in.

Townley looked around again and then asked, "So what you been up to, man?"

"Just living life on the coast. You know the Savannah and Charleston areas. The building and textile industry is booming, which yields a lot of work for construction."

"So, you foreman now, I heard," he said, looking at his cousin directly.

"Yeah, building contractor, they call it, but I don't plan to stay in it long, though. I should be contracting in commercial industry by the end of the year and doing architectural designs. Then I can live anywhere. Me and my girl, Niagara, that is." His voice tapered off, and Townley shifted in his seat, looked into his martini, and took another sip.

"How long's it been now?"

"Twenty-one months."

"You all right, man?"

"Some days I am. Some days it's still hard, though. It's like it just happened yesterday…"

> *Ari strapped her daughter, Niagara, into her seat and looked up. It was a gray day with overhung clouds. The trees stood leafless, unabashed in their nakedness. Their cold, bare beauty belied the coming sunlit season. Ari looked around, tightened her parka, and got into her car. She turned the key, and the engine fluttered and choked. She pumped the pedal and tried again, and the car started. If they hurried, they could see Momma and Pappa Sax before they left for the Orient. Almost three, Niagara bounced her doll up and down. She chanted, "Poppy, Poppy."*
>
> *Ari looked at her daughter in the rearview mirror and coaxed, "Agri loves Mom-Mom, too."*
>
> *Niagara echoed "Gri-Gri loves Mom-Mom too." She then resumed her animated, "Poppy, Poppy!"*
>
> *"She does love her grandpa," she thought.*
>
> *She entered the Route 96 ramp for the short drive to her parents' home. It had rained during the early-morning hours, leaving a light mist, lingering stark cold temperatures and crusty invisible black-ice patches in the yards and on the streets. To Ari, it seemed that the sky*

threatened more rain. The visibility was fair, but she was not too concerned because her parents lived just five exits off of the turnpike, and the ride would take less than fifteen minutes. As she drove forward, she checked on Niagara in the backseat. She focused on the road, her car, and what appeared to be a backup of cars ahead of her. As she slowed her pace, she was careful not to follow too closely to the car in front of her. Her car, however, sputtered, and the engine light went on. She then cautiously slowed the car and moved to the shoulder of the road. The car behind her clonked the back of her car and then hit her again. On impact, Ari overcorrected and spun on a patch of black ice, which sent the car spinning rapidly out of control. By the time she stopped in a road ravine, she had hit her head on the steering wheel, leaving her barely conscious. The subsequent sound of the blowing horn could be heard by passersby. Quick-thinking motorists pulled to the side of the road, just above the gorge and flagged down medical help. Once the emergency responders arrived, they moved Ari's unconscious body into the clear. Niagara was removed from the backseat, where she was crying hysterically but was unharmed. Sirens blaring, the two were driven to the Clearview Hospital emergency room. By the time they arrived, however, black ice had stolen Wyatt's Ari to Jordan.

Wyatt found out about Ari's demise a day later when he returned to their upscale Teakwood Trace address, following a business trip. He was devastated to see his lovely, brown wife lying lifeless. Her silkily-textured hair framed her once-vibrant face. Her repose in death radiated a rare, poignant lost beauty. He stared intently at her and wept. Later, he hugged his daughter,

Niagara, finding solace in the warm glow of her pecan brown eyes, and the thick, curly eyelashes, so much like her lifeless mother's. Her smooth, chestnut brown, flawless skin was the very replica of the recently departed Ari Saxton Fleming's.

The Saxtons were devastated by their loss and wanted to adopt and raise Niagara as their own. They hinted that this would give them life and Wyatt a new start. Wyatt did not agree with this but, instead, insisted that Niagara was his life—his beginning and his end. Although her grandparents clung to her, Wyatt decided he wanted Niagara with him to raise as he saw fit. He made sure she spent summers with her maternal grandparents and he arranged visits for most fall and winter holidays.

"I feel ya, man," said Townley with heart. "Your loss and all with Ari. But I'm glad for you too. 'Cause you got that lovely daughter, and she is yours always. You and yo' little princess are bound to find happiness again. Just remember what they say about time… 'It heals all'," he said with a quiet sigh. Heartened, he raised his glass. "To you, Cousin Wyatt. May all of yo' good days outweigh yo' bad days."

They both drank to his toast. The two sat for a few long moments in silence.

"You know what I like about you, cuz, is that you were always a mover, not stayin' in one place or position long. Regular cats like me dig that." He leaned over and said, "You remember your cousin Townley when you make it to the top," he said cheerfully. He reached his hand over the table and cupped it over Wyatt's hand. This brightened Wyatt's spirits and they turned their eyes to the stage, anticipating an evening of cabaret, jazz, and blues entertainment. At midnight, Wyatt excused himself for the night. Townley partied awhile longer.

After Ari's burial, Wyatt moved to the river town of Savannah with Niagara in tow. A chance encounter reunited the builder with his father, whom he had not seen since age five. While working on building plans for a casino in Barcelon, a tony enclave in the Golden Isles, Wyatt became reacquainted with Winston Taylor Barlow. His mother, the flaming Goldie Fleming, was visiting with her son and granddaughter in Savannah at the time. She traveled with them to Barcelon the summer of 1943. She and Niagara picked up Wyatt after a working luncheon with a client, and Goldie was mortified to see her son and former lover emerge from Spago's smiling and nodding. She broke the news to Wyatt late that evening, after they had put Niagara to bed.

"Mom, are you okay?"

"Why, yes, Wyatt. Why wouldn't I be okay?"

"I don't know. You just seem kind of quiet tonight. Like out of sorts." He glanced at her. "It's not your diabetes flaring up again, is it?"

"No. I was just taking in the coast," Goldie lied and tossed her blondish-red hair.

He looked askance at his mother, whom he had not seen so ashen in a long time. As she poured them a nightcap, she looked at him over the clear cylinder top.

"Who was the fellow you were with at Spago's today?"

"Oh, that was Mr. Winston J. Taylor Barlow. He's a businessman on the island. He got in early on the sight-seeing and resort business in Barcelon and wanted to see what kind of plans we could come up with for a new beachside casino and resort. There's not much going on now, but he thinks that after the war is over, things will pick up considerably. Seems like a sharp old man."

Goldie did not reply. She looked into her sherry and ran her fingers along the bottom of her lips, like she did when she was nervous about something. Wyatt noticed but said nothing. They sat for a while and visited.

Before the night ended, Goldie told Wyatt that Winston Barlow was his father, due to a casual relationship. Wyatt listened to his mother and then looked at her. He was stunned and skeptical at once. He took the news quietly and kept sipping his brandy. Not wanting his mother to know that he was doubtful, he expressed faux surprise.

Goldie looked at her son, glanced around the room, and then stared at him and quietly asked, "You don't believe me, do you, Wyatt? Son, I am not your girl—I'm your momma, remember?" she said in a sweet-and-sour tone. "I know that questioning look when I see it. He goes by Winston now, but I knew him by his christened-middle name. Before he was Winston, he was plain ole Johnny. I don't know when or how he came up with Win. The next time you see him, tell him Goldie said for you to say hello to 'Johnny Tee'."

The two conversed awhile longer, then, after their night cap, Wyatt announced, "It's been a long day; I think I will just turn in now. We'll talk about it tomorrow," he said.

He gave his mother a brief hug and checked on sleeping Niagara. Goldie watched her son as he walked across the room, entered into his adjoining accommodations, and closed the door. Taking his sudden detached behavior in stride, she walked out onto the balcony, lit a cigarette, and gazed at the harbor between puffs.

Wyatt did not sleep well that night. "How can these things be?" he pondered.

It was unsettling news because he had longed for his father to come back to him when he had been much younger. He fantasized about him showing up at one of his baseball games or even on graduation day with an explanation—even if it was not a good one—explaining where he had been all of his life. He had his doubts about whether his savvy business partner could really be blood. He did not say anything else to his mother about Mr. Barlow. He decided to launch his own private investigation into the matter, which he knew could take a while.

After a year of willful investigation and as incidents unfolded, he found out that it was true. The distinguished, gray-haired gentleman was his father and Niagara's grandfather. Winston was no less stunned by the facts than Wyatt and instantly wanted a close relationship with his son and granddaughter. Wyatt, however, demurred and decided to go slowly.

He quietly pondered the recently revealed facts and the impact of this new knowledge. He even tried to comfort himself with the thought that he had lost a wife but had gained a father. Deep inside, however, he acknowledged that he felt "some kind of way" about the revelation. He instantly knew he would need time and healing. Although Winston wanted much more time with his son, Wyatt was cautious in developing a relationship with the man he now called father. They still worked on the project together, but he usually took care of business and left Barcelon as soon as his work wrapped. Even though he was relieved to finally know who his father was, he made a conscious and deliberate effort to be distant in his contact with him.

He reasoned, "One does not absent himself from a son's life, not a son that he truly loves, and just walk back in over twenty years later and take up where he left off."

As the relationship wavered, he took the time to ferret out the many ambiguities that he felt. He admitted to himself that the whole scenario was awkward, at best, for him and his newfound father. Wyatt asked himself, "Where was he when I learned to ride a bicycle or threw my first ball? Why didn't he try to find me and spend time with me when I was in my formative years? What about my teen and early adult life? Can we really just pick back up from the time when I was five?"

These questions haunted Wyatt. Winston knew inherently that his son had every right to reject him and understood his many questions about his absence. He was, nonetheless, pained. Wyatt was his only son of four children. There was no going back and explaining all of his actions. He was away building a life of wealth that he now regretted had taken precedence over a relationship with his son. He wished he had done things differently and desperately sought to retrace the lost years. The fractious subject came up at the end of a business session at Tillerman's Wharf one late afternoon.

"I know I wasn't there for you and I can ask for nothing." He looked pleadingly at his son. Wyatt did not answer. "There's no way I can go back now," he said as he looked out over the wharf.

Wyatt just shook his head slightly and remained silent.

"I was kind of hoping that you would take my name, though."

"After all of these years? I would really have to think long and hard about that," returned Wyatt, a cold stare accompanying his icy words.

He carefully hid the fact that, down inside, he had always wanted his father's name and had toyed longingly with the idea during secret moments, but his anger about having been abandoned was real and palpable. Due to this, Wyatt was sometimes deliberately contrary toward his father.

Winston knew he would have to settle for the breadth of relationship that his son wanted. He knew full well that Wyatt was in the driver's seat and that he could make no demands nor rush his son into a relationship that should have begun long ago. Under no illusions, he made no excuses. At the moment he was just glad to behold his son with no promises attached, and he cherished moments with his delightful granddaughter. He decided to make the most of his time with Wyatt, even if it was mostly a business relationship, with scant family or social time.

From the time of this discovery, Wyatt visited Barcelon thrice a year. It was here that he saw his second cousin Townley, on a chance encounter.

On a balmy evening in August, Townley invited Wyatt to go to a night spot with him to celebrate old times. "What's buzzin', cousin?" he asked. With a twinkle in his voice, he mentioned he had a surprise. Wyatt had doubts about meeting Townley, because he did not want to get involved with any of his groupies. He knew his cousin. He was not interested in becoming a fixture in the nightlife; he wanted no part of it and was not shy about letting Townley know it.

"I am down for having a good time, but what about the groupies and the hangers on? I am not interested in that scene."

"Don't snap your cap, Y. Relax," he said. He further intoned, "Don't hate the playa, hate the game."

Changing the subject and with intrigue in his voice, he prevailed upon Wyatt to spend a night out on the town in Barcelon, playfully teasing him, "Man, I hate to tell you this, but you gettin' boring."

The words struck at Wyatt's core because it was true—he did not get out much. So, they agreed to meet at the Seashell Lounge that evening at ten o'clock. They had barely greeted each other and ordered their drinks when the lights dimmed.

As the pianist completed his opening reverie, Charlie Stokes, the lounge maître d', who doubled as an act presenter, announced the evening's headliner— "LéJenay"! As the curtains rose slowly to light applause, Jenay Morgan, dressed in a stark purple gown, appeared with her back to the stage. As she turned to the audience, she radiated in the low glow of the lounge's dim lights. She tossed her fluffy, mauve colored stole around her neck and paced the stage with a rousing, throaty rendition of "Stormy Weather". Each note was crisp and sung in a rueful, bluesy tone as one yearning for lost love. Her next selections were contemporary upbeat tunes.

Townley nodded his head slightly to the beat and stole a glance at Wyatt, who, obviously spellbound, tried to hide his surprise. He sat quietly and listened as she sang a ballad with a smooth tempo:

> The more I see you
> The more I want you
> Somehow this feeling
> Just grows and grows
>
> With every sigh
> I become more mad about you
> More lost without you
> And so it goes
>
> Can you imagine
> How much I 'll love you?
> The more I see you
> As years go by
>
> I know the only one for me
> can only be you...[4]

"How long has she been at the Seashell?" he finally asked Townley, trying to sound detached. His eyes were glued to her as she began another ballad, to light applause.

"Little over a year," Townley said as he lit a cigarette.

Wyatt said little else as he sat back in his chair, stared at the artist, and ordered scotch on the rocks. Townley instantly noticed his switch to a stronger drink but spared him any joshing because of it.

Townley popped the question to Wyatt, just as Jenay sang a signature, upbeat closing song.

"Well, Y, you wanna go backstage with me for a few minutes after the set?" he asked, clearing his throat.

"Backstage?" he asked hesitantly.

"Y, when have you known your cousin T to stutter?" He silently observed Wyatt. "Yeah, I said backstage. Been doing that for months naah. You know me, man. I cain't come this far, see a home girl, and not look her up. Some of these bougie southerners can do that, but I cain't. She knows that if I'm here, I will pay her a visit backstage. Last time we kicked it at the Blue Martini after her performance. We sat up until the wee hours of the morning talkin' about Troutdale and old times. Yeah, we talked. We talked, and I had a few. You know Jen ain't gone drink nothin'," he said between cigarette puffs. "That was until the bartender put us out so he could close the joint." He reminisced, chuckled, shook his head, and took another sip of his tonic water and a short puff of his cigarette.

Wyatt hated cigarette smoking, but obviously intrigued with the conversation, he hung on to each of Townley's words, oblivious to the circling smoke. He pondered the question but did not answer right away. Instead he looked around the room, deep in thought; took a swig of his scotch; and looked straight ahead at Jenay Morgan, who was singing a jazzy, upbeat finale. Wyatt never answered Townley. He just sat looking ahead as the crowd of patrons began leaving. Townley drank the rest of his drink, stood, put on his jacket, and patted his cousin on the shoulder. He said, "C'mon, Y, let's go."

After exiting the lounge, they walked along Mariner's Way, headed for the West End Bridge. After walking a few paces, Wyatt slowed down and asked, clearing his throat, "Ahem...

were you going to say hello to Jenay tonight? I know you said you usually…" His voice tapered off.

"Well, I wasn't sho' what you…I mean, if you wanted to talk to her or not?"

Wyatt looked around, and touched the back of his collar, before responding. "I can talk," he mused as he ran a cupped hand down his chin.

"Shore, man, shore," Townley responded. They retraced their steps to an area of dotty businesses near the Seashell.

"Let's cut through this side over here."

Wyatt followed Townley down a short, dimly lit alley and they entered the side of the Seashell. Once inside, there was a short row of mostly dark dressing rooms. When they arrived at a lit, curtained center room, Townley motioned for Wyatt to wait outside of the room for a minute. After leaning against the wall and waiting for the space of about four minutes, Wyatt paced for another minute, and then slipped inside the dressing room, with the side stride and the air of a paramour. Jenay was seated, brushing her hair. Townley was seated as well, sideways, on a counter near her mirrored dresser.

She turned her eyes from the mirror, looked at Townley, and stood uneasily. She turned to Wyatt and held out her hand in acknowledgement. She greeted him with a nod, a handshake and a glossy-eyed half smile. Her eyes burned lightly from the smoky ballroom.

"Hello, Jen," he said, accepting her hand.

Rising, Townley said, "Ummah go get a snack on the boardwalk. See you in a few, man." He tapped Wyatt on the shoulder. "Later for ya, Jen." He gave her a knowing look and exited through the alley.

"So, how've you been?"

"I've been good, actually, and you?" she asked, looking down at first and then glancing around the dressing room area. "I was just leaving for the evening, or"—she checked her time piece—"shall I say the early morning," she answered in a genial tone. She appeared to Wyatt to relax a little more.

"I'll walk you out, then."

As they strolled down the boardwalk and became reacquainted, a few pedestrians shot approving stares. They did make a striking couple: she, a honey-toned beauty and he, a bit taller, a shade darker, and handsome.

"I see the years have been a friend to you. Still a dish," he complimented her.

"Thanks, you look well yourself." She smiled, looking at the sidewalk and then at Wyatt. "What brings you to the 'Lon?"

"Well, I'm actually here in Barcelon working on a building project with my father."

"Your father? Why, I didn't know you knew him!"

Wyatt told Jenay about how he had met his father, and the conversation grew from there. She listened attentively with her ears and heart, as she always had when Wyatt spoke. He shared his last seven years with her: school, work, Ari's demise, and Niagara's birth. She expressed her condolence regarding Ari.

"Townley told me about Ari," she said compassionately. "Are you alright?"

He looked away from her. "Time has a way of healing all things, I guess," he said, without directly answering her question. He looked out over the harbor, with a glint of pain in his eyes and voice.

They walked along the riverfront in silence for a few minutes. Strolling leisurely and visiting, they arrived at her transit stop near the West End Bridge.

"Good night, Jenay. It's been great seeing you again—really."

She smiled and returned, "Likewise." She extended her hand,

which he brushed away and gave her a brief hug. They parted ways for the evening after they agreed to see each other again.

After the bus departed, Wyatt retraced his steps to the boardwalk. Townley caught up with him and asked, "Well, did you holla at your girl?"

Wyatt looked quizzically at Townley and then responded, "Yes, T, I hollered at my girl."

"Get a load of you," he said cheerfully. "That's a good thing," he nodded with a smile in his voice and on his face.

As they walked down the avenue, Townley raised two thumbs in the air and bobbed his head. He pointedly bounced in his stride as they walked toward the boardwalk and said in a raised tone, "Holla!"

Wyatt just laughed and shook his head.

A stream of glistening raspberry daffodils along the riverfront stirred in the dark and looked on.

22

Bells in Barcelon

After that August evening, Wyatt visited with Jenay whenever he was in Barcelon, which turned out to be often, as he worked toward completion of the job at his father's resort. His attendance at the Seashell was regular. After the show, they usually went for long walks along the riverfront. As they slowly rekindled their friendship, they revisited a time and a place in their past. Suddenly it was summer's eve again, a season of young love that they both longed to recapture. Their times spent in their Mulberry Ash neighborhood now seemed a recent splendor in the park. Memories of the fountains, along with shared clips of their lives, fueled endless banter.

In the fall of the next year, Wyatt took his mother and daughter with him on his trip to Barcelon. While Goldie visited with a childhood friend, he took Jenay and Niagara for a late lunch and ice cream. Lucky for Niagara, there was a kiddie carnival nearby, and she delighted in the rides and joy of it all. The couple took turns riding with her and marveled at the pure way she enjoyed life.

Jenay delighted in the winsome, graceful, fun-loving girl, and she was silently impressed with her and Wyatt's bond. Niagara reached out to Jenay and told her father, "Oohh, she's pretty," which brought a smile to the face of both adults.

"And so are you, my little beauty," was Jenay's cheerful response.

Wyatt was relieved that the two of them seemed to get along.

He reminded Niagara during their father-and-daughter time, that no one could ever replace her mother, Ari. He also gently explored with her the prospect of him marrying a new mom. After months of infrequent small talks regarding it, she gave her quiet approval. Wyatt then began planning his next move with his old flame. As their outing and the afternoon waned, Wyatt kissed Jenay on the cheek.

Niagara's eyes widened, and she asked, "Is Miss Jen my new mom?"

Her father suspensefully responded, "I don't know, Agri. You'll have to ask her."

Niagara turned to Jenay and questioned with the wonder of a child, "Miss Jen, are you my new mom?"

In matching bewilderment, she responded, "Why, I don't know. You'll have to ask your father, because after all, a lady has to be asked first," she responded coyly.

In memory of their early years in Mulberry Park, the two jovially took on the role and tenor of the statuesque English gent and lady, encircled by the park fountain. In playful, distinctly English tone and mannerism, Wyatt turned his back, reached into his pocket, turned back, and presented a small box, which he handed to Jenay. He bowed and stated, "For my lady." She playfully curtsied, and accepted the box. Niagara looked at the two in delight. When she peeked inside, she was stunned to find a diamond engagement ring. She looked at Wyatt and stared at the ring, frozen.

Wyatt removed the ring from the box, knelt and asked Jenay if she would marry him. Unable to contain her happiness; fast tears rippled quietly down her face as she hugged her husband-to-be. Niagara stood between them smiling and looking up at the both of them. The two instinctively circled her into their embrace.

"The lady hasn't answered yet," said Wyatt with a twinkle.

"Oh," said Jenay, composing herself, she returned, "Why, the lady says yes, and she thinks this would be a most agreeable arrangement."

Wyatt then placed the brilliant ring on her finger as Niagara clapped her approval.

While Jenay said she would be content with a December marriage, Wyatt reminded her of her youthful longing to have a May wedding. They spent a few weeks sketching plans for a spring Troutdale wedding but decided to marry by year's end.

~ ~ ~

As the snow fell softly in Savannah, Jenay Morgan, resplendent in a white satin tea-length wedding gown, embroidered with pearls and sequins, became the bride of John Wyatt Taylor Barlow on a mid-December day. The bride's stylish gown included a white taffeta silk bodice with crystal organza sleeves. She carried a full winter berry rose bouquet, accented with lacey green leaves. The stunning, veiled bride had adorned herself for her husband, and his eyes teared at the sight of her. They recited vows that were written by their hands, and the attendees felt their joy. The festive, late-morning wedding was attended by Niagara, and her little cousin Melody, who were flower girls; Wyatt's parents; his stepmother and half-sisters; and a few of his close friends. Jenay's friend Gaither, a showgirl whom she had met in the Golden Isles, was the maid of honor, and Townley was the best man. Rob and a few fellow musicians from the jazz quartet, who had performed nightly with the bride, attended. Later, they serenaded the couple at the wedding reception.

Winston Barlow hosted a lavish, afternoon luncheon at a Savannah riverfront hotel for the couple, where they were joined by more family, friends, and business acquaintances of the groom and his father. Winston wanted to fete the couple at his new resort in Barcelon, so he arranged an evening reception for the two at his retreat the week after the wedding. As a tribute to the newlyweds, he arranged for the bells atop his resort to chime, welcoming the couple when they arrived. The event was well attended, which brought joy to the couple and their father. A few weeks afterward, in the New Year, the Barlow's left for their honeymoon in the south of France, while Niagara remained in Savannah with her grand'mere Goldie, her cousin Melody, and her newfound relatives.

Upon their return and after many intimate talks about their future, the two decided to return to their native Carolina to begin their new life together. Wyatt left for Savannah to wrap up business and prepare for the move North. This gave Jenay four months to transition from her island lounge life back to Troutdale. The plan was that she would reach Troutdale by April, and her family would join her on Memorial Day. The family would then make their home in Charlotte by summer.

The memory of her journey overwhelmed her as she walked down the street toward the Seashell on the evening of her last performance. As the sun set, she looked at the picturesque bridge and the ever-active river with the backdrop of tall, urban buildings. She closed her eyes and took in the sounds of the rushing river, the feel of the moist air, the smell of the fragrant flowers; the distant sounds of boat horns near the harbor and the quiet chatter of tourists traversing the bridge.

After her final show, Rob, her loyal accompanist, walked her to the bus stop, and they said their good-byes. Rob, a dark figure who towered over her, had longed for a romantic relationship with his nightly lead, but it was not to be. He looked at her tranquilly, bade her farewell to night time entertainment, and wished her well with a cheek kiss under the street light. She thanked him for his friendship, his mentoring, the opportunities he made possible for her, and returned well wishes. She then boarded the bus for her last ride to the outskirts of downtown. Rob stared at her quietly as she ascended the bus steps, then turned and walked back toward the lounge.

Jenay took a seat near the middle of the bus, beside an open window. Just past the bus line, under the lamplight, she noticed a patch of radiant, blue, windblown water lilies and bright-mustard-colored sea daffodils laced with salmon tulips along the riverbank. In her mind, they seemed to gaze at her with an air of serenity. She took in the colorful sight and scent of the flowers and was comforted as she reflected upon her time in the Virgin Islands and in Barcelon. There had been cold, late, lonely nights and hard times as she had established herself as a singer. She had endured broken practice engagements with musicians, the betrayal of faux friends, been shortchanged by lounge owners, and often opened for acts that were far less talented than she. In all of the heartache and trials of her short life, she was jubilant that she had survived a winter season of her life.

In her struggles and between seasons, she was persistent in one thing. She prayed that a star would send true love back her way and into her life. Since leaving Troutdale, she had dated and had even been engaged once, but she never quite forgot the times she and Wyatt shared growing up at the Landing. In recent times, she had fastened her eyes on her sparkling wedding ring, leafed through the pages of her youthful upbringing, her heartbreak, her singing sojourn, her reunion with Wyatt, and the joyous, unbelievable occasion of their marriage. The magic of it all overwhelmed her at times, and she quietly shed cool tears and marveled at her reversal of fortune.

23

New Arrivals

Rap, rap, rap. Rap, rap, rap, rap. Faint knocking could be heard at 900 Mulberry Ash. Awake, but not dressed, Jinger, at first, continued to drink her coffee. As the knocking persisted, she listened closely, put her coffee down, and fastened her robe tightly about her. She looked at the clock, and it was barely 7 a.m.

"Probably a stray dog, scratching and tapping for an early bone. Or, then again, Lucky could be back," she surmised about her wandering dog.

She looked out of her window past her laced curtains and saw a lad standing alone at her door. She pushed the curtains back and thought it odd that a little boy would be out so early.

"Why would this child be out here this time of the morning, all alone?" she queried aloud.

She looked again and saw a slender, thirtyish-looking, attractive woman standing behind the young boy.

Jinger opened the door with a questioning look. "Good morning."

"Good morning, ma'am," said the lad, looking up.

The woman only smiled and extended her hand. "Hello. You must be Jimmie."

"Yes. I'm Jinger Rose," she responded in more of a question than a statement, as she shook the woman's hand. It had been over forty years since anyone had called her Jimmie.

"My grandson and I are visiting from up North; may we come—"

Before she could complete her question, Jinger heard a car door slam. She peered past her two visitors and saw Rustin helping an elderly lady out of the car in the driveway.

She paused and asked the woman, "Do I know you?" Her heart listened as the stranger introduced herself as Marie and the boy as Charley. As she looked on in confusion, her brother brought a frail but sturdy woman to the front porch.

"It's okay, J. R.; it's Mollie and Katy Marie."

Jinger's universe stopped and then twirled around her as she looked at Rustin and then Mollie, Katy Marie, and young Charley. Instinctively, her hands flew to her face and she stared in wonder and smiled broadly. She drew Charley to her, took his face in both of her hands, and hugged him tightly. In a rushed motion, she then stumbled to her sister and gave her a long, warm embrace, shedding tears. She wiped her eyes, stepped onto the porch and greeted Mollie with a hug and a kiss before she took her other arm. Her mother was darker and frailer than how Jinger recalled her.

"Can we go in?" Charley looked up and asked.

"Yes, child, go on in. You are family," she looked through moist eyelids. "Family that I never expected to see again," she said aloud. Jinger invited her guests to settle in the dining room, as she looked on between tears and awe.

"I've been knowin' about them for six months now," mused Rustin.

"Why didn't you tell me, brother?"

"Oh, I wanted to surprise you—that's all." Rustin beamed.

"Well, this is a surprise, an answer to prayer, and an absolute joy," she said as she beheld her kin.

Their sister, Katy Marie, was still a beauty, and seemed like a sweet woman. Their mother, Mollie, had aged quite a bit. She looked around with faint satisfaction; her distant mannerism took Jinger back to the time when she was a mere girl. As more breakfast was prepared, the four of them reminisced about Baywater and shared their pasts since their separation.

Brimming with questions, Rustin asked, "Mollie, how have you all been? It's been a long time."

"We alright," she said instinctively.

"Pretty good," said Katy, cryptically.

"So, you all have been living well?" asked Jinger.

The two women glanced at each other.

"Actually, we have lived from place to place," answered Katy. She looked at her mother and then looked down.

"When you two left, the city gave Katy back to me.It was only for a short while, though, and they took her from me again. Zoot wouldn't take her at first on account of he has another family. You all remember Miss Vera and her nephew? Well, I asked her, and she took her in until she was a big girl. Thirteen, I think."

"No, Momma, I was twelve."

"I didn't really have a stable place for Katy, so I was glad Miss Vera thought enough of me to sign her out of child haven and let her live with her and her nephew. I would see her a few times a year, whenever I made it back to Baywater. She took good care of Katy. At the time, I lived in Chicago with a man named Lodell Davis. After some years went by, and the project housing where Miss Vera stayed got so bad, Katy came to live with us. It was just too much goin' on for Katy to be safe, so Miss Vera sent her to me, and she and her nephew moved down South."

Katy sat quietly and looked steadily but somewhat sadly at Mollie.

Lodell didn't want her there, though, so I got in touch with Zoot and begged him to take her. He did. That lasted for a few months. Katy has two half-brothers and a half-sister. I think they got along okay. Didn't you, Katy?"

This question was met with a nonchalant shrug.

Mollie continued, "I don't think Zoot's wife, Adelaide, took it too well, though, so Katy didn't stay too long. I'll let her tell you herself what it was like living with the Carlisles'."

"It was mostly awkward. They treated me alright, but I always felt like an outsider. Adelaide's eyes were always red. My half-brothers really accepted me, but my sister basically tolerated me and did not want to share time nor space with me. Daddy was good to me, but it seemed like him and his wife argued all of the time. She would be nice one minute and then be going off and throwing things the next. So, it was hard, and I knew I was a big part of the problem. A few months after I went to live with them, Daddy's sister visited us and agreed to take me to live with her. I was so relieved."

"I know I done wrong goin' around with and havin' a child by that woman's husband, but that's what happened. Too late to take it back now. One thing about it, though: Zoot loves all of his chil'ren, but he had to have known that the situation would put Adelaide in a strain. I think it had an effect on all of the chil'ren, so it worked out when Katy went to live with his sister, Razella Rae, in Chi' Town. That worked out well, 'cause I was still living in Chicago then, and I had a chance to see my Katy from time to time."

"How did Miss Razella treat you, Katy?" questioned Rustin.

"Well, she couldn't have any children of her own, so she was glad for the company and a chance to 'raise somebody', as she used to say. Aunt Razz was good to me, though. I had a chance to go to school; wear nice, clean clothes; and live in a pretty nice little house. She taught me how to cook and clean. I got married in her backyard when I was seventeen. Too bad, nine months later, she died of a stroke. Bless her heart. I was sad to see her go when she passed."

"I heard she had the traits of a ho," said Mollie under her breath.

Katy gave Mollie a lasting ornery look and commented, "People can say what they want to, but she never put me in harm's way. She drank every now and then, and she had her friends, but she kept me under a watchful eye and didn't let anything happen to me. No, she wasn't perfect, but she took me in when she really didn't have to," Katy said wistfully. "I loved my aunt Razz," she said as she stared defiantly at Mollie.

"I'm glad she took you in, sister," Rustin said in order to give Katy time to calm her emotions.

"I know I wadn't the mother that I shoulda been to my chil'ren, but the good Lord let other people hep me to raise you all, and I'm thankful to Him for that," she said quietly after her tongue lashing from Katy. She paused, then solemnly added, "You all can call me Momma, now, if you care to."

It seemed to Jinger that she noticed a slight tremor in her mother's fingers when she gestured.

"My marriage lasted for about ten years. We divorced, though, and I took my maiden name back. I had a son, Charles Jr. He's in the army now, so I'm raising little Charley for him. After he stayed overseas for a while, his wife became restless and took up with another man. Some say she skipped the country and is living overseas with an airman. She dropped my grandson off for me to babysit one day, and I haven't seen her since. So, I'm keeping him with me for now. It's fine if Charles Jr. comes to get him and fine if he doesn't, 'cause he's just like mine now." She looked dotingly at her grandson.

"I don't want to live with anybody else. I jes' want to stay with you, Me-Me," he said as he laid his head on her arm.

"You don't have to go if you don't want to."

"You really shouldn't tell that child that, 'cause if Charles Jr. comes back for his son…"

"I know, Momma. I know." This prospect obviously pained the two, as Katy looked lovingly at her grandson, and he lingered and leaned on her arm.

"After Aunt Razz died Moll…Momma stayed on for a few days after the funeral. That turned into a few months. Come to find out, she really didn't have anywhere to go. Mr. Davis got sick and later died, but he had never divorced his wife, so that left Momma out in the cold, financially. She stayed with me for a while, and then we moved to Cincinnati after they took Aunt Razz's house. It was then that I thought about searching for you and sister," she said to Rustin. "We left Cincy and went back to Baywater. I looked up the Murdochs as soon as I got back to town and they helped me trace you all to Tessa Lee through some old papers that Aunt Katie had. It took me two long years, but I contacted her, and she told me how to get in touch with Rustin, which I did. When I told him that me and Mollie and my grandson were all together but with no stable place to live, he sent for us. We don't want to be a burden to anyone; we just need a little help until we can get on our feet." She looked at her mother and then at the floor.

Not expecting any company, Jinger did her best to spread her food to feed five instead of two. She had invited Miss Paisley to breakfast, but her neighbor had sent word earlier that she would not be able to make it.

Katy was anxious to hear about what had become of Rustin and Jimmie. While they visited, Flossie's grandson brought Jinger some peas and asked if Charley could come over to play. Katy looked at Charley in a protective way.

"You need to let that child go, Katy. You keeps him under

you too close. Let him play for a spell. Your sister here wouldn't let him go into harm's way."

"Believe me, it's fine sister. My friend Flossie runs a tight household. She'll keep them inside and watch them. He would probably get bored just sitting here listening to us talk."

"Can I go and play, Me-Me?" His eyes begged his grandmother.

"He looks a little older than my Charley, but I guess ita be okay."

"They're all chil'ren. A few years' age difference ain't gone make no never mind," said Ollie.

"He's not that much older than Charley. I'll tell you what. Gregory, go ask your grandma if you can stay awhile and play with my nephew," said Jinger.

"Yes, ma'am."

"Can I go with him to ask his granny, Me-Me?"

"Yes, go along," answered Katy.

"They'll be right back," assured Jinger.

Rustin and Jinger shared reflections about their journey from Baywater to the South and their life in Roxborough.

"The first thing my aunt Tessa did was rename me Jinger."

"Why did she do that? Ollie asked.

"Aunt Tessa said she thought the name Jinger sounded daintier than Jimmie. She said where she came from, girls weren't named Jimmie, just boys."

"I named you after my brother, though." Ollie paused and then said, "She had some nerve."

"Yes, I know, Momma. It didn't set too well with me either, so I just always called her J.R. or Rosie. I've been calling her that ever since, out of respect for our uncle Jimmy," said Rustin as he looked fondly at Jinger.

Rustin shared stories of their upbringing in the Maxwell house, their separate departures from Roxborough, his army times, and stories of his and Jinger's adult lives with their mother and sister. Jinger mostly listened and let Rustin talk.

Jinger showed the two of them her college diploma. Katy smiled brightly, and Ollie said, "Humph."

"So, you all had a chance to get book learning? I made it to the twelfth grade, but I got married before I graduated. I took typing and a business course, though, and worked as a secretary. I type and do shorthand, so I'm hoping to find office work," said Katy.

"I'll take you downtown next week, and you can put in some applications," offered Rustin.

Katy nodded and smiled at this prospect.

The boys returned and played in the parlor and in the backyard, as the adults continued their visit. Ollie wanted to see more pictures of Louis and Jenay. She and Katy commented on the pictures that hung in Jinger's small picture gallery in the parlor. She freely shared the memory of her husband and pictures of her doted-upon daughter.

"He was a good lookin' fella. Remind me a little of Zoot."

"Yeah, he sort of favors Daddy," said Katy softly.

"Y'all just had that one?" queried Ollie.

"Yes, just Jenay. We wanted more children, but Louis just wasn't here long enough. I was married to a man named Nathan Keys for a few years, but he was pretty much a rolling stone, so we never had any children together."

"We don't all come here to stay no long time," said Ollie softly. "I'm sorry you lost your husband at such a young age."

"She's beautiful," Katy said. "When can we meet her?"

"She and her family live in Charlotte. They usually come down once a month, so you can see her and her family next week, at Sunday dinner."

Ollie quietly studied pictures of her granddaughter and stated to Katy, "I have a picture of you when you were five. You two looked a lot alike at that age. It's funny how chil'ren ah sometimes take afta somebody in the family."

"You know, they do favor quite a bit," said Rustin with a knowing smile. Jinger nodded her head in agreement and chuckled in delight under her breath.

Gregory played with Charley until he had to leave to go to children's afternoon choir rehearsal. As the banter continued, Jinger put on a pot roast, rice, snap peas, yams, and rolls in preparation for dinner. Katy made gravy and put the finishing touches on an apple cobbler for the meal.

Jinger noticed how her mother looked around her kitchen expectantly several times. When Rustin went to his car for a moment, Ollie asked her if she had anything to drink.

"I have some soda water, juice, or ice-cold water in the refrigerator. Can I get something for you?" Jinger offered eagerly.

Ollie looked over her shoulder toward the front door and then asked, "You got any wine? If you do, I would like a small glass," she said in a hoarse, earnest voice.

"No. I don't drink, so I don't have any liquor in the house."

"Not even for ya comp'ny?"

"No, ma'am."

"Grow up."

"Ma'am?"

"Nothing."

Ollie resignedly leaned back in her chair and looked around for a minute. Jinger gave her a glass of cranberry juice, then continued making dinner for the family. Katy put the cobbler in the oven and then took Charley into the back room to relax before washing up for supper. When Ollie went to the back room to rest, Rustin joined his older sister in the kitchen. There, he posed a question.

"Mother and sister don't really have a place to stay right now. I was wondering if you could take sister and little Charley in, and I'll take Momma with me."

"You know you don't have to ask me that. There's nobody here in this house but me. I couldn't turn sister away, and after not seeing her for so many years," said Jinger. "While we visited, the one thing I did want to ask Momma was why she did not go to the train depot with us when we left Baywater, but I decided not to dwell on it. I am just so relieved to see her and sister." Rustin did not reply but nodded his head introspectively.

Jinger then added, "Sounds like they plan on staying in Troutdale for a while."

"Sounds like it."

"I was wondering how Momma is really doing, brother?"

"Like, how do you mean?"

"When you went outside to your car, she asked me for a drink, which you know I don't keep liquor in my house."

"She can't have anything to drink! Katy said her liver is about gone, now." Rustin shook his head.

"Looks like the lifestyle she chose has taken a toll on her."

"Yeah, me and sister talked a little about Momma's health and their living arrangement. She said she would take mother to live with her just as soon as she can find work and get her own place."

"How does Chérisse feel about Momma living with you all?"

"She said it would be fine. I told her it would just be until Katy gets on her feet. She said she doesn't mind helping family."

"You know sister and my nephew are welcome here for as long as they need to stay. It's so good to see her after so many years. It was always my secret wish to see them both again."

"Mine, too."

Brother and sister stood in silence. They looked out of Jinger's modest kitchen window past the half-drawn pearl white and apricot, ruffled curtains and outside window flower box. Both noticed the slow-moving clouds and the slanted rays of dwindling sunshine that seemed to dually portend the end of the day and the presage of a new day.

24

Celebration

"Naah, is this eighty for Miss Paisley?"

"Eighty-five."

"She's lived a long time. Past the three score and ten that was promised to us."

"And she has been such a support and blessing to us all."

"Don't fool yo'self; that Miss Paisley is smart too. She is as smart as a whip, and she will getcha if you get outta line."

"Yes. She's not afraid to confront and correct, if she needs to," said Jinger with a chuckle.

Jinger and her friend, Flossie, heard a commotion and looked up. It was Charley and his stepsisters. They ran through the house and burst into the backyard before Katy could correct them.

"Mmmm…smells good in there!" said Charley as he and the girls made it to the backyard. This was met with giggles from the little girls.

"Can we play on the swing, Mommy?"

"First, we do not run through anyone's house!" Katy marched her troop back through the house and to the front porch. She had them to walk outside, along the side of the house, through the gate, and into the backyard.

"Can we play now?"

"If it's all right with Aunt Jinger, you can play on the swing. But you all stay away from the tables and decorations."

"Can we, Aunt Jin?"

"Why, sure, sugar. Nothing here is for any special people.

Any little one can play on the swing. Play your little hearts out." She smiled broadly and chuckled, scanning Katy's five.

Little Charley had inherited four stepsisters when Katy married Hollis Dunbar. She and Charley had been in Troutdale for ten months when she caught Hollis' eye. He had four daughters by his first wife, Charlotte, who was what some called a mulatto. Although a black woman, she looked more white than black. She had callously announced one Saturday morning to her husband, Hollis, that she was not happy. She said she didn't want to let life pass her by and had made up her mind to do what most members of her family had already done: she decided to pass for white. She said she no longer felt fulfilled with her life in Carolina and was moving to California. She tightly hugged, and kissed each one of her little ones and then left Hollis to raise four stair-step girls alone. She had left on the bus that Saturday afternoon dressed in her casual best, carrying her belongings in the family's best suitcases.

Townley said he saw her passing for white in a chorus line on the island of St. John. He said she pretended not to know him when he went backstage and spoke to her. Her accent and her stunned look when he called her by her name betrayed her, though. He further stated that he was sure it was Charlotte, although she answered to Margo.

A proud man and a skilled tradesman, Hollis was from one of the established, founding families of Troutdale. He had looked past many daughters of the Creek for Charlotte. He and his girls disappeared from attending church for a few weeks, and church folks wondered out loud if Hollis would die from the embarrassment of desertion or at the prospect of doing all of those little girls' hair.

When Hollis and Katy became engaged, the townsfolk whispered. Some said they did not think the newcomer was particularly in love with Hollis but thought she agreed to marry him for companionship and ulterior motives. Katy ignored the naysayers and jumped at the chance to be with Hollis, to become a part of the influential Dunbar family, and to have a home of her own.

Hollis was a decent man and was clearly taken with Katy. He tried, in vain, to find Charlotte. After months of searching, he divorced her on the grounds of abandonment. So, Katy Marie Carlyle married Hollis Dunbar one Sunday afternoon after church services. Most of the church congregants stayed for the brief wedding and lavish Sunday-afternoon reception. She and Charley blended with the Dunbars, and they became one family. The four young girls, one of whom could barely talk, said they missed their real momma. But Charlotte never came back home, so they took to Katy, and she took to them.

Jinger delighted in seeing her sister and her little ones on the eve of her celebration. As the children played, Katy and Flossie placed the finishing touches on the backyard decorations. Rustin and Wyatt arrived and set up ten round tables and eight chairs at each table. The salmon tablecloths were accented with fall flowers. Fresh daisies, day lilies, and tangerine cone flowers with candles in the center, accented the tables. Katy dressed the punch table with a fountain, cups and napkins. As Jinger worked, she could not help but to think of times past when she and Louis had catered events together. She worked diligently on the tables, tying bows, curling ribbons, arranging napkins, and placing centerpieces, as Flossie checked on the layout for food preparations.

A teardrop fell. She wiped it away quickly and continued decorating, trying to hide her sudden recall. She worked on through a few more teardrops. Her brother, Rustin, walked over, stood beside her and, without saying a word, gave her a warm side hug.

"Let me help you with that, sister," he said softly.

Jinger did not offer an explanation. Rustin did not ask for one. They worked in silence for a few minutes. She was comforted by her brother's presence. Ever since they had left Baywater, he instinctively knew when she was happy or hurt. And most of the time, he knew exactly why. Rustin had been observant that way since their early days. He must have known that the happy occasion brought back memories of her Louis and their catering days. They kept decorating.

Drying her tears, after a while, Jinger glanced sideways at her brother's awkwardly tied bows. This brought a subtle smile to her face as she worked. She knew she would have her work cut out redoing those rail and table bows.

"There's someone here to see you, Mother," said Wyatt.

Jinger was surprised to look up and find Nathaniel Keys, her second husband, standing with her son-in-law. Rustin stared at him, looked at his sister and stood still. Jinger motioned that she was alright. She nodded, and her brother left the two of them to talk.

"Came back to Troutdale a few months back. Thought I'd come by and see how you're makin' it. How have you been?" asked Nathan.

"I've been doing pretty well. And you?" she said as she looked up.

"Pretty good. Looks like you plannin' a party. Is it somebody's birthday?"

"Yes. You remember Miss Paisley? It's her birthday, and we will be celebrating tomorrow."

Nathan nodded and looked around. "I guess Jen is 'bout

grown with kids of her own, naah," he said in a half question, half statement.

"And twins at that." Jinger' eyes opened widely, and her hand shot to her mouth. "Oops! I wasn't supposed to tell that part. Can you keep it under your hat?" she asked with pleading eyes.

Nathan chuckled. "Oh, I won't say anything about it."

"She will be here at the celebration, tomorrow night, at half past six," she said. Jinger thought for a moment. "You can come by if you'd like."

"I think I'll stop by then." He looked around. "Looks like you all still have a lot to do." He looked back at Jinger. "Think I'll just make myself handy, if it's alright with you," he said quietly.

Jinger was silent at first. She looked down at her place settings and looked awkwardly around her backyard. She then nodded in agreement.

Flossie showed herself to be a true friend. She and her grandchildren stayed until the early evening hours helping Jinger decorate her home and yard. She mentioned Nathan's presence but did not pry.

Shrouded in the planning, cooking, and decorating, was a curious undertone about Nathan. She wondered about his reappearance in Mulberry Ash, and she remembered how he had left. She wondered if he would show up at the celebration, as he was not always a person of his word. His presence that day in her back yard was not the first time she had seen him in recent times. One Tuesday afternoon, as she left the market, he saw her and asked if he could walk her home. She had hesitated at first, looked him over, and had then given her consent. They walked to her home mostly in silence.

They sat and talked on the front porch for about an hour, but she did not invite him in. She later confided in Miss Paisley about her mixed feelings on a midsummer evening during one of their long walks.

"Miss Paisley, how do you know if you should accept a man back into your life or not?"

"Well, I would probably ask myself if my life would be better with him or without him?"

"Yes, and that's what makes it difficult to decide."

"Who is it?"

"Nathan Keys."

"I saw somebody who walked like him down by the riverside last week. So, it was him."

"Yes. He seems to want to come back into my life, but I'm not so sure about that, after the way he left and all."

"Mmnh."

"I know I have to forgive him, or I won't make it past the pearly gates."

"Yes, we do have to forgive others—not just on their account but mostly on ours. That way we have a measure of peace in our lives and enjoy life better."

"Well, I think I'll just go slowly on this one. Try to see where he's coming from, first."

"That's wise. You have to watch some men. Sometimes if they're in financial straits or have an undisclosed illness, they'll choose to be with a woman on account of what she has and the comforts he can enjoy."

"You know, I hadn't really thought about that. I know it's said that two are better than one, but I was thinking not if it will make my life worse."

"I know that companionship is a good thing and we all desire it, but we have to be both patient and wise, which we all know is hard to do. I would keep an open mind and a discerning heart, take it one day at a time, and seek His direction."

"That sounds right."

"It's always good to weigh a matter but guard your heart."

"Um humn."

Jinger reflected on Miss Paisley's words on the eve of her celebration, but right then she just wanted to sleep. Pretty soon the sleep fairy beckoned her. Answering, she fell into a deep, sound sleep.

~   ~   ~

In what seemed like no time, she woke up refreshed for the celebration day. Aunt Tessa was the first to arrive. Jinger heard a knock at her door, peeked at her porch, and was surprised to see her aunt. She opened the door wide and said, "Why, Aunt Tessa, what a pleasant surprise," as she warmly hugged the woman who had raised her, hiding her wariness.

"Hello, daughter."

Jinger sensed there was something wrong right away but didn't mention it. Without asking a word, she brought three suitcases in from her front porch and set them in the parlor.

"You look well, Aunt Tessa. I am so excited that you came today, of all days, because tonight I am having a party. It's just perfect that you are here for it."

"It's good to have family."

"How's Uncle Max doing?" Jinger inquired quietly after comfortably seating her aunt.

"Max is not doing too well; he's been having a few sick spells. I'll tell you about it later. How's the family here in Troutdale?"

"Everyone is good. You'll get to see them all tonight. Come and sit here in the kitchen. We can talk while I cook us a little breakfast. Would you like some juice?"

Over breakfast, Tessa shared her troubles with her adopted daughter. Max had stayed in the house with her but was rumored to be having an affair with Hester Horsley, a young neighbor lady less than half his age. When he had become gravely ill, Tessa had nursed him, waited on him, cooked his food, and washed his body. He suffered several sick spells, and, although devastated about his alleged behavior, she had stayed with Max. Fred and Myrtle Jackson felt badly for their middle daughter but encouraged her to stay and try to make her marriage work. Although she loved her husband, she was deeply hurt and embarrassed by his behavior and lack of respect. She wanted more than anything to make her marriage work, in spite of her dire circumstances.

When it was discovered that Hester was with child, the Jacksons were silent. During a visit to their home, she overheard her mother say that if it was her, she wouldn't stay there and take it. Her sisters encouraged her to "smack that simple ho down", leave Max, and move in with them. They had said there wouldn't be a woman in Shady Grove who would blame her, including Hester's own mother, Minerva, who made it known that she did not approve of her daughter's behavior—nor had she raised her that way.

Tessa had listened to her sister's pout and hiss, but chose instead, to find Jinger and Rustin and make a life near them. Max, having regained a reasonable portion of his health, left for work a few minutes before nine o'clock the previous day, as he had for many years before his sickness. Tessa made her move. She packed her belongings. She asked her father to come by that morning, and he had arrived on time. He helped Tessa load her boxed and suit cased belongings into his Ford. They stopped at Violet's first and left a set of boxes, then headed to the bus station. The two rode along mostly in silence, but Tessa could tell that her father approved of her decision by the quickness with which he moved.

Before she boarded the bus, Fred had given his daughter a long hug, and asked for no explanation. Tessa gave him an envelope. She had written her parents a brief note, letting them know that she would be at Jinger's home indefinitely. She found her way to Troutdale and posed the question, over breakfast, regarding whether she could stay for a while.

Jinger, moved by her aunt's plight, said affirmatively, "You know you will always have a home with me, Aunt Tessa Lee. After you took us in from a life of neglect, when me and Rustin were on a pathway to certain despair, and you gave us a home, a proper raising, and a fighting chance at life, there is no way I could ever turn you away. There's nothing on this green earth that's too good for you, Aunt Tessa. You are welcome in my home."

The two embraced warmly. After a few moments, they dried their moist eyes, finished their breakfast and then reviewed the evening's plans.

~ ~ ~

By seven o'clock that evening, the party was in full swing. Rustin had encouraged his sister not to be too austere in the music, so he and his family arrived early and played light jazz tunes on the phonograph.

Jenay, Wyatt, and little Niagara arrived near sundown. Jenay wobbled in, looking radiant as a mom-to-be. Wyatt doted on his wife so until she became flustered and sent him to the store for apple cider. When Jinger found out about Wyatt's errand, she frowned at her daughter and questioned why she had sent her son to the market when there was so much punch and drink to be had on hand already.

She said, "Momma, I want to breathe, and he's smothering

me." This brought smiles from the older clan who were seated having lemonade at the kitchen table.

"Jes' let him be taken with ya. You'll appreciate that after a while," said Flossie in quiet amusement.

When she walked off, one of the seasoned guests remarked, "She gone be glad for her husband once them pains start stabbin' her." This was met with knowing looks, half nods, and a few repressed chuckles from the seated guests.

Katy and Hollis arrived with their clan. Charley and the girls walked politely into the house, spread around a few hugs, and then dashed out of the back door toward the swing set and punch.

Rustin, Chérisse, and their young adult children came next. They brought Ollie to the party. The younger people went outside into the backyard and began a card game with a few other partygoers. Jinger looked admiringly at the young set, as they sat under a spreading chinaberry tree. Inside, Rustin parked Ollie at the kitchen table. She looked tired but happy. She didn't say much at first, just beheld her children and grandchildren with a sense of satisfaction and joy. She was seen wiping tears from her eyes more than once. After settling in, she looked around thirstily for spirits; finding none, she asked her son, Rustin, to bring her a ginger ale. She resigned herself to this and cherry club soda for the remainder of the evening. Her countenance showed slight disappointment.

There was music, card playing, chatter, horseshoes, board games, and playtime for the children in Jinger's large backyard. Tessa had helped with the preparations right up until the time the guests arrived. Right before the sun set, she came out to be with the family. She looked striking; her silver, bobbed hair moved when she moved. She wore a stylish summer dress and a smile. Jinger had not told the family that she was there. Rustin gave her a warm embrace and invited her to sit with them. Chérisse greeted her jovially. Ollie eyed Tessa, looked at Rustin and her daughter-in-law, then managed a quiet, genial greeting.

Tessa, always the socialite, visited amiably with her family. She was friendly and made several attempts to chat with Ollie, who made little effort at conversational return. Feeling a cool draft from her cousin, Tessa excused herself and decided to check on the party outside. She made herself useful by icing and slicing cake and pouring punch.

Jinger grabbed her face. "Oh, I almost forgot. Wyatt, could you walk down a few doors and bring Miss Paisley? She is our guest of honor. I told her earlier today that I was having a few people over this evening, so she will probably be already dressed. Just tell her dinner is ready and try not to give away the surprise."

"I'll walk down with ya, Wyatt, just to keep you comp'ny," Hollis added.

"Sure, be glad to have you."

As they walked outside along the side fence toward the gate, two youngsters abruptly let go of their embrace and hurriedly walked into the backyard. Neither adult said anything to them, but Hollis wondered out loud: "That looks like Carlotta's girl, Floyd's granddaughter. Didn't know she was old enough to be courtin'."

"I think her name is Treelani. If her mother sees her, she'll get the switch for sure."

"Well, I might jes' mention it to Floyd or Carlotta, because I don't want to see no good girl go bad. 'Cause if it was one of my four, I would sure appreciate knowing so she could receive her correction."

"I hear ya, Hollis. The same for my Niagara, when she comes of age."

While they were gone, Townley arrived with a female guest.

Although he had not been formally invited, Jinger gave him a warm hug.

Shouts of, "Surprise!" could be heard from the partygoers welcoming the guest of honor when she was escorted into the backyard. She gasped, looked around, and tearfully expressed her joy. Ollie squinted when she saw Miss Paisley but said nothing.

"A party for me?" Miss Paisley said, half questioning, and half exclaiming.

"Yes, Miss Paisley, for you!" said Jinger. "I think you may have touched the life of everyone in this yard, and we want you to know that we love and appreciate you!"

"Oh, I haven't done anything," she humbly stated, shaking her head.

"Oh, yes you have!" Rustin exclaimed. "You've been there for all of us." In a disc jockey's voice, he asked loudly, "Everyone, give a shout out if Miss Paisley ever loved on you, encouraged you, or has been there for you!"

The sounds in the backyard swelled into claps, yells, and yeahs." Miss Paisley couldn't believe it, so she just cried some more.

Wyatt escorted her to a seat of honor, which was in front of a well-chiseled, ribbon-laced, ivory lattice panel that had been created by Nathan Keys and decorated by Jinger Keys. The Dunbar girls planted a hair wreath of ribbons, dusty pink garden rose buds, olive leaves, and baby's breath on her head. Charley gave her a bouquet of pale blush pink roses, along with a huge hug. Miss Paisley hugged him back and kissed the girls. The guests sang "Happy Birthday" to the honoree, and someone made her a plate of food. The party continued as well-wishers gathered around and wished Miss Paisley a grand and happy birthday.

The music was turned up a notch, and the partiers delighted in the sounds of Charlie Parker, Cab Calloway, and Sarah Vaughn.

The teenagers had brought a phonograph and played jazz and doo-wop sounds on the side of the house. They danced the jitterbug, the swing, and the hop. The noisy crew was asked, at times, by Rustin to turn the music down, as it was competing with the backyard music.

Nathan slipped in right after sundown. Jenay was pleasantly surprised to see her one-time stepfather, and greeted him warmly.

Jinger took the opportunity to stop the music and have everyone gather in the backyard to present Miss Paisley her gifts and share family news. First, she asked her daughter and son to come forward. Wyatt announced that Jenay would be giving birth to twins. This was met with loud claps of delight. On a personal note, he shared that he was running for alderman in the November election in Charlotte. He acknowledged the few Charlotteans in attendance and reminded them that he had assumed his father's name and would be running on the ballot under the name John Wyatt Barlow instead of Wyatt Fleming. This was met with nodding heads and round support from the revelers.

Rustin then took the floor and announced that he had been promoted to the position of branch manager of Cedar City Savings and Loan. Such an accomplishment was so rare that it was met with silence and then brisk claps. To an attentive group, he shared:

> "I got my first break in numbers when I was in the military. I had a sergeant who took an interest in me, and he made sure I was assigned positions in the counting room at the commissary, and I went from there. I took it upon myself to finish high school in the army and I took all the math and accounting courses that I could. I strongly

encourage all of you here to take advantage of any
opportunities to learn and better yourself that
come your way. I started at the bank when it was
called Savers First. I was a young fella then, just
out of the military. I could find no other work, so
I took a job as a porter sweeping the floor at the
bank and worked my way up. I say to the young,
don't ever be too proud to start at the bottom,
because more than likely, that is where you'll
start. So just get in where you can fit in. It took
me seventeen long years to rise up the bank ranks.
I trained thirteen tellers, who were all promoted
past me. Eight of them became branch managers.
It was really hard to see their progress and me not
be able to move. I went home disappointed many
days, but I chose to get up and go back, in the face
of unfairness. As a porter, I arrived to work on
time and did my best every day. After a while, I
was promoted to bank teller. By and by the bank's
management recognized my work. They said I
performed with such precision that they could no
longer deny me my earned and rightful place as a
branch manager. Every person of color who came
into the bank congratulated me for weeks on end.
All of this is good and fine, but make no mistake,
my words tonight are not about me, it is about all
of us. Jim Crow has really robbed our people of
opportunity, but we must not let it take away our
dignity or our hope. You must learn to persevere
through the winters of your life. And all of you
will have those dark and windy seasons. I want to
encourage the working among us, though—and

especially the young—to fight the good fight and keep the faith, because a change will come after a while, and you must believe that. Just the other day, the bank management offered me a position up north in Milwaukee. After talking it over with my wife, I think I'll take it, but that'll be next summer. I encourage all of you under the sound of my voice to remember that in order to shine in this world, you must be three times as good as all others. My uncle Max instilled this in me, and it is yet good advice today. The long wait I had wasn't fair, but then life is not fair. Just be excellent, do your best, hold on, don't stop, stay humble, and your change will come."

Rustin then took the occasion to ask his wife, Chérisse, to come forward. He proclaimed his love for his mocha sweetheart and praised her for standing by him through the good and bad times. He also recognized his son and daughter; Tressa and Rustin Jr. Ollie Jackson beheld her son and shook her head through tears. Jinger cried too. She had always believed that her brother's gift with numbers would present opportunities for him. Aunt Tessa smiled and nodded her approval. Katy looked proudly at her brother.

Jinger then gave Miss Paisley her gifts, which culminated with the presentation of a finely sewn quilt of many colors. It featured lifescapes of those who were close to the honoree. Jinger had invited family and friends to sketch squares for the quilt. She then hand-stitched it herself.

Charley and the Dunbar girls' square had their little handprints in different colors, and Jinger had a college campus building, with ivy crawling up two columns, in her square. Jenay and Wyatt's had an outline of their family with three little trees on it. Rustin's had a sketch of himself sitting in the bank, Pastor Brewster's square had a church steeple on it, Katy and Hollis' had a sketch of their home with six windows, and Flossie's had a silhouette of two friends. One quilt square featured Mulberry Park, replete with flowers in full bloom. There was a sewn sketch of Miss Paisley sitting on her porch rocking. This larger square was the center piece of the quilt. It had taken Jinger five long years to sew the quilt. She had decided to sew it after Miss Paisley turned eighty. This memento of the lives that she had touched was a moving time for the matriarch, as she had no biological family in Troutdale. The honoree was then asked to have words. The children were stilled; teenagers and young adults gave up their seats for older guests. All sat attentively in anticipation of what the seasoned matron had to say. Miss Paisley had the little ones make a semicircle on the lawn in front of her.

"My message to each of you today is simple. To the children, I say listen to and respect your elders. They have been where you are trying to go. To everyone under the sound of my voice I say seek wisdom and pursue it. Her value is worth far more than precious stones or riches. Treat others the way you want to be treated. Act from the good treasures of your heart. Don't be discouraged. If you fall down in life, get back up and try again. Whatever life brings your way, remember the sun will rise and shine again. No matter what happens, do right, and right will come."

"And now I have a surprise announcement of my own."

She stood up from her seat of honor and asked Ollie Jackson to come forward. Rustin rolled his mother forward and parked her beside the guest of honor.

"It's been a long, long time, but it's good to see you, Lola."

Ollie sat up in her seat. It had been years since she heard

anyone call her by her street name. She peered at the speaker, narrowed, and then bucked her eyes as if she had seen a ghost. She then fell back in her wheelchair with a knowing look.

"Most of you know me as Miss Paisley. My christened name is Veralene Coleman Paisley, though. And I have known the Jacksons longer than most of you would imagine and longer than some of them know. You see, I used to live across the hallway from Ollie in Baywater. It was me who babysat Jinger and Rustin when they were very young. Katy lived with me for a short time. Some may not have recognized me. One reason may be my appearance. Shortly after moving here from Baywater I became very ill with influenza and I lost 55 pounds. I almost died, but I became better and stronger as the years went by. I don't have much family left now, so I took the Jacksons as my family. And now, we have come full circle. I'm so glad we are all back together. Thank you, Ollie, for sharing your family with me."

Ollie sat with a glazed, teary look in her eyes. She wiped her eyes and then gave a pleasant nod to the honoree. Jinger and Rustin received their former babysitter with a sense of awe and disbelief. All four huddled in a group and hugged. Katy came forward and gave her former guardian a summery hug. Rustin's eyes were moist as he rolled his obviously surprised mother back to her table.

Jinger shook her head and marveled at this news. Her heart raced. She had always felt a kinship to Miss Paisley, and now she understood why. Now it all made sense. A few songs she had overheard her singing were actually flashes from her past.

She watched Miss Paisley as she celebrated. The elder woman made a silent wish, blew out the solitary candle that was on her cake and smiled broadly. This was met with claps of delight.

Aunt Tessa recruited several preteen guests to help her serve cake, punch and ice cream. The eating and merrymaking then continued. The party sounds and music could be heard throughout the Ash neighborhood.

One of the partiers arrived uninvited, but she was warmly embraced because of her date. She was Townley's guest. It was late evening when she took the yard. She walked to a colorful Sugar Maple near the middle of the yard. Several of the tree branches held low hanging lanterns which yielded a gentle, mellow light. She made the patch of grass underneath the tree her dance floor. She was tall, big boned, brown, and graceful. Her form-fitting, multicolored dress swayed as she danced solo, to her own inner music, under the light. A quick-thinking teenager put a slow jazz instrumental on the phonograph, and she danced smoothly to the rhythm in a steady trot. She needed no partner as she gently swayed her hips and careened her shoulders, torso, and feet in a syncopated, slow-swung, tasteful motion. She extended her arms in front of her, and finger popped gently to the music. Children, teenagers, young adults and mid-lifers, along with the seasoned, followed her movement and were struck by her poise and graceful, rhythmic motions. They were taken by the total oneness and wholly appropriate union between the woman and her music. After her jig, the mesmerized crowd clapped warmly and mixed awhile longer.

By ten thirty the crowd had dwindled. Rustin and Nathan began folding the tables and stacking the chairs. Jinger and Flossie refrigerated the leftover food and removed the decorations, while Wyatt walked Miss Paisley down the street and saw her safely inside of her home.

As Jinger closed her eyes after midnight, she thought of the magical evening. She was thankful for her home, family, and friends. She marveled at how far they had all come since leaving the city by the bay and she was grateful to have seen her mother and her aunt in her home. She reflected on the night's big surprise—that she had known Miss Paisley since the days of her youth. When she counted her blessings, she counted Miss Paisley as family...and she thought of Nathan Keys. He had labored in the backyard for the occasion and stayed until the last chair had been stacked. They shared a few reflections of the evening beside the lattice they had constructed and decorated for the occasion. Jinger thanked her former husband for coming. They said their goodnights and he left through the side gate.

She fell fast asleep that night with a sense of peace, newfound joy and a hint of anticipation.

25

Transitions

The air was fresh and crisp after the May showers. The rain left a trail of light, wispy, wet drops on the country porch rails. The clouds continued their pedestrian trek across the sky that was now a mixture of powder-blue and fluffy, white puffs.

Jinger sat on her familiar porch swing across from Mulberry Park, sipping her morning coffee and enjoying the view. Secure beneath the cover of her porch, she drank in the fresh, earthy aroma along with her coffee. Bespectacled, she beheld both the stark beauty of the sprawling park and her own lawn and perennials. Dewdrops rested on soft petals in her flower garden and on the richly adorned park flowers alike. She vividly remembered when her bulbs had been freshly planted, and she marveled at the growth and the morning's daffodil splendor. Several mini satins scampered about, bristling their white coats as they took cover under the clover. The cottony, furry creatures broke the stillness of the morning glory with their short jumps and dives.

The park fountain statues stood before a brimming bowl of water that circled their feet. Jinger noticed the stoic way they stood. Although time had brought about many adverse weather conditions, the English figures looked on undaunted. Bright yellow, windblown daffodils and pastel geraniums had stretched and swayed in the recent wind, but now stood upright and heavenly arrayed.

As she sipped her coffee in the morning quietness, Jinger

reflected on nature and the changing times. She thought about how she had been a mere girl when she had embarked upon her sojourn that led to Mulberry Ash. Watery reflections of the Bay Bridge crossing brought back rose-colored, if not rosy, memories of the way they had been: two young innocents headed for a place they had never seen, to live with people they did not know. It seemed to Jinger that she did not remember being a child, always a little lady, going from one destiny to the next. Looking back, she felt fortunate that things had not turned out worse for her, Rustin, and Katy.

She was proud of her baby sister, as she had always been since Mollie brought her home to their sparse apartment. Her mind went back to Katy's bright, innocent eyes and the searching way she would look for their mother when she had left their apartment for the evening. She sometimes wondered what really happened the night her mother and Aunt Katie quarreled, the same night they took Uncle Jake away. No one ever mentioned it, so she folded it into her memories and chose to think of the beautiful spirit who was her sister.

As she rocked on her porch swing, she thought of Katy and her new family and beamed.

"What are you smiling so about, sister?"

Startled, Jinger turned to see her brother coming through her side gate from the rear.

"How'd you…why, I didn't see you go to the side of my house, brother."

"Chérisse dropped me off on her way to the market. Somebody spilled trash in the street in front of your house, so I bundled it and took it to the trash can just before you came out."

"Why don't you sit a spell, brother?"

"Don't care if I do. Got any more coffee?"

"Yeah, black like always?"

"Yeah."

Jinger went into her house and brought back a pastry and fruit tray, juice, and coffee. They shared their continental breakfast and the morning ambiance.

"Still haven't told me what you were smiling so about."

"About sister. I'm so glad she now has a family and a home to call her own."

"Yeah, that was somethin' how it all worked out. How they all blended and became one family."

"I was just thinking that we three could have fared a whole lot worse than what we did, but the good Lord watched over us and brought us to this present time."

"Yes, He did, and now we're all back together again. My children really enjoyed meeting their aunt Tessa Lee."

Jinger listened and nodded. The two sat in silence.

"It doesn't look like Momma's going to be with us too long," Jinger said quietly.

"No, I don't think so, either. She talks a lot about her brother, Jimmy—the one she named you after. She told me earlier that he passed away sometime back."

"Wonder what that's about?"

"Don't know. She said for us all to stick together and love one another. And that whatever happens, not to worry, because things have a way of working out for the best most times. She talks a lot about the Lord and the good book now. But she still likes to poke a little fun sometimes," Rustin said with a smile.

"That's Momma for you. We waited a long time to be able to call her Momma, didn't we?" asked Jinger quietly.

"Yeah, we did. I thought about her a lot when we grew up in the borough and when I was in the army too. At times I shed a few tears, but I'll always love my momma. She gave us life."

"Me, too. Truth be told, I had misgivings for a long time

about Momma, and our early days in uptown Baywater, but I decided to just let it go. It was hard, but I had to move on. You had gone to Six Miles when me and Jenay took the twins by to see her. When she saw my little grand girl, Carmella Rose, she smiled really wide, and when she saw her twin brother little Wyatt, she looked over, and all she said was, 'That one's darker, but I love him jes' the same.' Jenay took a little offense, but I assured her that she didn't mean any harm. I think people say things sometimes because they don't know any better."

"Color shouldn't matter any."

"No. It shouldn't, and it doesn't. But to a lot of folks, it does, and it always will."

"Um hum, color struck. It doesn't make a lick of sense."

"You know, brother, there's something I always wanted to ask you."

"What's that?"

"Wonder whatever happened to Tandy Jean? You know, we went to Stony Brook with her and her brothers. Anybody ever say what became of them?" she asked gingerly.

Rustin was quiet for a moment and then looked out toward the river. "When I was on leave once from the army, I never told you, but I went back to Roxborough looking for Tandy."

"Was she still in Shady Grove?"

"Yeah, but the family had moved out a little way from the city. Not too far off, though. It was easy to find. Her brothers had married and moved away. She's there staying with her parents. At the time, she still looked pretty good, but you know age has crept up on all of us since we were kids."

"What did she say?"

"She was pleasant and all. It turned out that she had a couple of kids—the townsfolk said by different men. She never married that I know anything about. She was friendly, but she had a faraway look in her eyes. You remember how Mr. Jiles couldn't imagine Tandy with me? Well, I don't know if it was my uniform or what, but when I saw him, he was right talkative. It seemed to me that both he and his wife would have loved for me to have come for Tandy. When I went to throw my jacket into the back trunk, before leaving, I saw the three of them staring at me from the front porch."

"That's sad, really. I guess that's the reason people shouldn't get headed up thinking they're better than others. We can say where we've been, but we don't know where we are going or what life might hand us."

"That's true," Rustin said quietly and nodded.

Jinger could tell that this was still a touchy subject for her brother. "Are you, alright?"

"I'm good."

"You all getting excited about your move up North?" she said, changing the subject.

"Yeah, we are looking forward to a different way of life. I think a change will be good. Maybe someday you can move back up North too, and we can all be together again," he said wistfully.

Before Jinger could answer, Chérisse drove up. She smiled and yelled a hearty hello. Jinger waved back.

"I'd better go," said Rustin, gulping down the rest of his coffee. "We have a full day today, and I'm due for a haircut while in town. I'll see you and the family at Sunday dinner tomorrow. I'll bring Momma." Rustin leaned over and kissed Jinger on the cheek before leaving.

After her company left, Jinger busied herself with laundry and chores for the rest of the day. She also buttered a chicken for baking, picked garden vegetables, scalloped potatoes, and started on a chocolate cake for the family Sunday dinner.

After napping, she decided to take a walk to Mulberry Park.

She stopped by and invited Miss Paisley to join her. The two enjoyed the beauty of the fountains, the park grounds, and the summer annuals hedged along the magnificent riverfront.

"I was just reading this morning where it says 'To everything there is a season, and a time to every purpose under the heaven...'" (Ecclesiastes 3:1) KJV "It seems like I feel a change of some sort coming on."

"Yeah?"

"Right."

"Well, change is in the air. I think we have all been just holding on to the way things are. Holding on until our change comes."

"It's been a long time for all of us."

"Yes, my dear. Five generations in all."

"How's that?"

Let's see: me, your momma, you, Jenay, and now Carmella Rose."

"Oh, that *is* right."

"We've taken the sweet with the bitter and become better."

"Somehow, though, I'm hoping my grandchildren will have it better than we did."

"They might. I've been reading where there is political talk about removing all of the racial separation in public places. This new court case I've been reading about is questioning what they call 'separate but equal.'"

"So, with this case ruling there is a chance that segregation, as we know it, could end?"

"Not entirely, but it could open the door for more choice and equality if they adopt it into the laws."

"Then we would be able to drink out of any fountain and eat in any restaurant?"

"That's right. But it won't happen overnight. I think it will be a long process to change the laws, which is the only way real change in practices will come about."

"If lasting change does occur, it will be a happy day."

"And they say they want to carry it over into the schools. There's talk that the schools might become more open so that all children can learn together. If my memory serves me right, there is a case coming before the Supreme Court called Brown vs. the Board of Education. How this case comes out might determine whether all children will be able to learn together in the same classrooms and schools."

"It would be great if the court rules in the favor of integration. Then my grandchildren would be able to attend schools of our choice and maybe have a chance at a better life. You think it could really come to pass?"

"Yes, I do. It's been a long time comin' to even get to this point. But I believe it's entirely possible. All things are possible to them that believe."

As they basked in their private thoughts and the possibilities, the two focused on the fluid, blue-green water as it moved downstream.

They did not notice, but Wyatt had brought his family to the park. He held little Wyatt, and Niagara ran beside them. Jenay, holding Carmella, joined the two seasoned women.

"Look at that fine, fat-cheeked girl," said Miss Paisley with laughter and delight.

Jinger just smiled and looked at her granddaughter. Jenay looked on proudly.

"Uncle Russ is looking for you, Mother," said Wyatt, as he greeted the two women with hugs.

"Is he? Tell him to come over to the park," responded Jinger.

"Yes, ma'am. Be right back."

Niagara quietly watched Miss Paisley, Jinger, her stepmother, and her half-sister. She decided to run alongside her daddy. Rustin brought his mother, who strolled with a walker, and placed her beside Miss Paisley.

By this time, the sage, elderly woman stood with a cane on a short bridge overlooking the river in motion. Next to her stood Ollie, then Jinger. Jenay took her place beside her mother with her twin daughter, Carmella, in her arms. The five generations looked out over the tide. Instinctively, they decided to share their thoughts, dreams, and visions.

Rustin, Chérisse, Wyatt, Little Wyatt, Niagara, Flossie, Aunt Tessa, and Nathan Keys, along with a few park-goers made a semicircle around the bridge mates.

Miss Paisley was the first to share her thoughts. "I dream of a better day for all people; a time when man's inhumanity to man will greatly diminish."

"I'm hoping that my children and my children's children will all walk in the light. Because the night life? It ain't no good life," said Ollie. She coughed and shook her head.

When Jenay started to share her dream, Miss Paisley gently stopped her. "Old men and women dream dreams, but the young see visions."

"I see visions of little Carmella, Niagara, and Wyatt being free to be all that God intended for them to be. Free to learn all they can. Free to be themselves, aspire, and achieve anything they set their minds to. I see them running past fields and through open doors."

Jenay cradled Carmella, then held her up so she could see the running river water. The toddler subsequently winced, then leaned forward, smiled broadly and gurgled as she lay her head on her mother's chest. This brought smiles of joy from the gathered.

"As the middle link, Jinger Rose, what is your vision?" asked Miss Paisley.

"I see a shift in time, chance, and circumstances. I cast my lot with those who hope and believe in a tomorrow of opportunities for our children and for generations to come. A sincere hope of mine is that our people will learn to esteem and embrace all shades and hues within our race and that society, as a whole, will move toward judging every person based on the content of their character.

We still have many obstacles to overcome, but I believe a time of transition is coming." She sighed. "Just like the rolling river that streams before us, we must keep moving and cling to the hope of better days to come and never, ever give up."

Family and friends stood in witness and gently applauded. The statues gazed, motionless; flaming, jet-fire daffodils streamed in the gentle breeze and nodded their approval near the free-flowing river.

Epilogue

- Rustin retired as a bank executive in Chicago
- Jinger remarried Nathan Keys and they moved to Milwaukee, then Chicago with Rustin and his family; she worked as a school teacher
- Katy Marie and her husband, Hollis, raised their six children and stayed in Troutdale. They had one child, a son, together
- Ollie remained in the South and lived with Katy Marie and her family until her demise
- Jenay became a politician's wife as Wyatt thrived in Charlotte politics, rising to the position of mayor. They raised their three children
- Tessa Lee moved to Milwaukee with Jinger and Rustin. She remarried, this time to a pastor; she and her husband relocated to Rochester
- Miss Paisley remained in Troutdale and was cared for by Louis' sister, Inez, until her nephew reappeared and took her to live with him in Richmond

  — *Paisley Place*, a riverfront mixed-use youth tutoring, recreational and cultural arts center was named in her honor by the Mulberry Park community

I never saw daffodils so beautiful.
They grew among the mossy stones—
About and about them;
Some rested their heads upon these stones,
As on a pillow, for weariness;
And the rest tossed and reeled and danced...

Lady Dorothy Wordsworth

Endnotes

1   Negro Spiritual, "Certainly Lord," African American Heritage Hymnal, #678. http://hymnary.org/text/have_you_got_good_religion

2   James Weldon Johnson, "Negro National Anthem," 1899. Arranged by John Rosamond Johnson. http://www.naacp.org/oldest-and-boldest/naacp-history-lift-evry-voice-and-sing/

3   Wallace Willis, "Swing Low, Sweet Chariot," 1840. http://www.aaregistry.org/poetry/view/swing-low-sweet-chariot-wallace-willis

4   Mack Gordon, "The More I see You," 1945. Composed by Harry Warren. En wikipedia.org/wiki/ The_ More_ I _see_ You

5   Scriptures taken from the King James Version of the Bible.